NADINE LITTLE

Who the Monsters Are

Hunters & Dragons 1

LITTLE PUBLISHING

This book is dedicated to Stuart Kellett, my first true fan.
I only wish you could have read it.

Sign up to my mailing list for a free character sheet and discover the backstories and quirks not included in the novel. Members of my mailing list get other free stuff and exclusive behind-the-scenes material.

Members are always the first to hear about my new books and discounts.

See the back of the book on how to join.

'There are far, far worse things to be than a monster.'
Jim Butcher, *Ghost Story*

'They say dragons never truly die.
No matter how many times you kill them.'
S.G. Rogers, *Jon Hansen and the Dragon Clan of Yden*

1

The bleak and wind-swept Scottish coastline is a world away from the dusty heat of Black Rock City and the Burning Man festival in Nevada. It's been ten years but I can still taste the grit on my tongue, see the flicker as the Man burned, the stars captured in a bowl of midnight velvet. The view across the playa was magical.

Until it wasn't.

My hands tighten on the wheel of my Mazda SUV and I shift in my seat. My sword sheath digs into my spine. The white glow from LED streetlights bathes the roads of North Berwick, the streets familiar from visits as a teenager.

My parents sold their sculptures to the local gallery—the smaller pieces. We'd stop for ice cream or fish and chips afterwards, which was my favourite part.

Maybe they have a collection in a museum now. A tribute. Or maybe everyone has forgotten them. Missing for a decade, presumed dead.

But I saw them die.

"This is a waste of time, Raine," Nate says in my ear.

His deep, Nevada accent jolts me out of my thoughts.

I push the talk switch in my palm and speak into my shirt sleeve. "You said that already. Multiple times."

"Our orders are clear—gather intel. No hunting."

"But we are hunters, Nate. That's what Vanatori means."

A burst of wind crackles in Nate's microphone. I imagine him prowling the darkened cliffs of St Abbs in his black combats and jacket, a scowl on his face while the rest of the group listen in silence on their earpieces, scouting their own slice of coast.

"It's for our own good," Nate says.

"We've had enough 'mourning and recuperation.'" I make air quotes with my fingers though he can't see me. "Six months of additional training and three months of sitting on our butts."

"I know how long it's been, Raine. The Principal will decide when we're ready."

I mash the indicator and turn left at a mini roundabout onto Tantallon Road. The red and blue of a Tesco supermarket competes with the streetlights, closed now since it's almost 11pm.

"Nate's right," Rick says, his voice as bland as the rest of him.

Of course he agrees with Nate.

I accelerate out of North Berwick, night-cloaked fields replacing the bright lights and buildings. My eyes scan the low and scudding clouds.

A good night for flying.

"I have reached *mi destino,*" Sofia purrs in my ear, her Argentinian accent strong despite fleeing her country nearly twelve years ago. "Dunbar—it is quite drab, yes?"

Do I still have my Scottish accent? I've only been back in my homeland for five months and I haven't done much mingling with the natives. I suspect it's different to the happy, fifteen-year-old me who left ten years ago, excited to be going to my first Burning Man with my mum and dad.

Less happy. More Americanised.

"I'll wave to you from the castle in ten minutes, Sofia," I say.

"Sounds good, honey."

Nate huffs into his microphone. "I can't believe we're following a story in a goddamn tabloid."

A house and a block of trees flash by, interrupting the monotony of the flat fields of oats.

"If it turns out to be true, we can write *Supernatural Scotland* a thank-you note," Dustan says reasonably.

Nate snorts. "Flying horse, my ass. We all know what they are and none of them look like a goddamn rainbow. I bet they're not even here. This country is too small to hide in."

"They're fuckin' here, Boss, I know it," George growls. "That's why the rumours are increasing."

A smile tugs at my lips at the thought of George stuffed into his ancient Range Rover. With me and Dustan, he's the only other person in our group born in Scotland, though Dustan's ancestors are Dutch. George is also the only one of us who was ecstatic to return.

The blackness of the sea opens on my left, the lights of Fife twinkling on the horizon. I slow for a sharp bend, accelerate briefly, then turn left, my headlights sweeping an empty car park. The Mazda rocks along a single-lane road of speedbumps sandwiched between landscaped hedges.

Fabian, the last member of our group, stays quiet.

I enter another car park next to a small building, the dark shape of the castle ruins hulking beyond. I pull the handbrake and turn off the engine, letting my vision adjust. Metal ticks as the car cools.

"I'm at Tantallon," I say.

"Everyone—thirty-minute check in or sooner if you have trouble," Nate says. "Remember this is a fact-finding mission only. Not that we're going to *find* anything." He mutters the last.

I agree with him. The person who reported the sighting to a magazine that believes in selkies and unicorns was likely high or drunk or desperate for attention. Even if it were true, what are our chances of being on the right spot of coast at the right time for another fly-by? The Drakul are secretive bastards. Powerful, rich and untouchable. They're amused by the Vanatori, not threatened, probably because they're so hard to kill, except in their human form.

I slide from the car and ease the door shut. A Saltire flag snaps in the gusts next to the tourist building. The air smells of salt when the wind fails to snatch it away. My long, dirty-blonde hair whips around my shoulders and I scrape it back, brushing the pommel of my sword in its spine sheath, crafted for my small hands. I stand and breathe for a few minutes.

I don't care if we *are* wasting our time. I'd rather patrol the coast for the next month than sit and stare at my computer, saving files collected by other groups who are actually out hunting and fighting. Sometimes killing, especially in America where buying a gun is almost as easy as buying a pint of milk.

Fruitless patrolling is also better than thinking how far I am from finding the monsters that murdered my parents.

I leap a short wall next to the tourist admission building, my black trainers thumping on mown grass. My matching jeans and shirt blend into the night. I jog past a couple of picnic tables and the white glow of a tourist information board. Pale dirt marks patches of erosion in the grassy path. I cross a wooden bridge onto a strip of cobblestone between a towering wall then hustle across more lopped grass towards the castle, following the roar of the waves. An archway curves into a mouth of blackness. Wind plays a desolate tune through the passageways. My footsteps scrape on uneven concrete and my pulse trips, a shiver dancing down my spine.

I have a sword. I am a badass. I'm not scared of ghosts.

My breath comes easier when I exit through another arch into a wide, grassy space stretching to the sea, the waves pounding out of sight at the bottom of high cliffs. I glance to the right. The curve of the coast cloaks Dunbar to nothing but an orange hue in the sky. In the opposite direction, the Bass Rock appears white from the layers of seabird crap.

A shape huddles on a bench near the cliff edge. I take a backwards step, my hand closing on the pommel of my sword. My fingers flutter over the talk button in my palm.

What are the chances a normal human would choose this lonely stretch for a night-time sabbatical? Normal humans would have friends. Alcohol. Is he the monster with colours so unlike a typical Drakul? It's impossible to tell unless I make my presence known and he shifts and tries to eat me or attacks me in his human form. Or I get close enough to light him on fire.

I tuck my cold fingers into my collar and walk onto the grass. The figure tilts his head, glancing at me over his shoulder, his face in profile against the sea.

"I'm sorry," I say, keeping my voice soft. "I didn't think anyone came out here this late."

The man straightens and turns around. My breath catches before I can tell myself to be cool.

He's tall and lean, messy hair sweeping across his forehead

and flopping into his eyes. Darkness pools in his cheekbones.

Man, those cheekbones.

"I can leave," he says, his voice soft to match mine. His accent is Scottish with something mixed in—American?

It's sexy.

I give myself a mental kick. If the reason for our 'mourning and recuperation' has taught me anything, it's that the most beautiful face can hide the worst monster.

"Seems unfair to chase you from whatever peace you came to find," I say.

One side of his mouth curves. "It's fleeting, anyway."

Okay, he hasn't attacked me yet. That's a point in his favour. What do I do now—ask if he, on occasion, shifts into a winged and fire-breathing reptile? Not exactly subtle.

"What's your name?" I say.

He watches me in silence. Shadows cloak his wary eyes. My fingers tap my collarbone, half-aching to wrap around my pommel and half-wanting to tidy my hair.

No make-up, a shaggy blonde snarl to my shoulders—every man's dream girl.

My cheeks warm and I feel like I'm back in high school. I was a late bloomer. Scrawny, geeky and flat-chested. Then my parents got eaten and the size of my breasts wasn't so important anymore.

"Jay," he says slowly. "Yours?"

"Raine." I force a laugh. "My parents were hippies."

Loving, talented, amazing hippies I miss every day. Is he one of the monsters like the two that killed them? I should stop being polite and show him my sword. If he's human, I can apologise later.

Jay cocks his head, his expression serious. His eyes are a

light colour—maybe blue or green?

"I like the rain," he says.

Holy crap, is he flirting with me? I wish Sofia were here. She's an expert at cutting through bullshit and trickery. She'd know if his words were lies as pretty as his face. She likes to tease me, saying I'm too sweet and innocent—a lamb in wolf's clothing.

Maybe that's why my kill count is zero.

Before I can decide how to respond, a leathery flapping churns the wind and a chunk of velvet sky thuds onto the lawn beside us. A reeking chunk the size of a minibus.

The black dragon bares its teeth in a grin.

2

The Drakul is near enough for me to reach out and touch its slick scales. Its hide swallows the night and shimmers with a hint of rainbow, like oil on water, but you'd have to be drunk to mistake it for a flying horse. Goosebumps flare on my arms despite the smoky heat pulsing from the beast.

It's similar to one of the monsters that ate my parents, if a little bigger. The other was a gold—the most powerful. I'll never forget her crimson eyes. Even after that awful night, this is still the closest I've been to a Drakul without it smacking me out of the way or smirking at me from the sky.

They don't have many expressions in their dragon form but you can tell when they're mocking you—puny, pathetic human. Drives me mad.

The dragon swings its head towards Jay, its neck long and dainty, for a black. The eye I can see narrows, an elliptical pupil surrounded by paleness. The nostrils flare, sulphurous air huffing out and ruffling Jay's t-shirt. Its mouth opens slowly, lines of drool connecting sharpened teeth.

No way. No more people are getting eaten in front of me, especially not a cute guy who may or may not have been flirting.

Ignoring the canister of dragon's-bane in my pocket, my

hand closes on the pommel of my Celtic leaf-bladed sword, hidden by my hair. The familiar grip banishes the paralysis in my feet as I pull the blade free from the spine sheath beneath my shirt, loving the sound it makes. The sword whistles in an arc and a flash of moon between the roiling clouds burnishes the metal with silver fire. I put my whole body behind the blow.

Fabian, our bladed weapons specialist, taught me never to attack a dragon with a sword unless it's a last resort. Attacking them in their dragon form is suicide if you're not in a large, well-armed group. He said in the unlikely event of coming face to snout, spray powder in their eyes and run. But I love my sword and keep it sharp, dragon's-bane blended into the steel before it was forged.

Also, it's a little late now.

The blade slices between two spines on the dragon's neck and bites deep. Scalding liquid splashes my face and the beast roars, trying to rear but its legs flop and scour the grass. Fear, adrenaline and the voice babbling, *"I'm dead! I'm so dead!"* help me tug the sword free. I hack at the dragon's neck. The shrieking in my head is awfully loud until I realise it's no longer in my head. I scream and chop in great slaps of metal and flesh. My arms numb. The Drakul dissolves in a burst of white flame, the ash swirling in the wind and peppering my cheeks. I stagger back and the sword droops in my hand. Gore drips from my lashes and coats me to my elbow, plastering my shirt to my chest.

Holy crap, I killed a dragon. Holy crap, I may pass out.

Jay stares at me, eyes wide, his face ghost-pale. He swallows hard and raises his hands. They're shaking quite badly.

Dammit. How to explain to a normal human about dragon

shapeshifters and the Drakul? The poor guy—wrong place, wrong time. This isn't my area of expertise. Nate would be better—he was the one who told me the truth of the world in a grim and patient voice once I was coherent enough to listen. I remember the horrified disbelief, the fervent prayers for it all to be a dream.

But the nightmare is real and my parents are still gone.

I lick my lips and immediately regret it. A syrupy, metallic liquid coats my tongue. My stomach heaves and I vomit all over the grass.

This is really not helping my image.

I try to find something to wipe my mouth but no body part or scrap of cloth has escaped the carnage. There are globs of stuff I'd rather not think about in my hair. I settle for spitting.

Smooth, Raine. And sexy.

"Before you ask," I say, my voice a croak, "you're not hallucinating and dragons are real. It's a shapeshifter."

I take a step towards Jay. His gaze skitters to my sword and he backs away. I rip up a clump of grass, wipe the worst of the blood off the blade and re-sheath it. I pretend it doesn't take me three tries because, hey, look at that—my hands are shaking, too.

Jay releases a breath and his shoulders slump. "I know about dragons."

My fingers tighten on the pommel in the act of releasing it. My gaze darts around the bleak ruins and cloud-filled sky but we're the only ones on the cliff top. Just us and the scattered ash, for now.

"How do you know about dragons?" I say slowly. "Are you in the Vanatori?"

"I'm not a hunter."

He stops backing up—wise, since there's not much left behind him except a short topple over a fence and a long fall into the sea—but he eyes me warily.

"Then how do you know?" I say.

He bites his lip and looks at the pile of ash. His gaze darts to the sky but nothing moves among the clouds.

The Drakul are matriarchal and connected to their offspring. The mother of this one will have felt its death, though not enough to pinpoint the location. The thought of a grieving mother dragon out for vengeance terrifies me. Maybe she's not in this country. What was a black dragon doing in Scotland and how many more are there?

"My family," Jay says, his mouth quirked though it's not a happy expression. "It's complicated."

I force myself not to recoil. "Are you a Lesser?"

Now that would be too cruel if this hunk of male perfection is a filthy Lesser—a human bitten by a dragon either very carefully in their full dragon form or less carefully if the dragon is strong enough to change only their teeth. That and the name—Drakul—is how the vampire myth originated but they don't morph into bats or drink blood. They prefer to eat the whole lot. Lessers can't shift all the way but they get nifty benefits like rapid healing and morphing certain body parts. They are servants, soldiers and spies for powerful families.

"Not me," Jay says. "My sister."

I'll have to take his word for it. The only way to know for sure is to have him strip and search for the scars…

No. Probably not a good idea to get him naked when I'm way too dazzled by the parts I can see.

"What's your full name, Jay?" I say.

He gives me a sad, half-mouth smile and walks around me, staying more than a sword's length away.

Not the most trusting soul. Has he been hurt in the past? Maybe he's still being hurt.

I sidle around the remains, my shoes squelching on the grass, and follow him into the sanctuary of the castle. Ash dusts my trainers. My footsteps are loud in comparison to Jay's.

"Is your sister a hostage?" My voice echoes from the roof of ancient stone. "What family has her?"

Maybe they're using her to force him to do things. Or maybe she's happy to work for the flying, murdering reptiles but it doesn't sit well with him. What sent him to this lonely cliff and carved such sorrow into his face?

A man in distress who may need saving—be still my heart.

He walks at my side, staring at his shoes instead of answering. The wind buffets us as we leave the castle and aim for the gap in the wall leading to the wooden bridge. Questions bubble in my throat—who is he, where is he from, how deep is his family in it?

"If you're in trouble, I can help you," I say.

Yeah, just look at my track record—I slew the dragon and only threw up once.

His sad smile wriggles its way into my soft little heart. Damn Sofia for always being right.

"I wish you could," Jay says.

"Let me guess—it's complicated."

"My whole life is complicated."

Why does this make him more intriguing? I don't need complicated. I want simple, easy. I'm an orphan who hunts dragon shapeshifters for the Vanatori. I don't expect to reach my thirties. Who needs extra drama?

The path widens into the grassy picnic area, with the wall and tourist admission building beyond. The Saltire fights against the flagpole like a dog on a leash.

"Check in," Nate barks in my ear.

I flinch and trip over my feet. Warm fingers catch my arms and keep me upright. Jay releases me as quickly as he grabbed me, no doubt repulsed by the cooling tackiness of blood. He stares at the dark smears on his palms. The others call in through my earpiece.

Crap, I have to respond or they'll descend on the castle and spook Jay but I'm not subtle enough or spy enough to do it without him noticing. I need to get more information out of him.

I slowly raise my arm and toggle the talk button.

"I'm fine," I whisper into my sleeve.

Panic flits across Jay's face. "Your group are here? Are they listening? Are they close?"

His wide eyes dart from the long grass bordering the picnic tables to the wall as if my group are about to spill over the top and surround him. Tension sings through his shoulders.

"They're scouting other parts of the coast. They can't hear you unless I push this." I raise my palm and wiggle my fingers, showing him they're nowhere near the button and mic tucked into my sleeve. "No one's coming to get you, I promise."

He shuffles from foot to foot, his gaze not resting on anything for more than a second.

Dammit, I want to hug him. He's just so cute and skittish.

"Let me help you, Jay," I say.

His eyes fix on me. "What if I can help *you?*"

"How?"

He turns to stare off towards the castle ruins so I can only see half of his face—slender neck, the smooth line of his jaw.

"I can get you information."

"What kind of information?"

Excitement tingles in my belly. This could be the break we need. Proper intel from someone stuck on the fringes of Drakul society. Solid information could elevate us from mild nuisance to actual threat, especially here in Scotland where their presence has been dismissed.

We could finally make a difference.

"The name of the dragon you killed, for a start," Jay says.

Drakul society is notoriously secretive. Sometimes, only the female head of the family is known, the identities of the other members heavily protected. We learn names but never appearances. The locations of their residencies are also a mystery or impossible to approach.

I raise my eyebrows. "You don't know who it was? I assumed it knew you. Did it speak to you?"

"I'm not a Lesser so I wouldn't have heard it if it did," Jay says.

"Are you a dragon?"

Way to be subtle, Raine.

The sorrow returns to his eyes. "If I were a dragon, wouldn't I have hurt you already?"

"Some of them can be patient. Lessers, too." My turn to stare broodingly at the castle. "So how did that thing know we were there?"

"It probably knew me or my sister. Caught my scent. They make it impossible for anyone to escape."

I lean my butt on the edge of a picnic table instead of comforting him.

"What would you want for the name?"

"I want to feel useful," he says. "Like I'm fighting back."

"How will I get in touch with you?"

"We can meet. In two days? You choose the time and place."

Oh boy, I get to see him again. The excitement spreads to my fingers and toes. I squash the urge to flip my hair. My fingers touch the tacky mess.

Definitely avoid the hair thing.

"Well, not here since it would be stupid to return this millennium," I say. "Do you know the arcade on the pier in Portobello?"

"I can find it."

"Okay. Meet me by the carousel at 1pm in two days."

His eyes search my face. I try to exude an aura of professionalism and trust, which is difficult when I look like I've murdered somebody. I pray I don't have vomit on my shirt. The blood is bad enough though, if he's trapped in Drakul society like he says, he'll have seen his fair share.

He nods and walks towards the long grass. "Guess I'll see you in two days."

"Wait!" I mentally slap myself and lower my voice an octave. "I can drop you off somewhere."

"It's better if you don't." He throws a glance over his shoulder. "But thanks."

Is he a fugitive? I should bundle him into my car and spirit him home. I can make him hot chocolate and wrap him in a blanket.

I cast my eyes heavenward. This is not how a proper Vanatori behaves, especially after what happened nine months ago. And Jay's not a fugitive since he agreed to meet in a public place.

I watch him skirt the wall and hedge and slip into the long grass, enjoying how his t-shirt clings to his shoulder blades. The slight narrowing from shoulders to waist. And his *butt.* Lord have mercy. I drool a little.

The night swallows him and my brain cells return to normal function.

"I hope you know what you're doing," I mutter to myself.

Whatever or whoever Jay is, I need to be careful.

3

My Mazda sits in front of the tourist admission building, looking sleek, dark and predatory. A badass bitch drives this car, not a wimpy girl whose pulse gets all fluttery for a total stranger.

Raine Waller—woman of delusion.

I press my key fob and the lights blink on, shining like cat's eyes in the dark. I hurry to the rear and throw open the boot, rifling through my various hunter paraphernalia: huge first aid kit, spare knives, a backpack of essentials in case I need to run, a crossbow.

I don't use the crossbow. It's a better weapon to counter a monster built for the air but the last time I used it, I almost shot myself in the foot. Projectiles and I have an unpleasant history. It makes me less effective in a real battle but we only try to fight the Drakul in their human form, anyway.

Tonight not included.

I tug out fistfuls of lemon-scented wipes and scrub my face, my eyes scrunched shut. The dirty ones go in a plastic bag to be binned later, the boot light bright enough to show the red-smeared cloth. My hands are next, my nails circled by moons of crimson. Unfortunately, there are not enough wipes in the world to get me clean. I take a calming breath and toggle the talk button in my palm.

"Nate, so, uh, when I told you I was fine, I wasn't entirely truthful," I say in a rush, "because I found the flying horse and it was a dragon and I killed it."

I wince at the uproar and hook out the earpiece to avoid being deafened. Among the cacophony, George yells, "I fuckin' knew it! I *knew* they were fucking here!"

George likes to say the f-word a lot. He uses it as an adjective, punctuation and sometimes a noun. I never realised it was so versatile.

Nate's voice thunders for silence and I gingerly slip the earpiece back in.

"Everyone meet at the rendezvous," he says. "The sooner, the better."

I leap into my Mazda and gun the engine. My headlights sweep the hedgerows. Each speedbump on the single-lane road jolts my spine. I scan the fields for a lonely figure but Jay has merged with the grass and disappeared.

Where does he live? And by himself or is there a Drakul family close enough to reach their house on foot?

I shiver and scan the sky.

I'm lucky the black dragon seemed to be hunting alone. Another beast could have smelled the ash on the wind and easily found me while I picked the crud from underneath my fingernails.

I reach the abandoned runways of East Fortune airfield in twelve minutes thanks to my rally driving on the country roads. A red gate blocks the path but swings open when I pull the bolt free. A sign with an arrow pointing down the main runway says 'Sunday market' in faded letters. I motor onto the decaying concrete and park. A black Citroen with red trim pulls in a second later. Sofia slides from the driver's seat, her short, black dress paired with tights on account of the wind whistling across the exposed runway.

She and I are the only women in our group. It can lead to some awkwardness, particularly when the men get protective or decide ladies aren't equipped for fighting dragons—too soft and emotional. Mostly Nate since, as the leader, our actions reflect on him. And, nine months ago, certain actions slaughtered five of our group.

He would not be happy with my reaction to the mysterious, alluring Jay. I'm not entirely happy with it, either.

"*Dios mío*, honey," Sofia says, "you weren't kidding."

She grips a clump of my hair between her fingers. Dried blood crackles and the wind whirls the flakes away.

Sofia's weapon of choice, after her shotgun of course, is an axe, though she always has a couple of throwing knives pinning her glossy black hair. When she was seventeen, she killed a man who'd kidnapped and raped her and her sisters. Unfortunately, the man was the son of a Latin American Drakul cartel. They murdered her family and she fled the country, living illegally in the US until she tracked down the Vanatori using her considerable computer skills.

If she'd met Jay, she would've pressed a knife to his throat and demanded to know exactly who he was and what he knew.

"It was somewhat unexpected," I say.

She grins. "So the lamb becomes a wolf. I will wait for the others but do not doubt—I want every detail."

She perches on the edge of the boot beside me and swings her legs. Dustan arrives next in a battered VW Golf, hitching his jeans over his flat butt. He favours baggy clothes that hang off his skinny frame. Every day there's the anticipation of seeing what brand of boxers he's wearing. He is what the Scots like to call a weegie, though his Glaswegian accent has mellowed over the years. Apparently, he was a thieving little hooligan as a teenager and made the mistake of robbing the wrong house when on holiday in Alicante.

He punches me on the shoulder. "Way to go, Raine. That's pure genius."

Four vehicles enter the gate in a blaze of lights. Nate strides towards our little huddle, followed by George, Fabian and Rick.

"Explain," Nate barks in his Nevada accent.

He's dressed in black, just like I pictured, the material stretched over broad shoulders and bulging thighs. Scary black-ops soldier, that's Nate.

I describe my encounter with the dragon, minus Jay, ignoring a blip of guilt. I hate keeping things from my group but I want to test Jay's connections, see how deep his involvement goes before I tell them about him. He could be a major asset and I don't want to spoil it by scaring him off.

Mouths gape at my story, eyes widen. George whispers, "Fucking-A, fucking-A," his ginger hair and beard frizzing in all directions. Nate is the only other person present who's killed a Drakul but in their human forms. His count is three, all when he lived in Nevada. Weaker beasts but three is three—damned impressive.

Nate cups his elbow and taps his chin, lost in thought. "So they *are* here."

"Told you, Boss." George slaps him on the back and Nate staggers forward a step.

I hide my smile and scan the rest of the group ranged on the runway. Fabian lingers at the back, his albino skin glowing in the darkness, uninterrupted by a single strand of hair. A real walking genetic disaster but a pretty sweet guy. Rick, as usual, stands next to Nate. He's an ordinary, middle-aged man—brown hair, brown eyes and a face you instantly forget unless you're staring right at it. It's his superpower and means he's an excellent spy.

They're my family now.

Nate claps his hands, commanding attention. "We've lingered here long enough. I'll talk to Principal Cozma but until we get new orders, we remain intel-only. Rick, speak to your informants—see if there are any ripples on who the dead lizard was."

Rick nods. The group disbands to their various vehicles. I hop off the edge of the boot but Nate touches my arm before I can shut the lid.

"If there is a next time, don't be stupid—call for backup," he says.

"I'm sorry, Nate, that didn't sound like 'good job, Raine. Excellent work.' Do you want to try again?"

He frowns at me. "You surprised it. You got lucky. I never should have let you patrol on your own."

My fists clench and I slam the boot lid.

Sometimes I think he still views me as that fifteen-year-old girl he rescued in the desert.

Shaking my head, I climb in my car and drive away.

4

The Portobello arcade is only a street away from my childhood home. Will the house be untouched, like a tomb, or was it sold off, all evidence of my parents scrubbed from its walls?

I'm not brave enough to find out.

The arcade also reminds me of childhood—my mum and dad holding a hand each and swinging me through the crowd. The sweetness of popcorn and candyfloss. The screams of people on the rides, the floors sticky with spilled juice. The bells and flashing lights and gunfire of the games. It was a magical place.

It's lost some of its sparkle.

Children shriek and shove past me, thundering down the boardwalk. Slender-limbed teenagers, more make-up than flesh, drape themselves on every available surface, their cropped tops and ripped jeans flashing acres of skin. I fist my hand to keep from fluffing my hair.

I put some gel in it after my shower and let it dry, the lazy curls framing my face. My make-up is a subtle slick of pink lipstick and gold eyeshadow to match my buttery leather jacket over a silk top that may or may not showcase my breasts.

They were fabulous when they finally grew in. Sue me.

I drew the line at a skirt but my trousers fit tight, in a good way, and look great tucked into my black boots. Agonising over this outfit took me two hours so I'm running a couple of minutes late. It's not helping the fizz of nerves in my stomach.

I spot Jay before he sees me. All the strength drains from my legs and I grab a fortune-telling machine to steady myself. The robot gypsy tells me I could get lucky. I almost faint.

Jay is *hot*. Out-of-this-world smoking hot. I'm surprised he's not been mobbed by women, though knots of girls inch closer to him. Even mothers dragging ice-cream-smeared toddlers stumble in their sensible shoes. He appears not to notice, watching the swirl of painted horses in front of him, the breeze off the sea ruffling his chestnut hair.

It's unwise to date someone of above-average attractiveness. He's bound to be a narcissistic ass or a womaniser. Probably both. Plain men are sensible. Safe. They're grateful for the attention and you're less likely to find them humping a neighbour on your kitchen table.

Not that we're dating. He's a stranger, a potential asset. I can't trust anyone on the fringes of Drakul society, not even if he's just a gorgeous boy caught in events beyond his control. Our relationship will remain strictly professional.

I slip out my phone and take a couple of photos, though they're side-on and blurry, then suck in a breath and saunter over to Jay. He turns to face me and my brain cells scatter. One eye is the amber of warm honey, the other peridot-green with flecks of gold, both ringed by long, dark lashes.

"You look different," he says.

I gape. How long have I been staring?

God, he's so pretty.

"Raine?"

Crap. Say something—you were running late. You had to rush.

"Sorry," I gasp. "Late."

Speak in full sentences! You are a strong, intelligent woman.

The entire English language disappears from my vocabulary.

Jay tilts his head. "Are you okay?"

I fix on a smile. "I ran to get here. Guess I'm out of shape. You want to get a milkshake?"

What the hell is happening? I can run ten miles without breaking a sweat but one second in his company and I'm breathless.

I barrel through the crowd before he can answer. Women purr as he passes them. I lead him to a café near the end of the pier, the interior decorated in soft pastels, the furniture worn but clean. We order banana milkshakes and sit at a table in a corner of the bustling room. I feel calm enough to look at Jay directly.

He sips his drink. "Hey, this is nice."

He sucks harder on the straw. My heart has palpitations.

"Did you find out who it was?" I blurt instead of telling him how sexy he is.

Professional. I am a professional.

Two old ladies at the next table elbow and whisper to each other, watching Jay with identical hungry expressions. Maybe they want his milkshake, though he looks edible in a long-sleeved cotton top beneath an open shirt and stonewashed jeans.

He sits straight in his chair, his arms resting on the table on either side of his glass. "I did. You might want to brace yourself."

"Brace myself?"

He gives me the mouth quirk and serious eyes. "It was Lukas Romanov."

"The Romanovs are *here?*" I yell and my voice bounces off the ceiling.

The café falls quiet. I duck my head to hide my blazing cheeks.

"The Romanovs live in Scotland?" I say, quieter. "But… but their matriarch is always being spotted in America."

"She travels. They've lived here for years."

I sway in my seat. Thankfully, I'm already sitting or I would've collapsed on the floor. Jay tongues his straw for another sip of milkshake. I go from terror to lust in one millisecond and slump in the chair, suddenly exhausted.

Lukas Romanov. Holy mother of god. The eldest son of Evelyn Romanov, the matriarch of the Romanov dynasty, the most powerful Drakul family in America but apparently this country, too, if not the whole freaking world. Their roots are planted in the Russian royal family and the mafia. If I ever meet the woman, I'll pee my pants.

And I killed her firstborn. She has four more but that's probably no consolation.

I manage not to hyperventilate, inhaling half of my shake as a distraction. It curdles in my stomach.

She knows he's dead but the connection isn't strong enough to lead her to where it happened. Even if she does find the castle, what are the chances of her sniffing me out?

Slim, I tell myself with a comforting mental pat.

"Who the hell are you, Jay?" My voice quavers a little. Barely noticeable. "Is your sister a Romanov Lesser?"

He clasps his hands on the table and refuses to meet my

gaze. "I can't tell you, Raine."

I huff out a sigh. Okay, so association with the Romanovs is far deeper than I wanted to tread but the information Jay could glean would be invaluable. We've never had an asset like this. *Rick* has never had an asset like this and he's our master of informants.

I peek at Jay through my lashes. He finishes his drink and glances around the room, moving only his eyes. He seems stiff, holding himself carefully. I open my mouth to ask if he's all right but he leans in, wincing slightly. He smells like vanilla.

I *love* vanilla.

"Why are people looking at me?" he says.

Most of the women—and several men—filling the other tables either cast their eyes towards us then to their food or openly stare. There's many a flirtatious smile and hair toss.

I snort, the shock of the Romanov name fading. "Are you serious?"

"Why wouldn't I be serious?"

I squint at him but see no evidence of guile. He cocks his head and blinks at me.

"You're gorgeous, Jay. That's why they're looking."

His eyes widen before his expression slips back to wary.

"You're messing with me." He runs the tip of his finger around the rim of his glass and sticks it in his mouth. "I'm the ugly one."

"Compared to who?"

He seems to find his milkshake unduly fascinating. The bustle of the café fills the bubble of silence at our table.

I try a different approach. "What's your sister like?"

Jay hunches, his face guarded, and I fear he'll stand and

leave without answering.

"She doesn't deserve what they do to her," he says softly.

His controlled facade cracks and I glimpse the hidden pain. The humid air of the café becomes hard to breathe. He bows his head and it's gone. I want to charge outside, find his tormentors—his sister's tormentors—and threaten to slice off limbs.

"Jay, please, let me help—"

A hip bumps our table and rattles the glasses. A woman plants her hand on the surface and leans towards Jay, the deep-purple dress she's poured herself into screaming for mercy. He must have an uninterrupted view from her cleavage to her bellybutton. I get treated to her butt. The dress is so tight, it's obvious she has no underwear on.

"Hey there," she says, her voice a husky purr. "How 'bout you ditch the skinny blonde and let a real woman give you the ride of your life?"

I think about showing her my knives.

Jay's gaze darts to mine. "I, um… I'm with her?"

"I can bend my body into positions you wouldn't believe," she says.

Jay's fingers grip the edge of the table, his knuckles white. His panicked expression makes him more adorable. Other women start to circle. I hold out my hand and he lunges for it. His skin touches mine and an electric shiver zips straight to my stomach. His hand is warm, dry and tingles against my palm. He crushes my fingers but it's kind of sweet. I lead him out of the café to shouts of, "That's right, girl, hold on to your man," and less flattering things from the snubbed she-monster. We duck into the cool dimness of the covered arcade. Young boys yell and gesture at the video games, ignoring us.

Jay blinks at me. "What was that?"

"Seriously, Jay, you need to look in a mirror sometime. How has this never happened to you before?"

"I don't get out much."

I'm still holding his hand, his fingers tangled in mine. I force myself to let go, my cheeks hot, and nod at the closest machine.

"You want to play?"

"I don't know how."

"You've never played an arcade game?"

He kicks at the scuffed linoleum. A whoop of pre-adolescent excitement echoes from the confines of a racing booth.

"Are you a prisoner?" I say, failing to keep the outrage from my voice.

A beat of silence from Jay. Derisive mockery from the gathered youth.

"Only when I can't sneak out." His self-deprecating smile sinks hooks into my heart. "It's complicated."

In other words, he's done talking about it.

"In that case, grab a gun," I say, "because we are definitely shooting up some zombies."

5

Zombie Apocalypse 5 happens to be my favourite arcade game or Zombie Apocalypse 2 when I was a kid but it's basically the same. I explain how to play and Jay positions himself at the console, his legs spread, a sub-machine gun held in a two-handed grip.

He dies almost immediately.

I stifle a laugh but can't help ribbing him a little. He doesn't seem to mind. His shoulders relax, a frown of concentration wrinkling his brow. We walk through the shattered streets of an abandoned city, shooting zombies and fighting mutant animals. He takes down five in a row and we move to the next level—the sewers. He pumps his fist and grins at me, his face slightly flushed.

It's the first time I've seen him smile. A proper smile.

After a few seconds, I notice his hand waving in front of my nose.

"Raine, are you all right? You got eaten."

I snap back to myself, my mouth dry, my heart thudding against my ribs. "Sorry. Drifted off. Where were we?"

He seems oblivious to his effect on me and every other creature with a pulse. Unfortunately, it makes him more endearing. My fingertips buzz with the need to touch him.

I can't control it. It's maddening.

We play every game in the arcade, Jay feeding the machines an endless supply of coins. He laughs. I blush like a girl and not an experienced hunter. He teases me when he's better at air hockey. It's like he knows my moves before I do, firing the puck past my guard every time. But he doesn't touch me and I don't touch him. We eat ice cream standing at the end of the pier and looking out to sea.

"It hurts my teeth," he says on a shiver.

He's never had ice cream. How is that possible? What human hasn't had ice cream at least once in their life? He's obviously not lactose intolerant and avoiding it deliberately. Is having his sister held hostage enough to explain an unconventional childhood?

Or is he just not human at all?

I shudder and suck harder on my ice cream, the vanilla and cold flooding my mouth and freezing my brain.

He seems so young, excited about everything, except when the sadness fills his eyes with secrets. He's curious not cruel. There's no hint of violence or arrogance. Is he really as innocent as he appears or is he that good an actor? Our group has been burned before, though the monster in question didn't act all sweetness and light. I should question Jay. Be strict. Refuse to accept his silences or evasions.

But I don't want to chase the happiness from his face. Not yet.

Some of the light fades anyway when he looks at his watch and says, "I have to go."

Hours have vanished but it doesn't feel like enough. I squash the disappointment.

"When can I see you again?" Okay, maybe not squash... I

clear my throat. "I mean, how will you get in touch if you have more information? Can you get more information—names, locations?"

There. That's professional. Mostly.

His smile is tentative but not sad. He digs in his pocket and holds out a slim, grey mobile, the flashing lights of the nearby arcade reflecting off the large screen.

"I'll call you when I have something. Mine is the only number on it."

I casually accept the phone. My pulse stutters at the brush of his fingers. I scroll through the apps instead of meeting his gaze.

Sure enough, there's one number in the contacts, listed under a single letter—J.

* * *

Being an incorruptible member of the Vanatori, I resist calling Jay for a few hours. I dust and vacuum my house, clean out my fish tank, the brightly coloured betta squaring up to me, and cook dinner. I find the phone in my hand but put it face down on my coffee table and turn on the TV, settling on a *Game of Thrones* episode I've seen a million times.

I hate the dragons. Normal people love them. The fictional beasts are larger than the Drakul and can't shapeshift but they share some similarities—fire breathing, terrifying, a tendency to eat people. The Drakul are born shapeshifters, the standing of their family determined by the colour of their dragon form, with the most powerful being gold then black, silver and bronze to the weakest jewel-like colours. No rainbows. They can create as many Lessers as they want, each marked by the scar of their master's teeth. Even with the advanced healing capabilities, Lessers don't ever heal that mark.

For some, it's a slave brand.

My concentration drifts. The phone is silky smooth in my fingers. The thought of it being in Jay's pocket warms certain nether regions.

I am ridiculously attracted to the guy. Dangerously so. I barely know him. He could be anyone. But a few hours in his company and I want to pull off his clothes to see if the promise is as good as the reality.

And to check he's not a Lesser, of course.

Darkness creeps in and I draw my heavy, floor-length curtains, the lights of Peebles sparkling beyond.

Nate offered me a house in Edinburgh but I refused. Too many memories. Here on the edge of the Scottish Borders' town, it's rural and picturesque. Quiet and unknown. I can make my own memories instead of being haunted by the old ones.

My finger hovers over the call button on the burner phone. I toss the bewitched thing on the couch and check my doors and windows. All locked, with dragon's-bane painted on in a special coating as an extra deterrent.

It's an unassuming little plant with yellow flowers and white-veined leaves. The fruit is the most potent but all of it can be ground into a powder. The most powerful Drakul find contact with it excruciating, even in their human form. Weaker dragons don't seem to get the pain but if used correctly, say shoved deep in a wound or blended into handcuffs, it stops any of the Drakul from shifting. Contrary to the events of three nights ago, it's still easier to chop a dragon to pieces in its human form.

But catching them is a bitch.

The phone screen glows blue in the cosy dimness of my living room. I hide it under a cushion and peruse my floor-to-ceiling bookshelf. Nothing grabs my attention. Temptation wins after another minute. I flop on the sofa and stroke Jay's number.

It would be smart to test it. In case of an emergency.

Oh, crap, I've pressed the button.

The phone rings. Sweat pools in my palms.

"Hey. Are you okay?"

I shut my eyes. "I just wanted to see if it worked."

"Oh. You don't trust me?"

"No, I"—for the love of god, don't tell him the truth—"I wanted to hear your voice."

Dammit.

A blush heats my cheeks and I squirm on the couch. My only consolation for being a simpering weirdo is he can't see me.

This won't be how Rick acts with his informants—tongue-tied, gushing, picturing them naked. He'll maintain a professional distance, knowing they can't be entirely relied upon but keeping them happy to squeeze as much information out of them as possible.

"You wanted to hear my voice?" Jay says in his sexy accent.

Maybe this was a bad idea. It's too intimate—having him whisper in my ear.

No. I can do this. I'm building a rapport. The more he trusts me, the more he'll tell me. It's all for the Vanatori and nothing to do with my fluttery little heart.

"I had fun today," I say.

"Me, too." His words are soft, the warmth in them clenching

my stomach.

Damn body, always betraying me.

I sag into the couch cushions. "Where are you right now?"

"In my room."

Questions crowd onto my tongue—where does he live? What family is holding him and his sister hostage? Is his sister there? I swallow them all. Too personal and he'll close down, give me the 'it's complicated' spiel.

"What are you doing?" I say.

"Reading. And I have snacks."

"That sounds fun."

We end up talking late into the night, my ear hot from the phone. We have the same taste in books (medieval fantasy or grimdark) and music (classical or anything from the 80s, especially rock). He laughs, though his voice stays hushed as if he doesn't want to draw attention to himself. Maybe he lives with his tormentors or just with his sister and he doesn't want to wake her. We have a spirited debate about what song is better—*Mony Mony* by Billy Idol or *We Didn't Start the Fire* by Billy Joel. Jay favours the latter but I can't fault him. It's a great song. His justification is better lyrics and I can't argue. I sing the first verse, very badly, and he laughs.

I think I'm in love.

Dammit.

6

Sunshine beams through angled skylights onto shelves of books, the carpet the same navy blue as the rafters, the walls white. I inhale the scent peculiar to all libraries—the smell of pages and adventure—and stack the last pile of books in the romance section.

The Vanatori aren't poor but we're not Drakul-level wealthy so some of us need to work part-time. The library is peaceful with its rows of books and air of reverence, sharing a building with a museum and art gallery on Peebles' High Street. If the weather is nice, I take my lunch in a quiet courtyard next to a war memorial with archways and a bronze cupola flanked by beds of yellow tulips. If the weather sucks, which it often does, I'll wander the museum and eat my sandwich while examining the plasterwork friezes.

It's nice to do something normal.

I wheel my cart back to the desk, glancing around to confirm no member of the public has slipped in to peruse the books, and dial Sofia's number on my phone. My mobile, not Jay's burner phone. It sits snug in my pocket, set on vibrate. I resisted texting him this morning after our call last night. Too eager. I need to wait for him to reach out.

"*Hola,* honey," Sofia says. "Killed any more dragons lately?"

I smile and sit on the chair behind the desk. "Still just the one. I actually need a favour."

"Do tell."

"If I send you a couple of photos, could you find out who the person is and if they have any ties to the Drakul?" I fiddle with a pen on the desk. "I'd do it but you know the databases better than me."

"Of course, honey. Do you want me to pass the photos to Rick as well? He may get more details from his informants."

"No," I say a little too quickly. "Not Rick, um, not yet."

Sofia chuckles. "You do not want Nate to know? Are you vetting a potential lover?"

"He's not a lover," I wheeze.

Anything that goes through Rick inevitably reaches Nate and Nate has the unfortunate notion that he and I should be in a relationship. He's a great leader but not boyfriend material, not for me, anyway—too intense and controlling. And he's a grumpy bastard.

"Please, send me the photos," Sofia says. "I am intrigued."

"Hold on."

I take the phone away from my ear and navigate to my email, attaching the two pictures I snapped of Jay at the arcade. The message vanishes into my sent items. Part of me wants to snatch it back and keep Jay to myself.

"Got it," Sofia says, her voice muffled. She whistles. "Where did you meet this fine male specimen? He is *bonito*, honey."

I duck my head, though I'm alone. "He came into the library. We chatted about books. He asked me out."

Another blip of guilt. Sofia is my best friend. She won't go tattling to Nate about Jay so why am I lying to her? Maybe because what I'm doing with him, what I want to do to him, is wrong. I'm worried she'll be disappointed in me. Once I have more information, I'll tell her then the others. She'll understand the secrecy.

"One background check, coming up," she says. "After Mikala, we can never be too careful."

Not that a background check would have helped us or Mikala. We knew exactly who the monster was—a Lesser with an important position for a powerful Drakul, pretending to be on our side. An informant. Rick almost salivated. All our other informants are the lower class of Lesser—servants and slaves too afraid to do what's necessary to get decent intel.

And Jay? He got me the name Lukas Romanov. Is he pretending, too? He's not being entirely truthful, that's for sure, but is it for my benefit or his?

"Are you training with Fabian tonight?" Sofia says.

I slump in the chair and spin myself from side to side with my toes on the floor. "You know I am. George doesn't train me anymore."

"Sorry, honey, but I never tire of hearing the story."

The door beside me slides open and I sit up straight in my seat, cupping my hand over the phone. The woman barely registers my nod and heads straight for the horror section.

"Got to go," I whisper to Sofia.

"Wait to hear from me before you set a date with your hunk of male perfection," she says, "but then I want every filthy detail."

"Okay," I squeak and hang up on her throaty laugh.

The rest of my shift passes quickly. Being a librarian, it's not frowned upon if I'm caught reading when it's quiet or while I wait for people to select their books. I finish five chapters of my latest grimdark novel about a woman who's kidnapped and sold into slavery before I collect my bag from the staff room and lock up.

Outside, the evening is warm and pleasant. I leave the busy High Street opposite the church and head towards the River Tweed, turning onto a leafy residential road ending in Gytes Leisure Centre. I show my membership card to the man at the reception desk and change into leggings and a t-shirt, leaving my bag in a locker. Fabian is waiting for me in a room at the rear, the floor covered in thick padding, the walls mirrored.

"Hi Fabian," I say, kicking my shoes off near the door.

He nods his bald head in greeting, dressed in a black gi that makes his albino skin ghostly. He tosses me a wooden sword. My fingers curl around the familiar grip, worn smooth.

In the seven years I've known him, I've heard his voice twice. It's deep, a little nasally, but perfectly fine, he just chooses not to talk. When he does, you know it's important. I suspect it's spillover from his traumatic childhood. His genetic conditions attracted a lot of bullies but his family were also doomsday preppers on a Kansas farm. Unfortunately, they hadn't been prepared for a dragon apocalypse.

Fabian gestures with his sword. I widen my stance and he attacks, the loud clack of wood on wood echoing in the small room. The blow shivers down my arms. He tests my guards one by one, searching for a weakness. Our bare feet slap and squeak on the mats. I parry and block and lunge, Fabian deflecting my attacks. He catches my bicep, my ribs.

One thing for having a mute sword trainer—you learn fast to avoid the bruises.

He sweeps my legs. I slam my arms down to absorb the shock of hitting the mat. Fabian's blade whirls towards my face and my sword stops it with a loud *thwack*. I slash and roll, regaining my feet. After an hour, my breathing is ragged, my thigh and hip throb, but Fabian smiles at me, sweat beaded on his head and slicking his cheeks.

I've worked hard for those smiles.

I bow over the sword and toss it back to him. He snatches it from the air and it disappears into a cylindrical carry case.

"See you next time," I say.

He tips me a salute and I head for the changing room.

Everyone but me also gets a gun session once a week, led by George, our specialist, which is funny since he's a proper Scot from the Highlands. He developed his fascination with guns during his Vanatori training in America. He tried to teach me. I missed all the targets but hit him in the arm even though he was standing beside me. It was the shoulder the next time. I was banned from guns after that, for everyone's safety.

I check my phone. Jay's burner phone. No notifications. Disappointment swoops in my gut. I could send him a casual 'hi, how are you?' or a 'what did you do today?' or the bit more desperate 'call me!'

Rick rarely meets his informants in the flesh. Too risky. All their communication occurs via phone or encrypted email. Maybe this is why I'm little more than a glorified admin. I'm not the master of anything.

God, I hope Jay gets back to me with something good.

And soon.

Jay calls me three days after our late-night conversation. I shiver at the sexy rumble of his voice, though thankfully he can't see.

"Hey," I say, the word high and eager and damned embarrassing, "how are you doing?"

"I have something for you."

His words are hushed, as if someone might be listening. I stop myself from asking if he's all right, if he's safe.

The emotions he triggers in me are somewhat confusing. Half the time I want to mother him and the other half wants to do things that are definitely not motherly.

Who am I kidding? It's way more than half.

"There's a food shipment coming to the port at Dunbar," he says. "Do you know it?"

Dunbar—where Sofia patrolled five days ago and right down the coast from Tantallon Castle.

I jerk upright on the couch, my hand tightening on the mobile. "I know it. When?"

"Tonight—midnight. Sorry for the short notice."

"Don't be ridiculous. This is great news. Who's it for?"

A pause. "Several families, I think."

"Just how many families are in Scotland?"

"More than you want to know," he says softly.

How much is he risking to get this information? The thought of him suffering bubbles bile into my throat. "How can I pay you back?"

"You don't need to."

"I want to. Please. Name it."

Sexual favours. Ask me for sexual favours.

"Could you…?" He clears his throat. "Could you teach me how to fight?"

"Really? You saw me—I killed a dragon and threw up."

He chuckles and it warms me to my toes. I flop onto the couch.

"Not a shining example but I figure you know how to defend yourself."

I'm no slouch at hand-to-hand combat, true.

"Okay," I say. "I can teach you. Can you get away tomorrow night?"

"I think so."

"Meet me at Gytes Leisure Centre in Peebles at eight pm."

It's only a ten-minute walk from my house. I tell myself it's a test to see how mobile he is. Peebles is over an hour from Tantallon. If he has a car, that's nothing. If he doesn't, maybe he'll want to meet closer and I can start to triangulate where the hell he's coming from. And, since it's not far, I could invite him back to mine for a nightcap.

It's traditional to drink hot chocolate naked, right?

I rap my fist against my forehead.

Man, I have it bad. Teaching him self-defence will be interesting. Lots of touching and grappling. Maybe we'll fall and he'll accidentally land on top of me, his face inches away, his hands pinning mine to the mat, his—

"Raine?"

"Hmm?" I quietly swallow the saliva pooling in my mouth.

"Be careful. Don't try to follow the shipment. Lessers will have it for the first leg but then they'll switch with dragons. If they suspect a tail, they'll kill you. They'll also have guns."

Drakul with guns! How is that fair?

"We won't follow." I wait a beat, aiming for cool. "You be careful, too."

"I'm always careful. It doesn't make much difference."

Oh, damn, I want to hug him again. Maybe he'd feel better. I know I would. And maybe our clothes will magically vanish.

A girl can hope.

* * *

I call an emergency meeting at the club, aka Titan Group Headquarters. The converted office building sits in a run-down industrial estate bordered by garages and a biscuit factory on the outskirts of Edinburgh, an hour's drive from Peebles. The air smells like custard creams when I slide out of my car. I inhale deeply and enter the club through a reinforced door laced with dragon's-bane. The whole building is fireproof, the windows tinted and protected by rolling shutters if we need extra security. We even have a holding cell in the basement.

George was in charge of locating and refurbishing suitable headquarters once we were reassigned to Scotland. He was so confident that the Drakul were here, he had the cell built special to capture a weaker dragon and interrogate it for information on more powerful families. It hasn't quite worked out yet after we learned the full extent of our 'mourning and recuperation' period so the room stores emergency provisions.

Fabian was in charge of that.

I'm the last to arrive from our merry band of seven. Sofia waves at me from the couch in the communal area and pats the empty seat beside her. "I know this is going to be good when you call a meeting, honey. Look, I did not wait to get my nails done."

She wiggles inch-long talons at me, one half slicked in red, the other bare. I plop onto the sofa, shifting to get a more comfortable angle for my spine sheath. My shoulder bag clanks at my feet, the large can of dragon's-bane spray tangoing with my handcuffs.

Sofia's background check on Jay turned up nothing—no facial matches, no flags, though it was a long shot with only half a name and a couple of blurry photos. He remains as mysterious as when I met him on the cliff at Tantallon, except for his taste in books and music. I confessed to Sofia that he's an informant, though I let her believe I still met him in the library.

Maybe one day I'll tell her the truth. We'll see how it pans out.

"Christ, don't leave us in suspense," Dustan says, sprawled in the chair opposite Sofia, his baggy jeans paired with an even baggier hoodie. "You said you had news."

A grin creeps onto my face. "There's a food shipment coming to Dunbar tonight."

"Fucking belter!" George leaps from his stool at the homemade bar. "There's more of those fuckers if they have to order in to eat."

Ask an American tourist to draw a picture of a typical

Scotsman and I have no doubt the image would look like George—ginger hair merging with a ginger beard, sparkling blue eyes, broad shoulders. Put him in a kilt and he wouldn't look out of place tossing a caber.

"How do you know this?"

Nate's voice comes from a sagging armchair in the corner. George stops dancing around at the commanding tone and looks at me expectantly. The silence builds.

"I have an informant," I say, giving him my serious professional face.

Nate leans forward, wearing his typical black. "What's their name? How did you meet?"

"I'd prefer to keep that to myself for now."

His small, pinched mouth gets smaller. "This is not your area of expertise. How do we know the information is reliable?"

"It's reliable. My informant passed on other intel and I have no reason to doubt it."

"What intel?"

I run my eyes over the rest of the group ranged around the room. Fabian sits at the bar beside George and gives me an encouraging nod.

"The name of the dragon I killed," I say.

Nate cocks an eyebrow. My grin sneaks out again despite my best efforts.

Once I got over the initial shock of the identity, and the terror of possible ramifications, I realised it was pretty fricking awesome.

I lick my lips. "It was Lukas Romanov."

The room dissolves into uproar and the bedlam lasts a solid ten minutes. Sofia punches my arm and it immediately goes numb. George yells, "Fucking belter!" and crows about being right. Fabian and Dustan crowd around to slap me on the shoulder and I fear my arms will be black and blue by tomorrow. Rick materialises in front of me though he's been there all along, bland and forgettable in brown.

It's funny since he's originally from Los Angeles. He must have stuck out in the City of Angels—a plain man in a plain suit. His brother was the flamboyant actor—he was hired for an independent movie but it turned out to be a snuff film by a bunch of Lessers and Drakul. His final act was not pretty when played out on the big screen.

"I knew the death was something big," Rick says, wagging his finger at me. "There's been shockwaves rumbling but nothing specific."

Rick's informants are so terrified of their masters, their information isn't particularly relevant or up to date. Every now and again, we get a decent hit, so he perseveres. But none of them are based in Scotland.

"Just because this information is reliable doesn't mean your informant isn't dangerous," Nate says, sobering the room.

"He's not dangerous."

Nate frowns. "Your contact is a guy?"

Whoops. So much for being secretive.

"Yes, he happens to be male. Why is that important?"

"Are you fucking him?"

"Nate!" Sofia snaps.

I will myself not to blush. "Is that what you ask when Rick gets a new informant?"

"Answer the question, Raine," Nate growls.

I cross my arms. "I am not having sex with him."

The *yet* hangs in the air, unspoken. It's none of Nate's damn business. So what if I've thought about it every day since I met Jay? There's nothing wrong with a little fantasy.

"Pass his details to Rick," Nate says. "He'll take it from here."

"No!" I swallow and, in a calmer voice, say, "No. It's early days and he's nervous. He's not going to trust anyone else right now. We can't afford to scare off the only asset we have in this country."

Nate stands to glower down at me. "Again—not your area of expertise."

"It's okay, Raine," Rick says, his paternal smile a little grating. "I'm used to informants being nervous. I'll take good care of him."

I keep my gaze on Nate, my fingers gripping my knees. "So I'm really just a glorified driver and receptionist? You promised to help me find the monsters that murdered my parents. You *promised,* Nate. I've had the same training as everyone here."

"Except with guns," George says with a wink, "which is why *we're* still here."

His attempt to lighten the tension dissolves under Nate's scowl.

"Your handicap with guns is detrimental on a hunt, Raine," Nate says. "We use the skills we have to work as a team."

I jump to my feet, a coffee table between me and Nate keeping us from being nose to nose.

"I killed Lukas Romanov with a freaking *sword,*" I say.

"You got lucky."

"She is excellent with a blade."

Fabian's quiet voice stops the retort on my lips. We all stare at him for a beat. He draws a pattern on the bar with his finger and refuses to meet our gaze.

Nate shakes his head. "Nevertheless, that's not what we're discussing here. Rick is the master of informants—give him your informant."

"We don't have time for this." I lower myself back onto the couch, leaving Nate to loom. "The food shipment arrives at midnight. We only have a few hours to scout and plan."

"*We* are not doing anything. I'll pass the information to Principal Cozma."

"Oh, come on, Boss," George says, his beard bristling in consternation. "We're the only group in this country. No one else is close enough."

"The Cyhyraeth Group are in Wales."

"Fuckin' hours away! They can't mobilise in time."

"Our orders are to gather intel. No hunting."

"It's a rescue, Nate," I say, "not a hunt."

George nods vigorously and Nate sighs.

"I'll still have to ask—"

George slaps him on the shoulder. "Better to ask for forgiveness than permission, Boss. Fucking quicker, too."

Nate pinches the bridge of his nose. A grin splits George's face. Dustan bounces onto the balls of his feet and his jeans slip half-way down his butt. Even Rick, Nate's yes-man, looks excited.

"Fine," Nate barks. "Let's get to work."

The others cheer and scuttle for their laptops. I take a step to follow Sofia. Nate says my name in a low and serious voice. My shoulders hunch but I turn to face him. His dark eyes drill into me.

"You and I will be having a talk later," he says.

8

Water ripples against barnacle-encrusted pillars, the air heavy with salt and diesel fumes. Bright halogens light our target dock, the rest silent and dark. Creepy as hell. I hunker deeper into the shadows cast by a metal container, a telescopic cosh gripped in my fist. One flick and I'm ready to bash heads.

We didn't have much time to plan bar a quick scout earlier to scope out hiding places. Sofia and Dustan are sitting in a van in a lay-by near the entrance. Lift home or rescue vehicle, should the rest of us get into trouble. It took a bit of arguing with Nate to avoid me being Sofia's number two in the van.

My information, my operation.

A small container ship chugs into the dock and drifts to a stop. The ramp lowers, clanging on concrete. Headlights sweep across the latticework of cranes from the direction of the road. A flatbed truck reverses up to the ramp and stops, two men in black bomber jackets jumping out to hurry to the rear.

I dart closer through the maze of containers, flattening myself against the last one, a short strip of concrete separating me from the truck. My fingers touch each item on my belt for luck: spray can, stun gun, cuffs, knife.

A swarthy guy ambles from the ship and has a low conversation with the two men. Money changes hands. A crane moves into position, chains scraping on metal. A container swings from the ship onto the bed of the truck and the suspension groans. The two bomber-jacket men secure the container, working quickly. A different container is swung from the dock onto the ship and the boat chugs away, swallowed by the night.

Smooth.

The bomber-jacket men walk towards the cab of the truck.

"Engaging," I whisper into my palm, glad my balaclava has a mouth hole so I don't have to put up with damp material sticking to my face.

"Let George do the manhandling," comes Nate's terse response.

I roll my eyes. "I'm closer. On me, George."

"Got your fucking back, Raine," George says in an eager whisper.

The first man reaches for the door handle. I sprint towards him, my heartbeat loud in my ears. He turns, likely hearing my rapid panting or the slap of my boots. His shorn hair emphasises a scar bisecting his eyebrow. His fist aims for my jaw. I duck and ram the cosh into his stomach. It's like hitting concrete. My hand numbs and the stick slips from my fingers but the man drops and curls into a ball.

His eyes fix on me. "Cunt."

"Such language," I tsk.

His partner gallops around the cab, the beak of his nose preceding him by a couple of seconds.

"Do ye have any idea who you're messing with, chickie?" he growls.

George wraps him in a bear hug and the man's feet kick

air. His round face turns purple. I press my stun gun into his abdomen, well below George's restraining arms. The man thrashes and catches George in the shin, loosening his grip. The man's nose almost takes my eye out as he flops towards me. His hands claw at my jacket. Material rips. My wallet flies from the inside pocket and bounces on the concrete, scattering cards and coins. The man blinks at me before his eyes roll back and he goes limp. I dose the wheezing guy with the stun gun until he quiets down. Nate, Fabian and Rick converge on the truck while I scrabble for my wallet and its lost contents.

George holds his hand up. "Good job, *chickie*."

I grin and slap him a high five.

"I'll drive the truck," Nate says, shoving his balaclava up.

"No way," I say. "I'm driving the truck. Isn't that all I'm good for?"

"Shotgun," George says.

Nate frowns. He's a big frowner, is Nate.

I slip on my gloves, roll my balaclava to my forehead and disengage the huge bolt on the rear of the container, carefully swinging the door open. The halogens illuminate thirty pale faces, their bodies huddled together. The hot stench rolling out makes my eyes water but I force myself not to recoil.

If I were trapped in a container for days, I wouldn't smell so great, either.

"Does anyone speak English?" I say.

Eyes shine in the light, darting from person to person. A wiry man with a drooping moustache cautiously raises his hand.

"We're taking you somewhere safe. You're not going to be hurt but you have to stay in here a little longer. Can you tell the others?"

He nods rapidly. I smile and hand him my torch, rubbed clean of prints. He accepts it and touches it to his forehead, bobbing at me. I still feel guilty closing the door, the murmur of his voice cut off. George and I hop into the cab, George's gloves a size too small. I adjust the seat and wind the window down, yanking my balaclava into place.

I salute Nate. "See you at the pick-up point, *El Capitan.*"

He crosses his arms, a scowl on his face.

He really needs to lighten up.

The big diesel engine roars. A carved jade dragon dangles from the roof. I rip it off and toss it out the window then shove the truck into gear and release the handbrake. The vehicle judders.

Don't stall, for the love of god. It'll ruin my badass image.

I ease the truck away from the dock, the big beast lumbering up an incline onto the road. My knuckles are white through the gloves. I take the corner slow and breathe easier when the route straightens. No lights follow us in the mirrors. My muscles relax. George's whoop shatters the hushed interior of the cab and I jump in my seat.

"That was fucking brilliant!" His white teeth split the blackness of his balaclava. "Those Lesser fucks had no idea what hit them."

They'll be twitching to their feet about now, groggy and confused. We tend not to kill Lessers if we can avoid it. The Drakul have a stronger connection with their Lessers so they can tell when and where they die. Something to do with the bite. I guess it keeps track of the help. Lessers also don't burn into a tidy pile of ash after death like their masters. The bodies are harder to explain, especially if they're a little singed due to the dragon part of their metabolism going haywire when their hearts stop.

We reach the nearest police station after thirty minutes of uneventful driving, my passengers all well-behaved and quiet. Even George. I angle the truck into the car park, leaving the key in the ignition and scuttling to the rear. I open the container and flap my hand. My balaclava causes a bit of a stir but there's nothing I can do about that.

It's too complicated to answer any questions the police may have. Better they assume the human trafficking is for prostitutes and slave labour rather than the monthly meat shop.

"Everyone into the police station," I say, hoping my smile lessens the threat of the balaclava.

Bodies shuffle towards the door in a line of ragged, stoop-shouldered people. George and I bolt before they reach the entrance, keeping the truck between us and the police station as much as possible to minimise our time on CCTV. Several streets away, we slow to an easy jog. Residential houses, shuttered and dark, change to businesses then fields. We slip into the van parked in a gateway. Sofia starts the engine and pulls out. I slump onto the bench seat in the back, tug off the balaclava and shut my eyes, the happy babble swirling around me.

There's usually a shotgun clipped under every seat, just in case, though not tonight. If we were spotted, it'd be hard to convince the police we were out grouse shooting in the middle of Dunbar harbour.

I'd love it if the others could run around with bazookas and assault rifles like the Vanatori in other countries. Unfortunately, Scotland has a pesky gun control policy. It's probably why the Drakul are here. That, and the remote Scottish moorlands.

The van engine shuts off and I jerk awake in the garage attached to the club, the door rumbling closed, the fluorescents pinging on. Everyone tumbles out and heads straight for the bar.

Sofia links her arm in mine. "A job well done, honey."

"Don't you get bored driving the van?"

She shakes her head, her hoop earrings swinging. "All that running around looks exhausting and I have the most important job—getaway driver."

George lines up shot glasses on the bar and splashes them full of rum. We take one and toast our general awesomeness. I sip mine while the others knock theirs back, coughing and spluttering like the tough Vanatori we are. I slide my almost full glass to Sofia and she slurps it down.

She can hold her liquor. I get tipsy on half a glass of wine then float around with a soppy smile on my face.

Conversations flow around me. I respond to Sofia but my mind is on the phone in my pocket, hard against my thigh.

I want to call Jay, hear his voice, tell him everything that happened. I'm meeting him tomorrow but it seems ages away.

Nate plonks himself on the stool next to me, his elbows on the rum-soaked bar. He tips his glass and drinks the liquid down. No change in expression. Macho.

"Tell me about this informant who knows the name Lukas Romanov and where the Drakul get their meat shipments," he says.

I swipe my fingertip through a rum puddle. "His sister is being held hostage as a Lesser. Sounds like she might be with a powerful family, maybe even the Romanovs."

"Have you spoken to her?"

"No."

"Have you verified anything he's said?"

I shift on the stool. "Rick agreed the shock in Drakul society could be attributed to a death as big as Lukas Romanov's."

"Which is why Rick is best placed to handle your informant," Nate says almost gently. "Rick is skilled at infiltration. Don't let pride make you foolish. We can't afford any more mistakes."

"This isn't a mistake. Look at the intel he's got us already."

"And what does he want for it?"

"Nothing."

Nate scoffs. "They all want something—money, protection, a new life."

"He won't even let me help his sister. He's scared. He…just wants to feel like he's fighting back."

"Or she doesn't exist and he's setting you up," Nate says.

I open my mouth. Close it. Frown at the bar. Sofia sips her drink, perched on a stool on my other side. I rub my face and shove to my feet.

"My informant may be cagey but he's not setting me up. My gut tells me he's not dangerous."

Nate spins on his stool. "You're not experienced enough to make that call. Pass him to Rick then you don't have to worry about it anymore."

"Look Nate, I'm beat and have an hour's drive ahead of me. I'm going home."

"Don't be naive, Raine," he says, his eyes hot. "And don't be another Mikala."

Sofia walks me to the door, Nate's disapproval burning a hole in my spine.

"You are going to call him, yes—your contact?" Sofia says.

I casually pat my pockets for my keys. "Only to let him know how it went."

"Uh huh." She wiggles her perfectly plucked brows at me. "I think you want more from him than information. Like maybe a real close look at what he has in his pants."

I giggle and it sounds hysterical. "It's a platonic handler-informant relationship. You heard Nate."

"I trust your instincts, honey. Be careful and be sure but do what you think is right."

The right thing would be to keep Jay at arm's length. Use his information for as long as it lasts. It would be more professional than fantasising about undressing him. Slowly. Using my teeth. I bet he won't look sad if I sit on his face.

Jesus Christ.

9

"'Lo?" Jay's voice is muffled and thick with sleep.

The thought of him lying in tangled sheets, his hair tousled, his different-coloured eyes half-lidded, jolts my pulse into orbit somewhere around Jupiter. Maybe he sleeps without a top on. Or naked…

I speak in a rush. "Sorry. I woke you up."

Well, duh, genius. It's three in the morning.

I shake my head and stare at my bedroom ceiling in the darkness. The soft glow of a streetlight halos my curtains.

"It's okay," he says. "Did everything go all right?"

Cloth rustles. A strangely sensual sound.

"Perfectly," I say. "Thirty poor souls rescued from being dragon fodder, thanks to you."

Ooh, *fodder*. Look how smart you are.

I tell myself to shut up.

"Don't thank me," Jay says.

"Of course I will. We wouldn't have known if it wasn't for you."

I listen to him breathe. The silence itches my spine. Nate's questions burrow a tunnel of doubt into my brain.

"Is your sister there?" I say as casually as I can.

"She's sleeping."

"Can I talk to her?"

A pause. Covers shift. I grip the phone harder.

"I don't want to wake her," Jay says. "She doesn't get much rest."

"Can I talk to her later?"

"I'll ask." He sighs. "She finds it hard to trust people."

"What about your mum and dad?"

He hasn't mentioned them before. Is he an orphan, like me? Is that how he and his sister were taken in the first place— the Drakul murdered their parents and kept their children as slaves? My stomach swoops. Jay must be a Lesser. Why would they make his sister one and not him? It's a perfect way to keep them isolated from normal, human society.

"They got me into this mess," Jay says flatly.

His answers only lead to more questions—did they sell their own children to the Drakul or did they try to exploit a family and this is their punishment? Maybe his parents are Lessers, too, but content to work as goons or servants.

"I can help you, Jay," I whisper. "You don't have to stay there."

"Believe me, I wish you could, Raine," he says, the longing clear in his voice, "but it's too dangerous. They have spies everywhere."

"Or that's what they want you to think to keep you in line."

He chuckles, though it's a humourless sound. "It's true. I found that out the hard way."

My heart thumps hard. He sounds resigned. Wretched. No one can fake that.

"Do they hurt you?" I say.

Silence. My heart stops. I want to rip out my tongue but the damn thing is too slippery.

"How risky is this, Jay—passing information to me?"

He stays quiet and I curse myself. What a stupid question. Of course it's risky—life and death risky. Being an informant isn't a long-term career. Anyone caught tattling on the Drakul is liable to end up a tasty snack, swallowed whole after hours of torture. No body, no evidence. The thought of Jay broken and bloody and gone in a snap of teeth twists my gut in a cold fist. I open my mouth to tell him to stop then bite my lip and mirror his silence.

Maybe Nate was right—I am naive. I can't separate my emotions and view Jay as only a valuable asset. He's more than that. I want him to be more than that. But what if he's a Lesser?

God, I really don't know what I'm doing.

Jay wants to do this—he offered. If I get him to trust me, maybe he'll let me protect him. And his sister. Mustn't forget the sister.

"I'm sorry," I say into his silence.

At least he hasn't hung up on me. Time to move the conversation to neutral territory.

"Where are you?"

Brilliant, Raine—stupid question number two. Where do you think he is at this time of the freaking morning?

"In my bedroom," he says.

"What's it like?"

I slap my forehead. *What's his bedroom like?!* Hello, stupid question number three.

"Basic," he says. "The nicest thing is the bed. It's an ancient four-poster of black wood. Ebony, I think."

Does he mention the bed so I'll picture him in it? I'm way ahead of that—I'm picturing *me* in it.

"What else?" My voice tremors and I hope he doesn't notice.

"My clothes in cardboard boxes. A bean bag." His laugh is bitter. "Why waste furniture on me?"

I scramble for something different to talk about instead of offering to save him. Again. No other subjects exist in the known universe.

"Did you"—I clear my throat—"did you finish your book?"

He replies and I sag into my pillows. I listen, respond, laugh but can't stop thinking *they hurt him, the bastards*. Semi-prisoner, forced to sneak out for some peace. His sister held hostage and probably abused, too. Or maybe there's something else going on.

I should keep my distance. It would be stupid to get too involved. I'm too involved already and I've known him less than a week. His complicated situation is bad enough, not to mention the question of whether he's human or not. Better to keep it to the platonic handler-informant relationship like I told Sofia. I'll teach him how to defend himself but then all future contact will be over the phone. I'll gain his trust and pass him to Rick as soon as possible.

Safer that way.

10

Gytes Leisure Centre sits surrounded by playing fields, trees and an allotment to the north of the River Tweed. It's a low, multi-levelled building with red bricks and a green-trimmed roof. The membership is expensive but the facilities are excellent. I come at least three times a week, including Fabian's blade-training session. The front doors whoosh open as I approach, the reception area bright and clean and containing the faint, sharp scent of wintergreen. A woman wearing a blue polo-shirt smiles at me from behind the desk, her ginger hair in a ponytail. I loop my holdall over my shoulder and rifle through my wallet for my membership card, everything out of order since the Dunbar mission. A second search confirms the sinking feeling in my gut.

The card is missing.

"Don't worry," the receptionist says, smiling at my no doubt panicked expression, "I can find you on the computer. What's your postcode?"

I mumble something that must be right as she waves me through with a cheery, "If your card is lost, let us know and we can print a new one."

My feet drift towards the private rooms at the rear.

I must have left my membership card at the harbour after

the thug tore my jacket. It doesn't have my address but it does have a smiling photo of me and the contact details of the leisure centre. What if the Lessers found it? Have they staked out Gytes, hoping to catch me? No—they would've jumped me before I entered rather than wait. Maybe they didn't notice the card. It's probably in the sea by now or caught in the grass beyond the containers. The thugs would've been more intent on contacting their masters than examining a tiny rectangle of card sliding along the concrete.

It's fine. A careless mistake that Nate never has to hear about.

I scan both ways along the empty corridor then enter the private room where I trained with Fabian. My bag thuds on the padded floor, my change of clothes weighted down by my sword and a canister of dragon's-bane.

I'm early. And nervous, the lingering anxiety from my missing membership card not helping. Restless energy jiggles my arms and zips to my fingers.

I pace, watching myself in the mirrored walls. My legs are a blur beneath my red shorts and black tank top, my hair scraped into a high ponytail.

Maybe I'm showing too much skin. Maybe Jay will like it.

Platonic thoughts. Must only think platonic thoughts.

It doesn't matter what Jay likes, not that he's given me much indication of his feelings while I blush and babble over him. He made that comment on the rain and said he had fun at the arcade. Hardly a declaration of love. Or lust.

Which is a good thing, I tell myself firmly.

There's a hesitant knock on the door, not quite as loud as my knees banging together. I stumble over and open it to Jay. He's wearing a green t-shirt, the sleeves ripped off, and black tracksuit bottoms, a holdall slung over his back. The curve of his bare shoulder and the dip of his bicep distract me for a moment.

I forget what platonic means.

He sets his bag next to mine. "Promise you won't hurt me too much?"

I lick my lips, my mouth dry. "I promise."

We warm up, stretching our core muscle groups. Classical music plays softly in the background, a mixture of strings and piano—my choice. I peek at Jay every time he bends over.

Man, that butt.

I start to forget the missing membership card.

I take Jay through a vigorous circuit session—push ups, squats, sit ups, burpees, plank. I plan on working him hard so he can defend himself against the people who have his sister. We finish the circuits panting and dewed in sweat. Or I'm dewed in sweat. Jay just glows.

"You're fit," I say, smothering some of the awe.

He shrugs. "I jog."

I can tell—slim build, muscled but not heavy. Long limbs.

"Good. A fight may only last a few minutes but defending yourself is exhausting."

I spend the next hour going through basic combinations and the parts of the body to hit for a quick take-down. My skin sings whenever it touches his. The vanilla scent of him is subtle but hard to ignore.

Why does he have to smell so nice? Couldn't he smell like cigarettes or… sandalwood? I hate sandalwood. Smelling like vanilla doesn't help my desire to lick him.

We put on gloves and spar. I dance around him, aiming short punches at his head until he puts his guard up and copies me. He watches me intently, his gaze fixed on mine. I should tell him to focus nearer my chest as it's easier to detect movement but I stare at him instead.

His eyes are so pretty.

My guard droops. I catch his motion but the blow clips my ear and I sprawl on the mat, blinking at myself in the mirror.

"Oh, god, I'm sorry! Are you okay?"

He leans over me, his face distraught, and I sweep his legs. He hits the floor on his back with an, "Oof," while I jump to my feet.

"I know you won't do that in a real fight but never underestimate your opponent. Punch them in the throat and make damned sure they stay down." I stand over him and it takes all my willpower not to straddle his lap.

He narrows his eyes. "You tricked me."

"It's all in the learning process," I say.

His smirk dissolves half my brain cells. "You're a good teacher."

"Now I'll teach you how to fall properly, and how to get up when you're knocked down."

Okay, so maybe I'll straddle him a little. For training purposes.

* * *

We call it a night after another hour, especially since my drooling is really cramping our platonic relationship. We split up to shower in the side-by-side changing rooms further down the corridor. I try not to picture Jay naked and wet a mere span of brick away. Fail. We meet at the front door, the car park beyond almost empty. His damp hair flops into his eyes. He looks cute and innocent in a clean, white t-shirt and black jeans.

I don't invite him home for a nightcap.

Jay waves and cuts across the car park, avoiding the two lone vehicles. Maybe he parked a few streets away so I wouldn't see his car. Or maybe he got the bus.

I should follow him. Rick would follow him.

I scan the car park. No one else in sight. No thugs lingering beside an unmarked van. I skirt the playing fields, hop a wall and cross the main Innerleithen Road. The cool air soothes the heat and clears the lust from my brain. Some of it, anyway.

My dreams are going to be raunchy tonight. But that's all Jay and I can ever be—dreams and fantasy.

I enter a narrow road towards the Peebles Hydro Hotel. Trees replace the houses, arching above me and whispering their secrets in the dark. My shoes seem loud on the concrete. I pick up my pace. The night is thick with the scent of wild garlic. A footstep scrapes behind me. I glance over my shoulder. Three black shapes range across the leafy road between me and the main street, the shine of their eyes and teeth all I can see in the silhouette of a lone streetlight. I check in front of me but no one has blocked my exit so running is an option.

I'll defend myself against humans but it's harder. Needs more finesse. The authorities tend to ask questions if you leave a trail of sliced and diced bodies. Though the dread in my gut suspects these men aren't human.

A mocking laugh sends something scurrying in the under-growth. The men stalk closer. My hand tightens on my bag and I slowly open the zip. A white rectangle flashes between the fingers of the man in the middle.

"I like a woman who keeps herself trim," he says, "but your photo doesn't do ye justice, chickie."

Crap. Perhaps Nate *will* hear about my mistake, if I'm still breathing after this.

Two of the men are the ones we fought at Dunbar harbour. I'd recognise that scar and that nose anywhere. The other man has a suitable snarling expression for a filthy Lesser.

The Nose waves my membership card at me. "Not so tough without your big friend, are ye? Well, ye fucked with the wrong people, chickie."

"What do you want?" I say.

"I want ye to come with me all quiet-like. Maybe if ye treat me nice, I'll put in a good word for ye." The Nose grins. "Maybe ye won't suffer too long."

The goons crack their knuckles. I draw my sword from my bag and widen my stance.

"Put your blade away, chickie, before ye cut yourself. Or before I cut ye."

The Nose holds out his hand. The fingers lengthen, joints popping, the nails thickening to curved black talons. Golden scales slide over his skin, bright in the light over his shoulder.

A powerful dragon made him.

His buddies morph their hands into claws—silver and bronze. All powerful.

"Don't touch her," a voice growls.

Jay appears behind the men, his bag at his feet.

Where the hell did he come from? Was he following me?

The goons hiss and twist to keep us both in sight.

The Nose tilts his head, his brow furrowed. *"You're* going to stop us?"

Jay glances at me. The shadows hide his expression.

The Nose chuckles. "Oh, I can't wait—"

Jay tackles him in a blur of movement. Their tangled bodies disappear into the vegetation surrounding the road, leaves crunching, flesh thudding on dirt. The other Lessers pounce at me, their talons extended, forcing me to focus.

Please let Jay be all right.

I lob my bag at Scar-face and he gets tangled in the straps trying to bat it away. The third man lunges. I step to meet him and he stops abruptly, blinking at me. As one, our gazes drop to my sword skewering his chest. Dark liquid seeps into his shirt. I jerk backwards and he drops to his knees then collapses on his front.

Scar-face bares his teeth. "You'll pay for that as well, *Vanatori*."

Muffled cursing comes from the undergrowth. Bushes thrash and rustle. Scar-face reaches into his bomber jacket and pulls out a stubby cylinder that looks ridiculous in his taloned hand. One flick of his wrist extends the cosh. He swipes it in front of him and advances on me. Our weapons clash. We fight in silence but for the ring of metal and an occasional grunt of effort. I parry a jab. Scar-face stumbles. My blade slides easily between his ribs and he joins his partner on the ground, unmoving. Their hands change back to human.

Jay pops out of the greenery and floors the Nose with a hook, the smack of fist on flesh loud under the trees. I drag the two dead Lessers off the road, the Nose's body half-hidden in a clump of nettles, his neck at an awkward angle. Jay and I blink at each other for a heavy second of pounding hearts and panting breath. He wades clear of the vegetation.

"You're a fast learner," I say.

"Not fast enough." He grimaces, his fingers pressed to his side. "I think he tried to scoop out my liver."

Jay shifts his hand and I sway. Sparkly lights dance across my vision. Blood, black in the night, daubs Jay's fingers and seeps through his ripped t-shirt.

I've seen worse—insides on the outside, splintered bones, chewed meat. The light-headedness makes no sense.

I swallow hard and curl my hands into fists instead of rushing to his side and flapping at the wound. Definitely not professional. Or helpful.

"Come on," I say, a touch breathless, "I live nearby. And their masters will be heading for us."

There will be no report of a horrific slaughter in the papers tomorrow. The monsters will clean up the mess.

I scoop our bags, including my membership card this time, and lope down the path. Jay follows, uncomplaining.

Guess we'll have that nightcap after all.

11

Jay is in my house! Panic stations everyone!

It's a modest building set back from the others at the end of a narrow road and paid for by Vanatori legacies. A short, dirt driveway leads to a wooden gate that opens directly onto the street. Trees surround the house except for a small patch of grass bordering my covered porch. The woods extend up a hill to the top of Ven Law and beyond for about eight kilometres in the wider Glentress Forest. There are some nice walks, though much of the land is fenced off because of a quarry that collapsed into an undiscovered cave system a decade or so ago.

The neighbours still talk about it.

Inside my house, narrow uncarpeted stairs lead from the hall to the single bedroom and en-suite.

Jay ambles into the living room, his hand pressed to his side. He pauses at the bookshelf, bending to look in my fish tank on the cabinet next to it but he doesn't get far before he winces. I follow him through the dining room, past the sliding door onto the porch, and into my massive kitchen. Everything is stainless steel and gleaming.

Thank god I cleaned.

"You live here by yourself?" At my nod he quirks his mouth.

"Must be nice."

I bite my lip instead of asking him to move in. He eases onto a stool at the breakfast bar and I drag my huge first aid kit out from under the sink.

My voice manages not to wobble when I say, "Take off your shirt."

He does the guy thing of pulling it over his head in one smooth motion. I tried it once. Got tangled and couldn't find my way out.

I realise I'm frowning furiously at a cupboard door over his sleek, bare shoulder.

I've seen half-naked men before. Hell, I've seen fully naked men before. I can look at Jay and not act like a moron.

My eyes drop.

Oh boy.

Words like 'sculpted' and 'perfect' and *wow* flit through my brain. The vulnerable line of his collarbone and the hollow of his throat do crazy stuff to my pulse. Firm chest, flat stomach, that sexy V only men seem to get disappearing into his jeans, begging me to stroke it with a fingertip or, better yet, my tongue. Bet he'd forget about his injury if I—

"Raine?"

I jump and swallow a squeak. He seems unaware of my slavering adoration. No teasing smile or rubbing my face in how badly I want him. No signs of revulsion either, thank god. He sits completely still and watches me. Blood weeps from three puncture wounds below the delectable curve of his ribs.

Delectable? I give myself a mental slap.

No scars mar the intriguing lines of his chest or abs, the skin on his arms smooth and unblemished. Most Lessers are bitten on their shoulders, arms or legs. A few are marked on the torso with the imprint of teeth forming an arch across their ribs and back. Scars on the back only are unusual but I can't rule it out, though Jay probably wouldn't have been quite so happy to take off his t-shirt if he were marked that way.

So, really, I have to get him out of his trousers to be sure he's not a Lesser.

I take a few deep but quiet breaths and focus on his injury to keep from hyperventilating. The blood flow appears to be slowing but the punctures could be deep.

"You should go to the hospital," I say.

He shakes his head. "I'll heal. I've had worse."

But will he heal human-slow or as fast as a Drakul? Is he a Drakul? He can't be a Drakul.

I bite my lip again to contain the many questions bubbling in my throat. I don't want to spook him now he's half-naked and in my kitchen.

"How much worse?" Crap, one slipped out. I flap my hand. "Never mind. It's complicated, right?"

"Right."

His eyes darken when he's serious or sad or thinking a multitude of unreadable thoughts.

I concentrate on picking items from the first aid kit.

I'll patch him up and send him home. There's no need to mire myself in all his complications. He can protect himself. He's still alive, isn't he? He doesn't need me for that.

"Were you following me, Jay?" I say softly.

He ducks his head. "I didn't mean to. You must have taken a short cut. I reached the main road and you were walking into the other street. Those three men went after you. I wanted to make sure you were okay."

Sounds plausible, though I'm struggling to be objective when he has no t-shirt on.

I twist the cap off a plastic tube of sterile saline. "This is going to hurt but I need to clean the wounds. Who knows where those filthy claws have been."

At his nod, I hold a dishtowel against his lower belly and squeeze the solution into the punctures. Pink fluid swirls out to dampen the cloth. He doesn't flinch, appraising me with his amber and peridot and gold-flecked eyes. I stand between his slightly spread legs but tell myself I don't notice. He shifts on the stool, his elbows on the table edge, muscle sliding under skin.

Nope, don't notice that, either.

I use the whole pack of six tubes then pat the wound dry with gauze and smooth a dressing over.

It's all I can do. I don't have antibiotics, though he should definitely take some.

He tenses and sucks in a breath.

Damn, did I lean on his injury? What an idiot.

My gaze darts to my hand. My fingers have strayed from the dressing to stroke along his stomach.

Whoops.

God, he's warm and silky.

My fingers continue to explore the gentle swell and dip of his abdominals. They don't seem to hear my brain telling them this is a bad idea.

Jay shivers. "That tickles."

My willpower crumbles. I step into Jay, the stool adding another couple of inches to his height. My hand slides up his chest to his shoulder, my thumb in the hollow of his throat.

His pulse flutters like a trapped thing. He seems to have stopped breathing altogether. I melt in his vanilla-scented heat and wish he'd shut his eyes because they're making me dizzy. I tilt my head up. He's still not breathing while I'm practically panting in his face. On tippy-toe, I finally reach his mouth. My lips glide over his.

Maybe I have some willpower after all considering I want to climb his body and feast on his mouth. But I have no idea what he's feeling. Will he bolt or is he a raging storm of lusty hormones ready to slam me onto the table?

Maybe that's just me.

He kisses me back, slow and tentative. It weakens my knees, somehow worse than if he chose the slamming-me-onto-the-table option. At this rate, I'll puddle at his feet in about three seconds. My muscles have turned to noodles.

I guide him to the couch without breaking the kiss. He falls onto it and blinks up at me, his expression dazed. I straddle his lap, a smidgen of awareness left to avoid kneeing his injury. My mouth finds his—exploring, tasting, encouraged by his response.

Man, his lips were made by angels. Or maybe it's the devil's territory. No man should be able to kiss like this.

His tongue meets mine and electricity zips to my nerve endings, rebounding to sizzle in my stomach. My clothes brush hypersensitive skin. Every part of me throbs, heat pulsing off me. Jay strokes my hair, my back, his fingers hesitant. My hips tilt in invitation, my pants clinging to me, but his hands don't stray below my waist or anywhere near my breasts. The frustration heightens the arousal, the anticipation unbearably delicious. I rub myself against him and make small begging noises in my throat.

Jesus. It's been a tough few years. I love my Vanatori family but hunting monsters leaves little time for romantic entanglements, especially satisfying ones.

Jay rolls his hips and it pulls my mouth from his with a gasp. His lips are swollen, his face flushed. Beautiful.

Why am I not kissing him?

I lean in. His phone peals and we both jerk. He scrabbles for his pocket.

"Where are you hiding," the tiny speaker growls, "you little—"

Jay pushes the button and cuts the voice off mid-expletive. He swallows, his eyes darkening to the wariness he gets right before he tells me it's complicated.

"I have to go," he says.

Desolate words or I'm projecting.

The flush fades from his cheeks. I feel ridiculous straddling him. His phone bleats and he flinches. I climb off, find his t-shirt and see him to the door, all in a haze. He pauses after one step, the night cloaking his expression.

"You kissed me," he says.

"I did."

"Was it for a bet?"

"A bet?"

He watches me for a long beat, his head cocked.

"Do you want to kiss me again?"

Say something cool, alluring, mysterious.

I lick my lips. "God, yes."

Damn.

The flash of his smile—pure, sweet and unguarded— staggers me. I clutch the door frame. He's up the step in one bound, his mouth on mine, his hands pressed to my lower back, fingertips grazing the curve of my butt.

The desire, banked by the aggressive voice on the phone, roars to life. I may burst into flames. My charred carcass will be found the next day. Cause of death—spontaneous sexual combustion.

Jay disappears into the shadows between the trees, the warmth and scent of him lingering to torment me.

"Let me know you're safe!" I blurt.

Great, Raine. Way to show how desperate you are.

His voice drifts from the darkness. "I will."

12

"All we did was kiss but I've never felt more"—I glance around but there's only Sofia and me in my living room—"turned on."

"So he was good, then?" she chuckles.

I slump into the couch on a groan, almost spilling my tea in my lap. "He was amazing."

I told her the truth about how Jay and I met. My worries about his background. My angst at wanting to know who he is while also wanting to strip him naked and pin him to my bed. She was miffed I didn't tell her from the start but she understood—even the sex part. She's seen his photo, though he's a million times yummier in the flesh.

"Honey, it is about time you had a proper fling with a gorgeous stranger. You are a nun." She tucks her silky hair behind her ear, her hoop earring brushing the shoulder of her dress.

"That's not true," I say. "I've had flings. Some of them were okay-looking."

"Did any of them get your little panties sodden from one kiss?"

"Christ, Sofia."

"Well, did they?"

I slurp my tea and pout. "No."

75

"There you go, then." She grins and digs her elbow into my ribs. "Milk your contact for all he is worth."

Holy hell, sex with Jay. I'll faint as soon as he takes his clothes off. This level of arousal isn't healthy, especially knowing what he's mixed up in.

I peel my t-shirt away from where it's sticking to me and place my tea on the coffee table.

No more hot liquids. I'm burning up as it is.

"I can't," I say. "Nate already brought up Mikala. What if this turns out to be just like that?"

"Mikala was stubborn. And foolish. She probably ignored the warning signs just to spite Nate."

"*I'm* stubborn."

Sofia boops me on the nose. "You, *mi amiga,* are insightful, optimistic and trusting. And a little stubborn. Has the sexy Jay done anything to arouse your suspicions?"

"I've been too distracted by everything else he's aroused," I mutter, "but no—he's not aggressive or mean. He doesn't ask me about the Vanatori. He's secretive and I think it's because he's scared. But what if I'm wrong?"

"Do not be wrong—be sure. You said he had no Lesser scars on his chest." She wiggles her eyebrows. "What better excuse to get him naked? Then, if he is scar-free, you can burn him to test if he is Drakul."

"I don't want to hurt him," I huff. "He can't be a dragon. He's… sweet. He was surprised when I kissed him, like he had no idea I found him attractive. You should see how I act around him. It's embarrassing and definitely not professional."

"Then, out of professional curiosity, check his body for scars." Sofia smirks and sips her tea. "If he has none, take advantage when he is all naked and lovely."

"I shouldn't. His life is complicated. And he's my informant."

"So what? You are not getting married. It is sex—we all need it."

Butterflies clench my stomach and flutter outward. The damn things have been flapping around ever since I told Jay I wanted to kiss him again. The look on his face did something to me.

"I just want to see him smile," I say, and sigh. "He's so sad."

"Sweet Jesus, honey, you are supposed to lust after his body not fall in love with him."

"What? I'm not in love with him. That's ridiculous."

She cocks an eyebrow.

"It's only been a week!" My voice rises an octave. "I haven't even slept with him!"

"He must be special."

"Goddammit," I say, and cover my stupid face with a pillow. "I think he is."

* * *

Seven long, *long* days crawl by and there's no word from Jay, barring his brief call to let me know he's okay. I cancel my blade training with Fabian, blaming a stomach bug, in case the Lessers told someone about the Vanatori that goes to Gytes Leisure Centre. I hope they kept my details to themselves to impress their masters with the results rather than the methodology. Next week's session is another matter.

If Gytes is compromised then maybe Peebles is, too. I might have to tell Nate and get the others to monitor the leisure centre for unusual activity. Or he'll make me move house. But that's a problem for another day.

I bury myself in my normal job, which is difficult considering I work part-time in the library. Lots of quiet moments to think among the smell of books. And my thoughts are all of Jay. His smile, the proper one. The way he laughs out loud then seems surprised. The stunned expression when I kissed him. What he might look like completely naked and in my bed.

I've been having a lot of cold showers.

I can't sit still. I swing from worry to disappointment to worry again. Why hasn't he contacted me? What if he's hurt somewhere? How could I have fallen for him, let myself need him this badly?

What if he's dead?

A quick call or text might soothe my anxiety but I'm scared he won't respond. Maybe the Drakul caught him snooping. Maybe I'll never hear from him again.

I pace on the thick rug in my living room, sunlight streaming through the window and warming my bare feet. The burner phone is in my hand, my thumb hovering over the only number in it, as it has been for the past ten bazillion hours.

A tiny part of me is convinced he regrets our kiss and is avoiding me but I'm too proud and stubborn to ask, which brings me back to the worrying and the pacing and the praying for a message.

"You are a disgrace," I tell myself and fling the phone on the couch.

It rings. I dive for it, narrowly missing the edge of the coffee table. I jab the answer button and listen to him breathe. A wave of relief leaves me lightheaded.

"Raine?"

"Are you okay?"

"Yeah. Sorry I didn't call. Couldn't get any privacy."

He sounds genuine. Not flippant or like he's lying through his teeth but since I'm picturing him naked, I'm hardly at my sharpest.

"Can you get away now?" The words rush out before I can stop them.

What am I doing? He could've taken ten damn seconds this past week to let me know he'd not been eaten. He has to use the bathroom, doesn't he? I doubt people follow him in there.

"I think so," he says.

"I need to see you."

Oh, jeez. Lack of a sex life has scrambled my hormones.

I listen to him breathe some more.

"You do?" he says.

This can still be salvaged. Like Sofia said, I have to see him—*all* of him—to look for scars. And his wound. A human wouldn't have healed it that fast. I just need to phrase it right so he suspects no ulterior motives.

"Jay, I need you to come to my house and… fuck me. Right now."

Yup, that'll do it.

His breath catches. The noise swells heat between my legs and I squirm on the couch. I'm soaked and he hasn't even touched me. He started something the second he kissed me back and it's been building ever since, scorching me from the inside out.

Please, god, don't let him be a Lesser. I deserve at least one orgasm out of this.

"*Jay,*" I whine into his silence.
Wow. I've never heard my voice so desperate.
"I'll be there in thirty minutes," he says.
Oh, Christ.

13

Screw panic stations, I'm in full meltdown.

I can't believe I demanded Jay come over for sex. I should have been coquettish, playful. Get him begging to come round so I have the upper hand. He's probably in his car, slapping himself on the back.

Does he even own a car?

God, I suck at the seduction game. This is why I go for plain guys. I have all the power in those encounters.

I jump in the shower to quench the thoughts of a naked Jay in my house. The cold water goosepimples my skin but I still feel hot enough to sizzle. I open a new bottle of soap and furiously work it into a lather. Raspberry and vanilla. It's like Jay is wrapped around me.

I almost orgasm.

I dry my hair, run gel through to tame the curls and dress in lace, black underwear, shimmying into my only dress—a cheery yellow that suits my hair and hits mid-thigh. Sexy and easy access.

I put my head between my legs when I hyperventilate.

Why am I so nervous? This is ridiculous. He's just a guy. I'm not a virgin. We're two consenting adults. There's no reason for my heart to thrash against my ribs this way.

I leave my sword in its sheath and balance it on the grey fabric chair in my bedroom. It might ruin the mood if I answer the door armed. Jay is the one who'll be sticking something in me, anyway.

Oh, Jesus. Deep breaths, Raine, you're not going to faint.

This is a bad idea. What happened to platonic? I'm not like Sofia—I'm not confident and sultry. I'm more likely to embarrass myself by drooling then keel over when Jay takes off his trousers.

I consider running a cold bath. No time. I settle for ice cubes rubbed in strategic places. They instantly melt. Maybe I should sneak out the back and hot-foot it into the woods but I don't want to hurt Jay's feelings.

My whole body vibrates, some sixth sense attuned to his proximity. I yank the door open before he can ring the bell and there he is on my front step, every glorious inch of him. The sun highlights gold streaks in his hair and cuts shadows across his face. His navy, short-sleeved polo shirt has three white buttons open at the throat, the collar and hems light blue. His jeans sit low on his slim hips, a brown leather belt at his waist.

"You needed to see me?" he says.

I planned to act aloof, a little flirtatious, scope out his intentions and torture him a teensy bit for getting me so worried but his shy smile briefly stuns all brain function. When I can move again, I lunge for his hand and tug him inside. My skin tingles. I push him into the wall, my mouth on his, my fingers buried in his hair. I'm wild, aching, hot. I manage to break the kiss before I lose my composure completely. My pulse thuds on my tongue. Jay sags against the wall.

"Yes, Jay," I say, panting slightly, "I needed to see you."

His grin starts slow but is no less devastating. Real and unguarded. He reaches out—are his fingers shaking?—and brushes my cheekbone in a light, tickling caress. It takes all my dignity not to purr.

"It's Julian," he says. "J is for Julian."

"So secretive, Jay is for Julian." I roll his name in my mouth and like how it tastes.

He steps closer. "Say it again."

"Julian," I breathe, suddenly giddy.

His happy smile flares bright and I vow to say his name over and over if he'll keep smiling at me like that.

He lowers his head and kisses me. The tenderness cools the raw heat to a glorious burn. I take his hand and lead him upstairs, padding in my bare feet, his trainers almost silent. He stands in my bedroom, curious eyes taking it all in—the white painted wardrobe and thick, cream carpet, the grey silk bedspread and pillows. His gaze hesitates on the sword in the corner. Nerves and excitement battle in my stomach.

"I can't believe I'm going to see you naked." I slap a hand over my mouth. "I can't believe I said that."

Smooth, Raine. How did I ever think I was cool?

"I have to tell you something else," he says.

"Your middle name is J for Jesus?"

He laughs and, thankfully, it steals all of my air so I can shut up for a minute.

"No. I've, um, never done this before."

I blink at him. What is he talking about? He blushes and stares at his feet. My mouth drops open.

"Holy crap. Holy. *Crap*. How is that possible?"

He shrugs one shoulder. "I'm the ugly one."

How can he believe, for one second, he's unattractive? Are

there only blind women in his life? Are there *any* women in his life apart from his sister?

"You're not ugly, Jay—Julian. You're so gorgeous you scramble my brain. Which is why I'm babbling like an idiot. *Hell*." I huff and fist my hands in my hair.

"I can go," he says softly, frowning at his shoes.

"You're not going anywhere."

It comes out more growly than I intended and his head snaps up, his eyes wide. The startled look makes me want to chase and pin, and sink my teeth in him.

"Oh god, you're a virgin and all I want to do is throw myself at you and rip off your clothes."

"Well, I wouldn't say no." He gulps. "Just… don't hurt me too much."

I cup his face and my fingers trace the wonderful curve of his lips.

"I'm not going to hurt you at all," I say.

My mouth replaces my fingers. His arms circle my waist and hold tight.

Okay, I'll admit I'm a little disappointed. It won't be the spectacular sex I've fantasised about since it's unlikely to last longer than five minutes but we have the whole day ahead of us. I wouldn't mind testing his stamina. And I'm a pretty good teacher. Also on the plus side—he'll have no idea if the sex is rubbish since he has no frame of reference. It'll probably be amazing for him. I don't like to brag but I've had no complaints.

The power is back in my hands. His nervousness banishes mine. And it's adorable.

His hands slide down to my butt while I'm giving myself a mental high-five. The shock of the contact blooms heat in intimate areas and pulls a gasp from my mouth.

He jumps away. "I'm sorry! I didn't mean—"

"You can touch me anywhere you want." I capture his hands and place them back on my ass. "I plan to touch you everywhere."

He swallows hard. "Everywhere?"

I give him a wicked smile and his breath shudders out.

Oh, this is going to be fun.

14

Jay—I mean Julian—sits on the edge of my bed, watching me, his pulse fluttering in the hollow of his throat. I ease his polo shirt off and he raises his arms to help. I take a moment just to look.

He could be a freaking model. Get women to do whatever he wants just by taking off his clothes.

The three puncture wounds on his stomach are scabbed and slightly red but dry, with new pink skin around the edges.

"That's—healing—good," I manage to croak.

It's healing, not healed. Healing human-slow. He's not a Drakul, thank you god. Unless there's an exception to their healing ability… Would a weaker dragon heal slower? No. There's no way Julian is a Drakul. He's shy and innocent. There's no such thing as a shy and innocent Drakul. I don't think he's a Lesser, either, but some of them don't get the rapid healing ability. Needs more investigation.

Julian's fingers hover over the marks. I guide him onto his back, one hand on his shoulder. He's so warm, I want to roll around on top of him. I keep my eyes on his and lower my mouth to his belly, kissing each scab.

He shivers. "Shit."

"I've barely touched you anywhere yet."

"Oh, shit. This is really happening."

I laugh and trail my lips across silky skin and taut muscle, savouring each little quiver. His nipples surrender to my teeth and his quiet moan tightens everything south of my waist.

Who knew teasing him could feel this good? I wonder how far I can push him.

I step back and he props himself on his elbows. I get distracted for a few minutes by the bunch of his abdominals. My dress puddles at my feet in a flap of yellow. I straddle Julian in my underwear. He touches me, tentative at first, smoothing his fingers up my thighs to trace the edge of lace at my hip. He leaves a trail of goosebumps in his wake, though I'm not cold.

Parts of me are very, *very* hot.

The bra follows my dress. Julian seems to have trouble swallowing, which is a nice boost to the ego. His hands slide higher, his eyes flicking to my face as if he can't believe he's allowed to do this. His thumbs brush the swell of my breasts and my heart rockets into my mouth, muscles clenching in places I really want him to touch.

The gentle caress is unbearably erotic.

His fingers play across my nipples, sending a bolt of fire between my legs. My head falls back, my breath catching. Frantic need clutches my throat and hollows my stomach. I climb off him to steady myself and kick out of my underwear. The nerves return at the hunger in his eyes, his gaze heating my bare skin.

This is when people are at their most vulnerable—naked in front of someone for the first time. Nowhere to hide, too late to run. Best to even the score, though I probably should have undressed him first. What if I find a scar? Would I even care enough to stop?

I remove his trainers and socks. Slim, delicate feet I may nibble on later. My fingers tremble when they unbuckle his belt. He's breathing quickly but keeping very still. I slide his jeans and boxers down his hips—

Oh boy.

Crap, I'm staring.

His jeans hit the floor.

Well, since I'm already on my knees…

I widen his legs. He definitely stops breathing.

This could get very messy and result in me getting a shot in the eye but I can't resist. I lick him. He makes a cute whimper and squirms on the bed. I suck him into my mouth. His hands fist in the covers, his spine bowed. The sight of him is almost enough to drive me over the edge but he's not yet undone. No accidental spurting or singing hallelujah.

"You have excellent self-control for a virgin," I say.

"Years of practise," he hisses through his teeth. "But please, have mercy."

What do you know—I can't wait any longer, anyway. I climb into his lap and press his hands to the covers above his head, his body arched beneath me. He tangles his fingers in mine.

"Just move with me," I whisper, and slide myself onto him.

Oh Christ. I may be the one singing hallelujah in about two minutes.

He matches me, his mouth on mine. I roll until he's on top, pressing my hands into the bed, the angle and weight driving him deeper. His lips brand my throat, his body gliding in and out as he takes the lead. The pleasure builds, swelling my skin and pushing my heart into a canter. I tremble on the edge, so desperate to have an orgasm, I may immediately pass out. Julian eases his pace, my climax dancing just out of reach. The rhythm is slow, punishing. Extraordinary. The sensation builds, peaks. I stop breathing. All I can hear is my pulse. Julian holds back again.

How is this happening? I was in control and he was the one overcome. It's like he knows the second I'm about to climax and eases off. It's excruciating.

In a way that has no doubt ruined other men for me.

He takes me to that glorious edge again and again. No man should have this much power over a woman's body. I may go insane. Each crest is more intense than the last. Every part of me throbs, begging for release. I've been saying his name over and over for the last ten minutes but can't seem to stop.

"Oh god, Julian, how are you doing that?" Wow, I sound husky.

His rhythm falters. We're both panting and shaking and slick. He drives himself deep and I blast off into the stratosphere. Float around there for a couple of lifetimes. The smile on my face feels huge and goofy. When I drift back to Earth, Julian has collapsed on top of me, his heart thrumming against mine.

"Julian. Jesus."

"Did I do good?" he mumbles into my neck.

"You—you were... You are..." I've forgotten every adjective in the English language. None are potent enough, anyway. "Yes," I finally sigh.

He cuddles into me and I stroke his smooth back, tracing patterns on his spine. My body is fluid. I'm surprised I've not soaked through the mattress to drip on the floor.

"Can we do it again?" he says.

My finger pauses mid-stroke. "Right now?"

He raises his head and smiles at me, a stunning mix of wicked and shy. I gape in adoration and find myself nodding. He circles his hips. My eyes roll back. His body is lithe, strong, graceful. *Hard.* He has muscles in places I can't imagine, moves like no man I've ever been with.

Oh, Christ, I'm moaning his name already.

I'm definitely going to faint this time.

* * *

Later, much later—the guy has the constitution of the Duracell bunny—I usher Julian into my walk-in shower since we both need hosed down. He stands under the waterfall from a shower-head the size of a dinner plate. I wash his hair and he squints against the bubbles. My soapy hands glide over every firm and unblemished inch of him. He squirms when I get to his toes.

Ticklish. So cute.

I stay on my knees. He seems pretty happy for me to be there so I take him in my mouth. All the way in. He groans and sags against the wall.

"Raine," he says, his lovely eyes desperate, "I used up all my self-control."

I murmur soothing assent, my lips wrapped around him. He bucks on the tile, his fingers gripping the grooves between them. I explore him with my tongue and he makes eager noises, his thighs quivering under my hands. I suck hard and he cries out, spurting deep in my throat. He slides to the floor and blinks at me. I wash myself while he recovers, his half-lidded gaze following my movements.

"Can I use my mouth on you?" he says.

My fingers clench, squirting conditioner up the wall.

Holy hell yes.

I shut my mouth and bob my head. He holds out his hand and leads me back to the bed, both of us dripping on the carpet, hot and slippery and wet.

It may only be me.

"Lie down and spread your legs." His confident tone falters and he ducks his head, a flop of hair hiding one eye. "Please?'

As if I would refuse. Best not to let him know I'd do anything right now.

I obey his command, my heart thrashing against my ribs, anticipation pooling in my belly. He laps the water from my skin, leaving me just as hot and wet and slippery as I was when I stepped out of the shower. He teases me, nibbling my thighs, tracing lightly with his fingers. I claw at the mattress and try not to thrust my lady parts in his face. Somehow, he's attuned to when I've reached my limit. The moaning his name and whispering, "Please, please, please," may be a clue.

He kisses between my legs and his mouth is as skilled as the rest of him. I burst apart and reassemble myself minutes—hours?—later, wrapped in his arms.

I do believe he's a keeper.

15

The doorbell startles me awake. I have a very warm male pressed to my spine and double the number of arms and legs. The scent of vanilla makes me drool. This could lead somewhere interesting, if it weren't for the damn person leaning on my bell.

Hopefully, they'll take the hint and go away.

I wriggle around onto my belly. Julian blinks sleepy eyes at me, his hair tousled, though there's a tension in his body like he's waiting for me to react. I steady my hand on his chest. His heartbeat jumps against my palm.

"Morning," I say, and kiss him.

He relaxes and his arms pull me close. The buzzing of the doorbell fades into the background. I have a pleasant ache in every muscle, including some muscles I'd forgotten about. I'm still high on the endorphins. I angle myself on top of Julian. His hands slide down to cup my butt. He grins and it takes my breath away.

Every day should start with a Julian-induced orgasm. It's only fair.

My phone rings. I pause in my exploration of Julian's mouth, the rest of me rubbing against him in a way that makes it hard to think about anything else. I huff and glance at the screen.

Sofia.

"Oh, crap," I say. "What day is it?"

Julian also seems to be struggling with his mental faculties. "Sunday?"

"Crap!" I leap out of bed, fall to my knees—seriously, the guy makes my legs weak—and heave myself upright. "It's my turn to host the coffee morning."

He props himself on his elbows, watching as I scramble into clean underwear, jeans and a red shirt.

"Coffee morning?" he says.

"It's supposed to help us bond—no Vanatori talk, just coffee and biscuits so our lives aren't all about hunting the Drakul." I roll my eyes. "Not that we're doing much hunting."

Julian's gaze flicks to my sword. I scoop it up but don't put it on. No one here is going to attack me but I like to keep it in easy reach.

A key scrapes in the lock of the front door and shoes clatter into the hall.

"Raine," Sofia says, "I hope you are not naked because we are in your house."

I'm not naked but there is a naked man in my bed.

Stupid coffee morning, ruining my sex life.

"I'm coming," I shout to keep them from rushing up the stairs to check on me.

I catch Julian's eye and heat blazes into my face. I yelled that phrase quite a few times yesterday, usually prefixed by, "Oh god."

My heart skips at his slow smile and the look a man gets when he has intimate knowledge of a woman—dark and predatory and possessive. Sexy as hell.

I find myself unbuttoning my shirt. I sigh and it comes all

the way from my toes.

"I can't believe I'm going to say this but you need to get dressed. There's no guarantee they'll stay down there."

Julian looks slightly alarmed and hustles into his clothes. Watching him dress is almost as erotic as taking his stuff off. Almost. Nothing is as good as a naked Julian.

"Do you want to meet them?" I say.

He hops around trying to put on his trainers. Everything he does is adorable. I want to tumble him into bed and play with him until he gets the dazed expression that makes my head light.

"Um, no," he says. "I'll pass."

"We may have more weapons than your average civilian but we're a friendly bunch."

"You're the only one I want to see."

Uh-oh, I have a goofy smile again. Julian matches it and I get a little dizzy. There's no hint of wariness or panic, no melancholy bowing his shoulders. He's happy and he trusts me. I want to rescue him, keep him safe in my house, not release him into the great unknown where someone could hurt him.

"Honey, you have two seconds then I am coming up there! This *muchacha* needs her coffee."

Julian's eyes widen.

"Yup," I laugh. "She'd eat you alive."

I shove my window open and wave at Julian. He climbs through, pausing with one foot on the sloping porch roof.

"When can you get away again?" I say, not caring if it sounds needy.

"I can try tonight."

"I'd like that." Damn, I'm doing the husky thing.

I kiss him hard—tongue, teeth, everything. When I pull away, we're both flushed and he seems close to sliding bonelessly into my back garden.

It's a wrench, watching him go, but it's probably bad form to handcuff him to my bed. Though he may enjoy that…

Something to think about.

He waves before he disappears into the trees. I compose myself—fix my hair, mop up my saliva—and pad downstairs to cater for my hunter family. I'll tell them I slept in. Had a tough night cleaning my house.

Totally believable.

Sofia is poised in my leather recliner, her hourglass figure poured into a strapless black dress, a gold belt cinched at her waist. Dustan slumps on the couch next to George, sneaking glances at her. Ralph Lauren boxers today. Nate, Fabian and Rick perch on uncomfortable chairs from the dining room I never use. Nate taps at the glass tank on the cabinet next to my bookshelf. My betta flares his elaborate fins, giving him the fish equivalent of the finger. Sofia scans me from head to toe and tries to hide a smirk but Nate catches our silent conversation.

"What?" he says.

I bat my eyelashes and say, "Nothing."

Dustan coughs into his fist. "Why are you all flushed?"

"Yeah, you look real fucking mellow, Raine," George says with a grin.

A knowing smile passes between Dustan and George. Even Fabian has a twinkle in his eye. Maybe the words 'I've just been royally shagged to my satisfaction' are stamped on my forehead. Nate frowns at everyone then his head whips back to me so fast I'm surprised it doesn't twist off.

"Who is he?" Nate says, almost a growl, his grumpy face firmly on.

I glance at Sofia and my blush betrays me.

"Your contact?" This time it is a growl. "You said you weren't fucking him. Is that why he gives you the information?"

"No, Nate, I'm sleeping with him because he's gorgeous and I want to."

"Is he still here?" Nate jumps to his feet, fists clenched, as if he's going to storm upstairs and drag him out.

"He left. Funnily enough, he didn't want to be paraded in front of everyone."

Rick shifts on his uncomfortable dining chair. "Oh, Raine, you should never get that close to an informant. None of them can be trusted, as eager as they may be to help. If they get a better deal, they'll betray you in a heartbeat. They're tainted by association with the Drakul, whether they realise it or not."

"Leave her alone," George says before my happy little sex bubble deflates completely. "It's hard to meet people doing what we do. I'm sure Raine was careful."

Nate throws up his hands. "She has no idea who this guy is. Did he know we were here? He could be giving our location to the Drakul right this second."

"He's not a Lesser or a dragon—I know what I'm looking for," I say. "He's human, Nate."

"Humans can still be the Drakul's lap dogs," Nate barks, and Rick nods sagely.

"Not him," I bark right back. "He's nothing like them."

"Hey, this is our coffee morning—no work talk!" Sofia sits forward sharply, the leg rest of the recliner clicking into place.

"What we really want to know is, how was he?"

A sigh slips out and I flop onto the arm of Sofia's chair. Nate's scowl isn't enough to dampen the flashback of Julian above me, pressing my hands to the covers, the slow, sweet stroke of his body, the excruciating ebb and flow as he danced me on the edge.

"Absolutely goddamn amazing," I say.

16

My house is fairly small but when you decide to have sex in every room, it still takes a while. I may not walk for days. The bath is my favourite—a huge, claw-footed tub in its own room downstairs, the walls tiled in swirls of blue so it's like being in the middle of the ocean. We get all flushed and slippery and limp.

Well, not every part is limp.

Julian came round last night like he said he would. I vowed not to jump him as soon as he showed up. That vow lasted until I spied him in the driveway and hurled myself into his arms before he could reach the front door. In between kisses, I told him I missed him and he seemed surprised.

He has no idea what he does to me.

When I stopped snogging him long enough to let him in the house, we watched a movie as if we were just two normal people on a date, not handler and informant or Vanatori and whatever Julian is. I managed to keep my hands to myself then made the mistake of feeding him popcorn. He sucked the sugar from my fingers and I climbed into his lap, the bowl thunking on the floor, forgotten. We ended up among the scattered popcorn, the sex hard, fast, breathless.

Today, after our energetic morning of sexually christening

my house, we're playing board games because Julian never has. A niggle of doubt tries to ruin the moment—who's never played a board game? How long has he been trapped with the Drakul that has his sister? Maybe he has Stockholm syndrome and is sympathetic towards them. Maybe he'll do anything they say—like lure a naive and trusting Vanatori into their clutches.

I tell myself to shut up. He had the perfect opportunity to act yesterday when my group were in the house. The rest of the coffee morning was tense with Nate checking out the windows every five minutes for a horde of descending Drakul.

But Julian didn't betray me.

Maybe I am naive, though it's better than being a cynical bastard.

We play my favourite games—*Escape from Atlantis*, *Cluedo* and *Monopoly*. Julian is funny and sweet and terrible at winning. My pulse trips every time he laughs. His happiness makes him more beautiful.

Hell, he's beautiful when he's sad. He's beautiful when he's asleep. Okay, I only watched him for a minute. Times twenty. It's not creepy.

I let my fingers wander over him—collarbone, jaw, lips, nose. He's wearing a long-sleeved, white top under a slim-fitting, grey t-shirt and jeans that hug his glorious butt. The tingle of his skin on mine is addictive. He likes to hug and that's fine with me since I can snuggle close and inhale his intoxicating scent.

We play strip poker and get distracted from games soon after.

My fluttery little heart wants him to be more than a fling. The sex is fantastic—mind-blowing, let's be honest—but sometimes I catch him watching me, his tender expression completely unguarded, his eyes dilated and dark with something close to awe.

No one has ever looked at me like that.

Nate was right on one thing, though—I barely know him. My emotions are too tangled in the intimacy.

I lie with my head on Julian's stomach, both of us sprawled on my living room rug in a semi-sexcoma, Vivaldi's *Four Seasons* on my stereo. I like *Autumn* the best. *Spring* is a little overplayed.

"What were you doing at Tantallon that night?" I say, keeping my voice soft.

His muscles tense. I force myself to breathe.

"It's quiet—no one goes there," he says. "It gets too depressing to stay in the house."

"Can't your sister sneak out like you?"

A little bubble of guilt lodges in my chest. I hardly give his sister a thought—too distracted by her captivating brother. I don't even know her name. She might as well not exist.

"She's too scared. They watch her too closely."

"What about your parents?"

He shivers underneath me. "I don't want to talk about them."

He still doesn't trust me. My throat closes. I trust him, foolish little lamb that I am. I've let him into my house, into my bed, close to my hunter family despite the huge warning of what happened to Mikala nine months ago. I shouldn't trust anyone outside the Vanatori—every face could hide a monster.

"What happened to your parents?" Julian says tentatively. "I figured they're no longer around the way you spoke about them when we met."

Only my hunter family know the truth about their deaths. Nate saw the aftermath when he was part of a group in Nevada. Rescued me before I could meet the same fate. I was sent to train at a secret Vanatori compound in Montana, where I met the others. George is the only one of us who's never witnessed the slaughter of a friend or loved one as an introduction to a world with dragon shapeshifters. He still talks to his family in the Highlands as often as he can. They think he's a managing consultant.

I roll my head to look up at Julian, bobbing along to his gentle breaths. From this angle, he's all cheekbones.

"I'll tell you about my parents when you tell me about yours," I say.

I wait for him to frown or look hurt.

He gives me a shy smile and says, "Deal."

"Can't you run away? You and your sister?"

"There's nowhere else I—we—can go."

"You can stay here." The words are out of my mouth before my brain realises what's happened.

He goes still. I forget how to breathe. My heart hammers my ribs.

"You'd let me live with you?" he says.

I prop myself up. He seems to be struggling with his expression.

"Of course I would," I say.

And suddenly he's on top of me, kissing me like he'll die if he doesn't. If I thought he was skilled before… Wow. He ups his game and I almost slip into a full coma. He buries his face in my neck, a fine tremble running through him.

"Let me help you, Julian," I whisper into his hair. "Please."

He holds me tight, almost crushing, and nods.

We lie like that until the classical CD on my stereo ends and my belly rumbles in the silence. I order Mexican take-out and whip up a couple of piña coladas. It would have been margaritas but tequila goes straight to my head.

Julian splutters on the first sip. "Are you trying to get me drunk?"

A little, though I don't tell him that. Hopefully, the alcohol will lower his inhibitions and he'll start talking now that he's finally agreed to let me help him.

"I think I could beat you in the lightweight stakes," I say, "though I may have gone overboard on the coconut rum."

I challenge him to who can drink theirs fastest. I win and forget what I'm supposed to be doing. The room swirls, happy bubbles lodged in my gut. I climb into Julian's lap and tug at his grey t-shirt.

"It's a crime for you to be dressed," I say. "It should be a rule—in my house, you always have to be naked."

My smile slops around on my face. I'm fairly sure one of my eyes is closed, the other not far off.

Definitely too much rum.

My hands slip under Julian's top and scurry up his ribs. He giggles and I pretty much fall in love. And asleep. He carries me to bed easily, my head on his shoulder. He tucks us in and we nap as the sun sets, snuggled together, sated and tipsy. Thankfully, the tipsy stage passes fairly quickly since I have a great metabolism.

"Sorry," I say. "I got a little drunk."

He stays quiet. I squirm until I can see him frowning at the ceiling. His fingers stroke my arm but he seems preoccupied. I roll on top of him and he blinks at me.

"Are you all right?" I say.

He quirks his mouth and the return of the sadness hurts my chest. "This day has been amazing—my only amazing day. Except when that Lesser tried to scoop out my liver, and you kissed me."

"So what's wrong?"

"I'm ready to talk." He fixes his gaze on the roof and swallows hard. "You're not going to like it."

"Crap," I say.

"Yeah."

"Is this going to turn out too good to be true?"

Another sad smile. "That's up to you."

I sit up but stay on top of him, a knee on either side of his chest. His arms are straight, his palms flat on the bed, not touching me. He glances at my sword in its position across the chair. He seems nervous, vulnerable, but makes no move to get out from underneath me.

"You can tell me," I say. "You're safe here."

"Can I have a cuddle first?"

The sincere request scares me. Maybe I don't want to know his secrets. He can stay irresistible, mysterious Julian as long as I get to play with him all day.

I snuggle into him, burying my face in his shoulder to hide my stupid, welling eyes. He strokes my hair, my back, and holds me close.

He's shaking.

"How bad is it?"

"Pretty bad," he says.

I sit up reluctantly and scrub my face, trying not to cry.

He takes a deep breath. "I—"

My phone rings. We both jump. My heart zips around the ceiling somewhere.

"Ignore it," I say. "If it's important, they'll leave a message."

The noise stops. Julian opens his mouth. The phone peals.

"Christ's sake." I swipe my mobile off the bedside table. "*What?*"

"Are you alone?" Nate says.

"If that's all you called to ask me, Nate, I'm going to be seriously pissed."

"Are you?"

Julian watches me, his amber and peridot eyes unreadable. He seems still, calm, but the pulse in the hollow of his throat flutters like a trapped butterfly.

"No, I'm not alone. So what?"

"We have a situation. You need to get to the club ASAP."

"What is it?"

"I can't tell you over the phone."

I fist my hand in my hair. "Goddammit. It has to be right now?"

"You know I wouldn't ask if it wasn't an emergency."

He's right. He may be a grumpy bastard but he doesn't fool around with the Vanatori stuff. He cares about the group, in his deeply controlling way.

"Okay. Give me an hour." I hang up on a sigh and focus on Julian, who hasn't moved. "I have to go—hunter business. Can you give me the summarised version?"

He shakes his head, looking a little relieved.

"You don't want to tell me at all, do you?"

"No," he says, "but I will. I hope that matters."

The walk to the door is heavy with silence, each step painful. It's like a horrible break-up. Like I might never see him again. A cold sweat pops out on my hairline. Julian turns to go, his smile sad, his shoulders slumped. I grab his arm and pull him into a kiss. He hesitates then melts into me, his hands pressing me against him, his mouth frantic on mine. The tears well but I fight them back. We're both panting when we stop trying to inhale each other.

"Whatever it is, we'll work it out," I say with more confidence than I actually feel.

"I hope so."

"I'll call you as soon as I'm done. Even if it's late."

He fiddles with the cuff of his top and doesn't meet my eye.

"I doubt I'll be sleeping." He walks a couple of steps down the path and glances over his shoulder, his voice soft in the gathering dusk. "I had the best day."

It takes all my willpower not to run after him, drag him back to my bed, forget about the last ten minutes and make him smile again. Why did I have to push him to talk? Now I'm dreading what he has to say. He's not a Lesser—I've seen every inch of his body and there are no bite marks. None I didn't make. His wound healed slow so he's not a dragon. What the hell could it be? Are the Drakul going to make him a Lesser like his sister? My stomach clenches. Then he'll never be free of them. He'll have a connection to his master for as long as he lives. Maybe it's not that bad. Maybe his captors are fleeing the country, frightened by Lukas Romanov's death and the increased Vanatori activity. Maybe they're selling him and his sister.

My fingers rub my breastbone but they don't soothe the ache underneath.

It can't be over. I've never felt this strongly before and I've only known him a couple of weeks. He's tender, innocent somehow. I love his delight at the little, everyday things— ice cream, beating me at air hockey. His sweet surprise at discovering someone can miss him, want him, be attracted to him.

The vulnerability.

Jeez, he's not an injured bird. But maybe he is—fragile, wounded and beautiful.

I roll my eyes at myself and force my feet inside, strapping on my sword and locking my house.

I should have stayed with the uncomplicated guys.

17

Nate is not at the club, despite the urgency of his phone call. I pace in the communal area, my anger building until it seems like the top of my head may blow off. Sofia sits cross-legged on a stool, tapping her manicured nails on the bar. She's stunning in a figure-hugging red dress that will get her arrested for indecent exposure if she so much as bends over.

She had a hot date and is not too happy with Nate, either.

"You have no idea why he called us in?"

"Not since you asked me five minutes ago," she says.

I huff out a breath and keep pacing, my fingers tugging my hair. "Sorry. Where the hell is everyone?"

"Probably off doing macho shit too dangerous for us delicate *señoras*." She blows a curl of silky black hair out of her eyes and examines her nails.

I've seen her wield an axe. Sofia is anything but delicate when she gets a good swing going.

"He has two more minutes, then I'm leaving."

"Why?" She flashes me a smile. "You did not give me the details."

"It's complicated."

Dammit. Now I'm doing it.

The thought of Julian and the secret he wants, but doesn't

want, to tell me sits like a bowling ball in my stomach. Where is he right now—lying on his four-poster bed of ebony thinking about me?

My brain is still spinning by how fast our day went from spectacular to crummy. Maybe it won't be so bad. Maybe my imagination is blowing it out of proportion.

Christ, what if he *is* being forced to become a Lesser? Most of them are thugs but even the ones who are abused and kept as slaves can't be fully trusted. Like Rick said, they all carry the taint of the Drakul.

Boots thud down the corridor from the rear of the building. My fingers wrap around the sword hilt behind my head. Sofia slinks off the bar stool and rams her hand into her matching red shoulder bag. Her crouched position gives me an eyeful of her underwear. There's not a lot of it.

Julian liked my lace bra and pants but maybe I should get a thong. Racy.

Mental head slap. Perhaps I won't feel like showing him my underpants after he tells me his secret.

And that makes me sad.

Nate appears in the doorway and raises a brow at our battle readiness. He lingers on Sofia but I can't blame him. He's a guy and she's flashing a chunk of prime real estate.

His dark eyes fix on me. "Come down to the basement."

The knees of his black combat trousers are dirty, with drops of something on his equally black t-shirt. He spins on his boot heel. Sofia and I slot in behind, his tone silencing any complaint.

The basement is accessed through a metal door at the rear of the building. It opens onto a flight of bare concrete steps lit by a buzzing forty-watt bulb.

"Nate, is that blood on your knuckles?" I say, following close down the stairs.

He stops and I collide with his broad back. He turns slowly, his face devoid of expression, and stares at me for a full minute.

"Yes," he says.

He continues down the steps. I widen my eyes at Sofia and she shrugs.

This is intense, even for Nate.

The stairs end in a short corridor and another metal door. There are scuff marks through the dust on the floor. Nate throws the entrance wide and marches into the cell-cum-doomsday-supply-room, courtesy of Fabian's hoarding. Unease replaces the bowling ball in my gut, racing outward to prickle my skin. Nate's large frame blocks my view of the room. Behind me, Sofia breathes quietly and exudes clouds of Chanel No. 5. I shuffle forward.

The assorted equipment has been shoved to the edges of the wide space—pallets of tinned food, batteries, spare weapons and ammunition. I bump into a table to one side of the door, wobbling the large screen perched on the surface. It takes me a second to process the shape in the centre of the room because it's so unexpected.

Here I am thinking I may never see him again and here he is, standing in the middle of our holding cell, his arms stretched out, his wrists and ankles shackled to the walls by heavy, silver chains. There are ragged holes in the knees of his jeans, his grey t-shirt ripped at the collar, a splotch of red on his white sleeve.

I open and close my mouth for a second before the words tumble out. "What the hell is this? Let him go."

"Is it Jay?" Sofia says, crowding in and peeking over my shoulder. "Damn, honey, he is *muy bonito* in real life."

Julian raises his head and his hair flops into his eyes. My heart skips.

He is pretty, if a little battered. A bruise darkens his cheek, blood dribbling from a split eyebrow and the corner of his swollen lip. He swallows hard, his expression so tightly controlled, the strain shows on his face. His eyes are as wary as I've ever seen them.

I rush forward only to come to an abrupt halt. Nate's arm across my chest bars me as effectively as a steel gate.

"Get out of the way, Nate, and answer my question. You better have an excellent reason for hurting him."

Nate's eyes glitter, his pupils dilated. I shove past his arm and plant myself in front of the monitor on the table so I can see both Nate and Julian. My body aches to hug Julian, comfort him, but I have no clue what's going on and the disquiet helps me keep my distance. Fabian, Dustan and Rick peer cautiously around the door frame, Sofia sandwiched between them and Nate.

No George. Where's George?

Nate glances at Julian and curls his lip. "Tell her your name."

"Julian," he says.

"Your full name, asshole."

Julian's lovely, different-coloured eyes slide to me. "You know how I said you wouldn't like it?"

Panic clenches my stomach and claws upwards. I want to scream, "*Don't! Don't tell me your—*"

"I'm Julian Romanov," he says.

18

Julian, Aged 15

Today is Julian's birthday and it's not going too badly, considering, until his mother commands his presence in her throne room. He hates the throne room—a huge stone cavern buried deep under the house and lit by flaming sconces despite the access to electricity. A staircase wide enough for ten people to walk abreast spirals down to the room, the steps too large for human feet. It's where his family shift into their dragon forms without worrying about being seen. It's also where his mother conducts business, throws lavish parties and occasionally tortures her youngest son.

But no one ever defies his mother. He imagines normal, human mothers can be a bit scary. Lucky for him, his mother is the chief of all the Drakul.

She can eat him if she wants to.

The long walk to the throne room gives lots of thinking time. Lots of time to remember he has no pleasant memories of being summoned by his mother, be it to this place or anywhere when they lived in America. They've only been here a few months but he already has nightmares. His heart thunders against his ribs when he pushes through the heavy, metal door at the bottom of the staircase.

He hates that, too. The problem with heightened senses is everyone knows when you're afraid.

His four older brothers stand at the base of the dais, his mother poised on her throne, his father in his usual position cowering behind it. Five pairs of predatory amber eyes watch Julian cross the room. His father stares at the floor. The air smells of copper and stone.

A tiny part of Julian hopes there will be presents. Some kind of cake. You'd think after the first fourteen years he'd get the hint.

But he still wants his family to love him.

His brothers crowd around, the youngest two years older than Julian. All of his brothers are huge and muscular, the only resemblance in their chestnut hair and eye colour. Half of it, anyway. Julian is slim in comparison—the runt. He tries not to cower like his father.

His mother rises from her throne, flipping her hair over her shoulder. Everything about her is sharp—her face, her eyes, the slash of her mouth. Julian has heard people say there are few more beautiful than the matriarch of the Romanov family but he suspects they're just trying to get in his mother's good graces. Better her good graces than chained and at her mercy.

"Strip him," she says.

It's not exactly, "Happy birthday."

He struggles. He always struggles but his brothers are bigger and stronger and he always gets hurt. They pin a panting, naked Julian to the cold, rough floor, blood oozing where he scraped against the bedrock. His mother pulls a knife from the folds of her flowing, red dress. She floats down the dais steps and kneels between his spread legs. Black sparkles dance in Julian's vision, his harsh breathing echoing in the room. He can't get his heartbeat under control. His brothers sneer at the panicked rhythm. Their fingers bruise his arms, his ankles.

"You are reaching the age when young men have certain desires," his mother says, touching the blade to the tip of her finger. A bead of red wells and she licks it. "I cannot have you mating. Any child would be more of an abomination than you are. I doubt any female will have you but it's an unacceptable risk. So I have come up with a simple solution." She twirls the knife in the direction of his privates. "I'm going to slice all this off."

"*No!* Please, *please* don't."

His brothers laugh at the high pitch of his voice.

Lukas, the eldest, punches him in the mouth and says, "Shut up, runt."

His mother eases forward, the blade steady in her hand. Julian fights, kicking, thrashing, biting. It earns him another punch in the mouth, from Dominic this time. Kester and Blane are restraining his feet and too far away to do more than crush flesh against bone.

"Please," Julian says, tasting blood, his eyes blurred by tears. "I promise I won't."

The icy blade touches the inside of his thigh and he freezes. A hot line traces upwards. The horrible need to pee clenches his bladder. His balls have disappeared so high into his abdomen, his mother probably won't get them on the first cut.

A hysterical giggle lodges in his throat. "Please. I won't touch anyone—they won't touch me. You don't have to do this. Mother, *please!*"

She moves until they're almost nose to nose. Hatred burns in her amber eyes. The tip of the knife pierces the skin under Julian's jaw and a scalding trickle of blood runs down to pool between his collarbones.

"If you ever sleep with a female, or I have any reason to suspect it, I will turn you into a eunuch before you can blink. Do you understand me?"

"Yes," he whispers, holding his head very still.

She slides the knife deeper until he whimpers then she stands and snaps her fingers. His brothers' hands disappear from his legs, his arms. They leave Julian curled in a shivering, shaking ball on the floor.

And that birthday treat suppresses any urges he may have towards the opposite sex.

For a while.

19

Julian, Aged 19

The run isn't burning off the excess energy like Julian hoped it would. His trainers pound on the frozen ground and crunch on the frosted grass, following the line of the twelve-foot security fence hidden from sight of the house. This is his fourth circuit. His breath tears his chest and puffs out in clouds of white but he still can't get her out of his mind.

Libelle Della Valle—Libby to her friends.

Julian isn't anywhere on her radar but he noticed her when he was seventeen. Right about the time he took up jogging. Ball-shrivelling fear dampened any reactions the two years before that. Then the running, tai chi. Frantic masturbation.

He sprints the fifth circuit of the fence and stretches to warm down, his vision furred by black. He walks on wobbly legs into the cherry laurel maze, collapsing onto the stone bench in the centre. The bare branches of a hawthorn tree claw at the grey sky.

It's peaceful here. Safer than staying in the house to risk bumping into Libelle, though he's getting better at hiding. Simple when there are forty million rooms to choose from and the security cameras have blind spots.

The Della Valles are visiting his mother. Negotiating deals and bartering their children—four perfect, blonde-haired, blue-eyed daughters. The youngest are only ten, and twins, though not too young to promise to his brothers. Libelle is twenty-one and will probably be mated with Lukas in a couple of years. Her sister Madisyn, at sixteen, is also too young for mating but is likely to be promised to Dominic. Julian can't control the heat he feels when he sees Libelle and Madisyn. Somehow, the temptation gets harder to control, not easier, even with the threat of losing his testicles.

But no female gives him a second glance despite the weight of the Romanov name. In his society, power is the only thing worth mating for.

He wipes sweat from his forehead on his sodden, dark-green t-shirt, drying his palms on his jogging bottoms.

Dragons only sweat under extreme conditions. Lucky for him, his body temperature runs hot so there's little danger of freezing to death even if he sits out here for hours. Which he might. Just until they're gone.

Footsteps crunch on the icy path. Julian holds his breath, praying it's not one of his brothers, though they usually move in a pack. He can't run since there's only one way in. He could shift but then they might chase him.

"Hello, Julian."

His breath catches. "L-Libelle?"

Cue internal screaming.

She sashays over to the bench, dressed in a fitted, fur-trimmed cream jacket that ends mid-stomach and leaves inches of pearly skin to the low-cut waist of her designer jeans. The furry boots match her coat. White-blonde hair curls over her shoulders and frames her lovely, oval face.

"Call me Libby," she says and plops onto the bench beside him.

The warm curve of her breast presses into his arm. He gulps and casually clasps his hands in his lap, his jogging bottoms way too loose for what's going on down there.

"Okay. Libby. What are you doing out here?" He gives himself a mental pat on the back for not stuttering.

Best not to think about how fast his heart is racing. Maybe she'll think it's from the exercise.

She rolls her eyes. "It's so stuffy in there and if Lukas flexes his biceps in my face one more time, I may throw up."

She laughs and he joins in, a little dizzy.

"Most girls like his biceps."

"Well, it takes more than bulging muscle to interest me."

She places her slim hand on Julian's thigh. Squeezes. His mind goes blank. She walks her fingers up the inside of his leg and his pulse attempts to climb out of his skin. He grabs her wrist before she gets higher.

"Don't be shy, Julian," she giggles. "I've seen you watching me."

God, his mouth is dry. He really should speak but the words are lost somewhere.

No one ever touches him, not gently and especially not girls.

"Don't you want to kiss me?" she says.

He's still gripping her wrist. She angles herself on the bench, bringing her face close, her eyes as blue as the inside of a glacier. Her lips are shiny and full.

He should say no. He *has* to say no. If his mother finds out, she'll neuter him.

But he's so fucking lonely.

"Because I want to kiss you," Libby whispers against his mouth.

Her lips are sticky and taste of peaches. The fur on her jacket tickles his cheek. He copies her, slowly moving his lips. His first kiss. She opens her mouth wider. Her tongue touches his and he makes an involuntary noise low in his throat. She pulls away and he swallows a growl, mostly at himself.

He ruined it! He's such an idiot. A stupid, repulsive idiot.

She jumps to her feet and his hand drops limply from her wrist.

"Come on," she says. "Let's go to your room."

She pulls him upright and her gaze falls to his crotch. The obvious tent in the material. She grabs his hand before he can cover himself.

"You want to go to my room?" he says, his cheeks blazing hot enough to melt the ice on the cherry laurel.

She raises her eyes to his face. "Oh, yes. I can't wait for this to happen."

They wind through the maze, Libby tugging, Julian stumbling on numb legs. They cross the rose garden, the rockery and climb a tiny lawn beneath scattered trees to the colonial mansion, two black Mercedes parked in the semi-circular drive. Julian scavenges enough sense to take the lead and sneak her inside, creeping upstairs to his room on the third-floor wing, far from the opulent rooms of the first and second levels. He locks the door and slides the shiny new bolt, the jamb below it splintered and held together by wood glue.

Libby prowls through his bedroom, trailing her fingers along his chest of drawers, one missing, the others wonky.

Lukas stole the drawer. It had Julian's underwear and he never got it back. He imagines what Libby sees—a rickety chair, worn carpet and a green bean bag that looks like it's been stabbed (it has been stabbed). The bed is the only nice piece of furniture. She wraps her hand around an ebony post and arches her spine, shaking her hair so it tumbles down her back.

Julian thinks he may faint.

She releases the bed and runs her fingers across his pecs. "You're all sweaty. Why don't you jump in the shower and come straight out? I'll wait for you in bed. Naked."

She whispers the last, her body pressed against his, her lips brushing his ear. He tries to put his arms around her but she skips away. She makes shooing motions at him and he fumbles for the handle of the en-suite. She perches on his bed and slowly unzips her jacket, shrugging it off. She's wearing a silver bra underneath, something with lots of thin straps. The mounds of her breasts swell above the cups of the material. Her heart is a steady throb. His is hammering at about a thousand beats a minute.

She tilts her head and smirks. "Don't be nervous, Julian. I'll only bite if you want me to."

He falls into the bathroom, shuts the door and collapses against it. After a second's hesitation, he twists the lock.

Coward. He should be confident, forceful. Command her to join him in the shower or at least leave the bathroom door ajar, daring her to come in.

He drops his damp clothes on the floor and turns the shower on. He braces his hands on the tile and lets the cool water batter his shoulders and bowed head. His legs aren't quite up for full support. He waits until he's calmer then washes quickly, dries and steps out. He swipes a hand across the mirror and stares at his fogged reflection.

Tousled chestnut hair darkened by water flops into his eyes—one amber, one pale-green. Another sign of weakness. His nose is too small, his lips too feminine. The cheekbones don't help. His brothers have strong faces, manly jaw lines. They can grow a beard in about two minutes. All he gets is ridiculous wisps of light hair.

So what is Libelle Della Valle doing in his bed?

He pinches himself. Ow. Maybe she's rebelling and wants something different to the usual Drakul she associates with. Does he care as long as she sleeps with him?

Nope.

He turns both taps on, the sound of rushing, gurgling water hopefully enough to stop her listening to him.

"You can do this," he tells his reflection. Shit, his eyes are huge and dilated. "It's just sex. Everyone has sex. How hard can it be?"

He watches porn on his phone at night. It doesn't look too difficult. Lots of thrusting and moaning. Women seem to like mouth stuff. He can do that.

Oh, god, will Libby want him to do that?

He splashes water on his face. "Be cool, for fuck's sake. Act like you know what you're doing. Don't make her wait any longer."

His fingers hesitate on the door handle. He glances down at himself.

Yup, naked, his penis sticking straight out like a divining rod. He's never felt more vulnerable, even when his mother waved a knife at his balls.

Wrong moment to think about his mother.

He sucks in a breath, holds it for an eternity and lets it whoosh out. The door creaks open. A mound wriggles under his covers.

Holy shit, Libelle Della Valle is in his bed. She's going to have sex with him. He can't believe this is happening. Maybe they can run away together.

The Della Valles will protect him from his mother.

He approaches the bed. His heart slams itself into his ribs. The lump under the duvet stops moving.

Julian licks his lips. "Libby?"

The covers fly off. Instead of the lithe form of Libby, Lukas takes up most of the mattress, a black t-shirt stretched over his chest, black jeans encasing bulging thighs, his shit-kicker boots dirtying the sheets. Julian backs up so fast his bare ass hits the chest of drawers and knocks it into the wall. Lukas surges to his feet. The door bursts open. Libby struts in, fully dressed, crowded by Kester, Blane and Dominic.

"My friends and my lovers call me Libby." Her lip curls in a sneer, her icy eyes scanning Julian from head to toe. "You are neither of those. Just kissing you made me feel weak."

Julian hunches and covers himself with his hands. Lukas slings an arm around Libelle's shoulders. She cuddles into his side, looking up at him with an expression of adoration, her frame dwarfed by his.

"Did you really think you could bag a Della Valle, runt?" Lukas says. "Are you stupid as well as ugly?"

Kester and Blane stalk towards him. There's nowhere to run. There never is. They grab his arms and force his hands away.

"Aww, look at the little thing, it's all shrivelled." Libelle arches herself into Lukas and purrs, her hand slipping down to rub his crotch.

The large bulge gets larger.

"You don't have to worry about size with me, babe." Lukas bends his head to kiss her and it's all slurping and sucking and tongues. They disengage with a wet pop. Lukas grins at Julian. "I won the bet on how far you'd go if Libby came on to you. That means I get to go first."

Blane slaps Julian on the back of the head, almost hard enough to drop him to his knees. "I thought you'd be too spineless to go anywhere so I'm last. You nasty, horny little fucker."

"Of course he's horny—he's a virgin," Kester says, giving Julian a shake that rattles his brain. "I bet all he does in here is whack off and pretend it's Libby."

She wrinkles her nose. "Gross."

They mock him, shove him around. Lukas releases Libby and punches Julian in the nuts. He squeaks and crumples to the floor, cradling himself. All he can hear through the crushing pain is their laughter. Bile scalds his throat. He lies still and tries not to choke on his own vomit.

"Don't worry, runt, we'll go next door so you can hear since that's the closest you'll ever get." Lukas's boots appear on the edge of his vision. "Shit, you're so pathetic, I want to stomp you til you stop moving."

A glob of something hot and wet hits his arm. The rest join in the spitting. Julian struggles to care, concerned with checking his testicles haven't ruptured. It's not like he could be more humiliated. Dominic drags Julian's chest of drawers through the doorway, stealing the rest of his clothes. Boots clomp away on a swell of laughter.

Lukas pauses at the threshold. "You better do what we say

from now on, runt, or I tell mummy-dearest exactly what you were planning on doing to Libby. Then you can kiss your tiny todger goodbye. Fuck, you don't even need it. You're never going to use it."

The door slams. Julian drags himself into the shower to wash off the saliva and scrub his jogging clothes. He drapes them on the radiators to dry, his movements hunched and tentative. Something bangs against the wall from the room next door. Rhythmic thuds. Bed springs squeal.

"Yes!" Libby moans. "Oh, Lukas, yes! That's it! Harder, Lukas!"

Julian wishes someone would scream his name like that.

He crawls into bed and wraps himself in the cold sheets. Silent tears dampen the pillow he puts over his head.

He'll run away tomorrow. It has to be better than this.

20

Julian, Aged 26, Present Day (an hour and 30 minutes ago)

It was nice while it lasted, Julian thinks. He should have told Raine who he was immediately but then he'd be ash, like his brother.

Julian manages a tiny smile, his eyes on his trainers shuffling through fallen leaves. The woods are dark but his night vision is perfect.

God, he wanted to kill Lukas for years and she did it right in front of him. The asshole never saw it coming. Julian thought he was next but then she threw up and that was kind of cute.

When his brothers kill something, they roar and roll around in the blood.

He shouldn't have met her again but she was also cute. A small, bright spark in the wasteland of his life. And he was curious. He'd not spent much time with humans. Their servants are a mix of humans and Lessers but they avoid him in case any hint of association angers his mother. If Raine hadn't come along, he would have thrown himself off the cliff at Tantallon Castle.

He was psyching himself up for it.

But now it's over. She'll not want to see him after he tells her how much he's been lying. Maybe it's better he does it over the phone, like a coward. Otherwise, she may ram her sword through his chest.

The way he feels right now, it would actually be a relief.

He doesn't want to go home. His mother has been on the warpath since Lukas died, sending them out every night to search for where it happened so they can sniff out who did it. He's managed to keep them away from Tantallon, covering the area himself and saying there was nothing. He can't let them find Raine.

An owl calls from the trees to his left, probably searching for prey. Feathers whisper when it takes flight. Julian picks out the shape arrowing through the canopy. His gaze returns to his feet.

Raine is amazing. She misses him when he's not there. He loves how she says his name. Maybe one day, she'll say his full name. He loves how her heart trips around all over the place when she's nervous. His does, too, but he doesn't think she can hear it. When she looks at him, he doesn't feel ugly or weak. He feels like he could do anything. He doesn't want that to end.

Maybe it won't. She'll be shocked, angry, hurt at being lied to. She might need some time alone. And then? Maybe she'll forgive him. He'll never hurt her or her friends, though they're Vanatori. He's quite happy to never meet them. He'll make up for deceiving her by doing the things that make her breathe really fast and wriggle around and whisper his name.

Twenty-six years of dashed hopes, you'd think he'd realise how futile it is. Maybe he is as weak as everyone says.

And if, contrary to every other relationship in his life, she wants him, what then? He can't be a normal boyfriend or move in with her, even though she said he could. His family will find him. He ran away once when he was nineteen. Roughed it for three days before his mother's network of friends, allies, spies and people who are too scared shitless to oppose her spotted him. His brothers dragged him home. What they did still gives him panic attacks. He was injured so bad, even with the rapid healing, it took him months to recover. And they made it clear if he ran again, they'd repeat the torture but worse, then kill him.

His suffering is their entertainment. God forbid, he could be happy.

He sighs and kicks a pine cone. It spirals off into the undergrowth. Heartbeats close in. Loud. Slower than any of the woodland creatures. The air pressure shifts behind him. He ducks without thinking and something whistles over his head. There's movement in the trees all around. Torches click on. Julian whirls. A huge man with a baseball bat snarls at him, his ginger hair frizzing in all directions and covering most of his face in a beard.

"Fucker," the man growls and twists for another swing.

Julian punches him in the throat and blinks, amazed, when the man collapses, choking, his boot heels furrowing the dirt.

Raine really is a good teacher.

A metal collar clamps around Julian's neck.

Oh, shit—dragon's-bane. How do they know what he is?

The collar nips his skin and stings his nose—not excruciating but it stops him from shifting and flying away. A solid blow smacks his shoulders and he falls to his knees. The collar is attached to a long pole and the person holding it rams it forward, driving his face into the mud. Boots thud into his ribs. He tries to get up but his hands are wrenched behind him. Cold metal circles his wrists. More dragon's-bane so he can't break them. The pole handler yanks back, throttling Julian until he struggles to his knees. A man steps into his field of vision, his eyes as black as his clothes. He looks like an assassin.

"You killed him, you motherfucker," he says.

For a second, Julian doesn't understand who he's talking about. Then he finds the man who attacked him first, lying in the dirt, his eyes wide, lips blue.

Oh god, oh no. He killed a Vanatori. He killed one of Raine's friends.

Julian sucks in a breath. "I didn't mean—"

The man in black punches him in the mouth and again in the face. Blood drips into Julian's eye, stinging like the dragon's-bane. The man rams his bat into Julian's stomach and now Julian can't breathe. Wheezing, he curls around himself, his mouth filled with the taste of metal.

"Just wait til she finds out what you are," the man sneers, looming over him, the bat raised. "She'll castrate you, you reptily fuck."

What the hell is everyone's fascination with chopping off his nuts?

The bat swishes through the air.

There's a thud, then nothing.

21

To say I'm stupefied is an understatement. I gape at Julian—Julian *Romanov*—with no awareness of time.

Facts click into place and make his mysterious background clear—the evasions around his family life, knowledge of Drakul society, the lack of a normal (human) childhood. Then there's the nervousness around my sword. Christ, I bet the stamina is part of it, too.

I had sex with a dragon.

My head floats somewhere at the ceiling, each heavy beat of my heart sending a sick pulse to my stomach. My butt hits the edge of the table and I slump onto it before my legs collapse.

"That's right, ladies and gentleman," Nate says, spreading his arms and gesturing towards Julian. "What we have here is the youngest son of the Romanov dynasty—the worst and most powerful Drakul family in history."

He seems to be enjoying this. His gleeful tone grates in my jaw.

"You can't be a Drakul," I find myself saying to Julian. "You're too nice."

And gentle and tender and gorgeous. Amazing. Affection-ate. More words than I can think of.

"He's a Drakul and a goddamn Romanov. He tricked you

into sleeping with him."

Nate spits and the glob lands at Julian's feet. The toes of Julian's trainers are scuffed.

Of course Nate focuses on the sex, not that he's jealous or anything. But was it a trick? It didn't feel like a trick. I threw myself at Julian.

Silly little lamb.

I manage to swallow the vomit before it gushes out.

"But what about the dragon's-bane?" My hollow voice echoes in my ears.

He touched my window frame. My door. The fact he's not screaming right now.

"He's either fucking stoic or weak as shit," Nate says.

Julian shifts his feet and the chains clink softly. He watches me but I'm not sure what he expects—hysteria, anger, nothing at all? I can't unscramble what I'm feeling. It swirls through me, leaving me dizzy.

Shock. Shock is a big one.

This is what he was going to tell me. The big bad secret that had him worried. What would have happened if Nate's call hadn't interrupted? How would I have reacted? It's impossible to picture.

Hell, I'm living it and still can't picture it.

"He killed George before we could take him down," Nate says into the suffocating silence.

Sofia gasps. The news is a blow to the chest and sorrow bleeds from the wound. No matter how many you lose, it always hurts. Poor huge, f-word loving George. What will we tell his family? He was going to visit—some kind of highland games they hold every year. George was so excited.

Julian winces. "I didn't mean to. He attacked me."

"Did you punch him in the throat?"

Julian's sad smile hurts almost as much as George's death.

"You're a good teacher," he says.

Oh god, this is on me. I told him to go for the throat. To make sure they stayed down.

I shut my eyes so I don't have to look at his beautiful, terrible face.

"I told you you couldn't trust him," Nate says with a tad too much smugness. "I told you he was dangerous."

"How did you find out his name?"

"I hid in the trees and took his photo when he arrived at your house yesterday evening. Posted it on a forum Rick knows is used by Lessers. Someone recognised him."

The news of Nate scoping out my house—*spying* on me—sluices off and puddles at my feet, my brain too full with everything else.

"And they just told you?" I say instead of screaming.

Nate shrugs. "Maybe he pissed them off."

"So the emergency phone call, getting me to the club—that was to lure him out so you could jump him? That's why you took so long to get here?"

"Jump him? He's a Drakul, Raine. He could have jeopardised our whole group."

I slide off the table, my legs steadier. I can't say the same for the rest of me. My head reels.

"Probably, Nate, though it seems this is the first time he's met or thought about any of you at all. He could have attacked you when you were in my house for the coffee morning. He could have told the Drakul where we were after he left, just like you thought he would."

"What are you trying to say—he's a good dragon?" Nate

snorts.

"I don't know. Maybe."

"Fuck me, Raine. Are you listening to yourself? Just how great was he in bed?"

"Don't be an asshole, Nate."

"Clearly, you're not thinking straight on account of the embarrassment. Take a minute while I see what his mummy thinks about her precious son in shackles." Nate shoos me away from the table.

Embarrassment? I'm not embarrassed. Julian showed no hallmarks of Drakul behaviour. He wasn't violent or cruel. He didn't try to eat me or roast me in my bed.

Huh, look at that—now I have the anger. For Nate's attitude.

Unfortunately, I do feel a teeny bit ridiculous. Some Vanatori I am. I invited a Drakul into my home and didn't have the slightest clue. Maybe I *should* burn test all future boyfriends. Dragons are immune to fire, surprise, surprise. Problem is, normal guys are unlikely to stick around after I set them alight.

And I don't want another boyfriend.

Oh, jeez.

Nate fiddles with a video conferencing unit plugged into the base of the monitor. The screen blinks on bright blue, a small rectangle in the bottom right corner revealing a close-up of Nate's black t-shirt. He scoops the remote and steps away, adjusting the unit until Julian is framed in the tiny screen, standing spread-eagled in his chains. Battered and bloody.

Give him an hour or two and the superficial wounds will have healed. I shudder. So what about the punctures inflicted by the Lesser? There should have been nothing there, not even scabs.

"Julian?" I say, and he raises his gaze from the floor to meet mine. God help me, my heart still skips. "Why was the injury you got from the Lesser not healed after a week?"

Nate pauses but goes back to prodding buttons on the remote. Sofia and the others watch the train wreck of my evening like spectators at a tennis match.

"It was but… you would have realised something wasn't right so"—he lets out a long sigh—"I did it to myself."

"You skewered yourself so it would look like you healed human-slow?"

He nods and avoids my eyes.

Nate barks a laugh and cocks one dark brow at me. "How deceitful."

"I just wanted to see you again," Julian says, so quietly it's almost lost in Nate's gloating. "I'm sorry."

Nate raises his fist and takes a threatening step forward. "Shut it, lizard. She doesn't want your apology."

"Don't touch him." The words rush out, suspiciously close to a growl.

Nate stares at me for a beat and shakes his head, though he relaxes the fist. "Can't you see what he's doing? He's playing on your sympathies, acting wounded and repentant and shit. You're falling for it. This is why women shouldn't be on the front line—you're too emotional."

That's one way to describe it. I'm so emotional, I don't know what to do with myself.

Throttling Nate sounds like a good idea.

"Is it too emotional if I hit you upside that thick skull with my purse?" Sofia plants a hand on her hip, her shoulder bag hanging almost to the floor.

It sounds like a girly threat but knowing the hardware she's packing, it could give Nate a concussion.

"Let's try to be professional in front of the dragon, ladies," Rick says from the doorway.

Sofia whirls on him. His head disappears into his shoulders like a frightened turtle, his brown suit rumpled and streaked darker brown in places.

"Quiet, everyone," Nate says. "The call is going through."

"Who are you calling? You can't possibly have a direct line to Evelyn Romanov." I glance at Julian. Unless he gave Nate the number.

"No, your wonderful informant didn't give me any information. He's been pretty tight-lipped about his family. Taking the fall, like a good son. Rick did some digging through layers of shell companies and thinks this investment firm has ties to the Romanovs."

The conference unit rings. 'Connecting…' appears in the centre of the blue screen. Nate presses a button and the image of Julian vanishes from the corner.

A pleasant-faced, middle-aged woman answers although it's nearly midnight. "Hamilton Investments, how may I direct your call?"

"I'd like to speak to Evelyn Romanov," Nate says, his voice calm and forceful.

I have to give it to him—he's cool under pressure. I'd be stuttering like mad.

"I'm sorry, no one with that name works here," the woman says, her accent something with an American twang—maybe Texan. "Do you have anyone else I can direct you to?"

Julian appears on the screen, his hair flopping into his eyes, a leaf behind his ear, the bruise on his cheek swelling and blue.

"Tell her I have her son. I imagine she'll want to speak to me before I get bored and chop pieces off."

Chop pieces off? We're not the freaking mob. We're the good guys. Good guys don't chop people into bits. It's a bluff, right? Nate's bluffing. The thought of even a little part of Julian being chopped off swirls uneasily in my stomach. I've touched every piece of him and like them just the way they are.

"Hold, please," the woman says, no change in inflection.

The screen fades to grey, white letters saying 'on hold' in the centre.

"She's probably calling the police."

Nate glances at me. "She's not calling the police."

"We're not chopping him into bits."

"I thought you'd be first in line to relieve him of his balls for how he fooled you."

"We don't torture people."

"He's not people."

Nate's dark stare sends a shiver down my spine. What am I supposed to do if it comes to that? Stand against my group, the only family I've had since I was fifteen? Sofia won't go for this. The others might since they saw him kill George. What if they all join in, hacking away like serial killers? Blood splattering, Julian screaming, the hands that held me so gently reduced to gore.

What the hell am I supposed to do then?

22

It takes thirty minutes. Thirty minutes of being passed from person to person, Nate giving flashes of Julian in shackles for an incentive. Julian stands there, looking resigned, waiting for whatever we decide to do to him. The skin around his wrists is red, like a mild scald.

I try to master my emotions while Nate plays pass-the-phone. I can't let them torture Julian. I don't want him to be hurt. But he's a Drakul. I hate the Drakul. They killed my parents and threw me into a terrifying world where humans are no longer top of the food chain. And he's a Romanov. From the little I know about his brothers, they're as cruel as his mother. Maybe Julian is the odd one out. Maybe he is a good dragon.

Fucking Christ.

The call recipients start blocking the video feed. Their voices get angrier, incredulous, threatening then, finally, there she is—Evelyn, matriarch of the Romanovs. Grey streaks her chestnut hair, pulled into a bun, her cheekbones sharp enough to pierce her skin. Everything about her is severe. The woman is scary. And a gold, the most powerful.

Nate toggles to the image of Julian. "I believe we have something of yours, Mrs Romanov. The question is—what

135

will you do to get him back?"

Glittering amber eyes focus on her youngest son. Julian swallows hard but straightens his spine and raises his chin, his face unreadable.

"Did you murder your brother, you traitorous runt?" Evelyn's voice is a deep growl at odds with her angular frame.

Nate frowns, clearly unhappy with being ignored, though it's the status quo. Humans barely register above trifling annoyance to the Drakul.

"No," Julian says softly, "but I saw him die."

Male shouts burst over the speakers. Evelyn snaps her fingers and they fall silent.

Holy crap, that's right. I killed Julian's brother in front of him and he didn't retaliate. He didn't seem all that grief-stricken.

"You're lucky you didn't come home last night. We found where it happened. Your stink was everywhere. It was my idea to tell the Vanatori your name when your picture was brought to my attention." Her cold smile drops the temperature in the room. "That's how worthless you are. I'd rather give you to my enemies than touch you myself."

Her words settle on Julian. There's real pain in his eyes.

And now I understand where the sadness comes from.

My throat closes. I want to hug him. I take a step forward and Nate scowls, shaking his head.

Evelyn sneers at the camera. "So kill him slowly, hunters. May you enjoy his screams as I have over the years."

I don't know what happens. Maybe it's the aura of defeat bowing Julian's shoulders, making him look beaten. Broken. One second I'm standing at the side of the room, arms wrapped around myself, and the next I'm in front of Julian, my sword drawn, facing the camera, a fire roaring in my chest.

"*I* killed Lukas, you bony old bag. And I'll kill the rest of your sons. Except your youngest—I actually like him."

I slam the flat of my sword on the video conferencing unit. There's a spark, a puff of smoke and the monitor fizzles to black. Everyone gapes at me, my harsh panting the only sound. The heat of Julian warms my back. He seems to have stopped breathing again.

"Oh god, I can't believe I just did that," I say.

I squared up to Evelyn Romanov. She saw my face.

I'm a dead woman.

I brace my hands on my knees, my sword tip brushing the floor, and tell myself I don't need to faint despite the bright flashes in my eyes and the wild flapping of my heart. I suck in air instead of vomiting. Big tough dragon hunters don't vomit. They threaten the top Drakul lady without blinking.

Okay, so we also vomit.

"Well, that didn't go quite as expected," Nate says, sounding happy even though I trashed the VC. "We'll still have one less dragon by the end of the night and we can pick off the rest of them later. Great thinking to show your face, Raine. We can set a trap."

"What are you talking about, one less dragon?" I manage to heave myself upright, though I still sound like I've run a marathon.

"Dustan, pass me my crossbow," Nate says.

Dustan heaves an evil-looking contraption into Nate's hands. The crossbow holds bolts of hollow-point steel that fire with enough force to skewer a Drakul in flight, the dragon's-bane solution in the centre designed to rush out into the target. Nate is just as comfortable with a shotgun or a rifle but he prefers the crossbow. I tried to lift it once and couldn't get it off the ground.

Nate slots it easily against his beefy shoulder and sights down the shaft. "Move, Raine. I'll make it quick and painless, which is more than he deserves."

I back up so fast, I slam into Julian, stretching the chains to their full extent. His breath huffs out and stirs my hair. His heart hammers against my spine. He smells of dirt and metal and vanilla.

"We're not killing him," I say.

"He's a dragon."

"A good one."

"There are no good ones. They all have a sob story when they're staring down the barrel of my crossbow."

"Like the three you killed in their human form?" I cover as much of Julian's body as I can with my own, the point of Nate's loaded spear winking in the overhead light and giving me palpitations.

Nate's eyes narrow. "Exactly. They'll say anything to survive. Anything for another chance to rip out your heart and eat it."

"Or they were innocent. You saw how Julian's mother acted—he's hardly in cahoots with his family."

Did I just say cahoots? Cut me some slack, I'm panicking here.

"It doesn't matter. He's a Drakul. No Drakul is innocent. Now, step aside and let me do my job. *Your* job."

"He could be our ally."

Nate's eyebrows disappear into his dark hair. "There's not a single mention of a dragon ever being an ally in all of our history and you know why? They're monsters. You seem to have forgotten that."

"Julian isn't a monster."

"Really? Ask him how many people he's eaten."

Julian goes very still against my back. I hold my breath but don't move from guarding his body. My stomach rolls.

What if he thinks snacking on people is perfectly normal?

Julian clears his throat. "There was only one but—"

"One is enough," Nate barks.

The chains rattle, tension vibrating through Julian. I'm still holding my breath and the sparkles have returned. If I faint, I'll wake up to a pile of ash in the middle of the room.

"You'd eat anything, too, if she tortured you," Julian says.

"Is that a threat, lizard?"

"The truth. You'd be luckier than me, though. She won't be able to keep you alive as long. Maybe you'll die first."

Horror blunts Julian's voice. An ache starts under my ribs.

He told me his sister didn't deserve what they did to her. But the Romanovs have only sons. Was he talking about himself? What has he suffered at the hands of his family?

"Why didn't you run away?" I say and my voice wobbles.

There's too much emotion to squelch down. This big tough dragon hunter is at her limit. All I want to do is cuddle the dragon behind me and make sure no one hurts him ever again.

"That was my punishment for running away," he says.

Jesus.

"Are you happy, Nate? He's not a monster."

"He ate someone."

"Were you not goddamn listening? I'd probably eat my own hand if someone tortured me and don't give me any of your macho bullshit. You'd break, too."

Nate seems ready to shoot us both, his eyes narrowed, the

muscles bunching in his jaw. If the spear hits me at this range, will it go all the way through into Julian? I send a pleading look at Sofia—my only hope in this testosterone-saturated stand-off.

She slides herself between Nate and me and raises her hands. "Why do we not all calm down? It is not beyond possible that a good dragon exists and it is this one. Let us go upstairs and talk about it like rational adults."

"This is un-fucking-believable," Nate mutters but the crossbow lowers and I breathe again.

"I'm staying here. Sofia, can I count on you to be the voice of reason?" I hate the thought of them discussing Julian's fate without me but I can't leave him battered, alone and vulnerable. The urge to protect him still blazes like a fire in my chest. No way am I going upstairs for Nate to sneak down and shoot Julian while he's helpless.

"Sure thing, honey," Sofia says.

Nate glowers but he follows when the others troop out of the cell. He slams the door behind him and the lock clicks. The small, barred window opens and he peers in at me.

"We can go talk all you want but I'll tell you my final decision, the decision any proper Vanatori would make." His black eyes flick to Julian. "The dragon doesn't leave this room alive."

23

I sheath my sword after a couple of shaky attempts, praying Nate won't barrel into the room as soon as the blade is gone. Could he shoot a crossbow through the small window in the door? From what I've seen, his accuracy is awe-inspiring but I can't shelter Julian all night. I have to look at him eventually.

But not quite yet.

"You had to be a Romanov," I sigh into the silence, the warmth of him and the slight clinking of chains the only evidence he's still behind me. "You couldn't be a Morrison or a Vanderbelt."

Two of the weakest Drakul families and nowhere near as psychotic.

"Believe me, I've spent my whole life wishing I wasn't a Romanov."

I face him with no memory of turning around. His head is bowed but he peeks at me through the hair flopping over his forehead. There's something different in his eyes, some new light I struggle to decipher.

"So, no sister, huh?"

"I'm sorry I didn't tell you sooner. I was happy and"—his shoulders lift and drop in a heavy shrug—"I wanted to be happy a little longer."

"But you were going to tell me—if Nate hadn't interrupted?"
Julian nods and stares at his scuffed trainers.

"Even though I could have run you through with my sword?"

"I was hoping you wouldn't."

A pressure builds in my gut. I need to huddle in a quiet corner somewhere and get my equilibrium but I can't leave Julian alone. Every time he sneaks a glance at me, a whisper of tentative hope, something fractures in my chest. It's too much. He's been abused by his own family and yet it's me he trusts.

The Vanatori.

I stroke the manacle at his wrist. "Does it hurt?"

"It's not so bad." He manages a sad, half-mouth smile. "I'm weak as shit."

And, suddenly, the pressure bursts in a flood of tears. I throw myself at Julian—nothing new there—and hug him tight, sobbing into his shoulder. He curls around me as far as the chains allow. The feel of him, the smell of him, is comforting. My crying fades to snotty blubbering and I scrub my nose on my arm instead of his t-shirt. My turn to stare at his shoes, my hands on his shoulders, a little space between us. I try to stop shaking then realise it's him.

"You still like me?" he says, his voice thick and raw enough to snap my gaze upwards.

A single tear trails from his peridot eye and traces the curve of his cheekbone. I catch it on my fingertip. The bead of moisture wobbles around all over the place.

Guess I'm shaking, too.

"I don't just like you," I say, "I love you, Julian Romanov."

His smile shatters what's left of my heart. My hands slide up to cup his face and I kiss him, meaning for it to be gentle but the glide of his lips against mine, the way he strains to get closer, stretching his arms at an angle, dissolves any decorum. I feast on his mouth, my fingers tangled in his hair, my body arched into his. I forget my name, where I am, the date. Julian is all there is. I don't care that he's a Drakul or a Romanov. I want him to hold me so badly, I ache. I kiss him until I'm breathless. We blink at each other, dazed and panting and flushed. He licks his lips. Swallows a few times. His tender expression turns my legs to noodles.

"I love you, too, Raine," he says.

My laugh is watery, my cheeks somehow wet again. "God, we're so screwed."

I'm kissing him. I don't remember moving. My hands slip under his top to the warm silkiness of his skin and trace the arch of his ribs. The groove of his spine and the angle of his shoulder blades are as familiar to me as the dusting of light freckles across my nose. The kiss deepens, our bodies melded together. My fingers pop the first button on his jeans.

He jerks away. "Oh, fuck."

My cheeks heat. What am I doing, pawing at him while he's chained and helpless? The poor guy's been attacked, threatened, and all I can think about is humping him. Hardly the most romantic place, either. Nate or one of the others could walk in on us.

Not to mention George, whose body is barely cold because of the man in my arms.

"My brothers are coming," Julian says.

The words don't make sense for a couple of heartbeats.

"How can you hear them?"

"They must be close enough in dragon form." He winces. "They're describing what they're going to do to me. And you."

"Can you talk to them?"

"Not like this." His gaze darts away, his chin tucked down.

"Oh. You have to be a dragon?"

He nods, still not looking at me. I tilt his chin until his eyes meet mine. Then I kiss him. He hesitates for a millisecond but kisses me back.

It's not his fault he turns scaly at will. If we could choose who we were born to be, we'd all be rich, tall and beautiful. He's a Drakul but he doesn't act like one. He's sweet, generous, gentle. He's never hurt me or anyone else, not deliberately.

That's what matters.

"How far away are they, can you tell?"

He tilts his head, his eyes unfocused. "Ten minutes. Maybe less. My mother must have traced the call."

"Oh, fuck," I say.

I throw myself at the cell door and hammer it with my fists, screaming for Nate, my face pressed to the edges of the little window. He appears at the top of the stairs, arms crossed, a smug expression twisting his features.

"You finally realised that thing in there isn't human?"

"Nate, the Romanov brothers are on their way. Ten minutes out. We have to run."

The others crowd in behind Nate, Sofia muscling through to stand next to him. He frowns at her but shifts to give her room.

"You scared to meet his family?" Nate's lips lift in a sneer.

"Of course I am. Any sane person is terrified of meeting the Romanovs." I glance over my shoulder, my face softening. "Most of the Romanovs."

"Hear that, lizard? You're not scary."

"I don't want to be scary," Julian says to Nate's mocking

tone.

"We're wasting time. Let us out."

"He's not going anywhere. I'll let you out, Raine. Give you the benefit of the doubt. You had a lapse in judgement. But he stays."

My shoulders tense and my nails scrape the metal of the door. "They'll torture him. Kill him."

Nate shrugs, no flicker of emotion in his black eyes. "He's a Drakul."

As if that justifies everything.

It did, once.

"He's coming with me, Nate," I say, my voice a low growl, "so open the damn door and unchain him."

"Then you both stay."

Fabian, Dustan and Rick shuffle their feet, the noise loud in the vacuum left by Nate's statement. Sofia pivots gracefully on her heel, slaps her arm across Nate's chest and slams him into the wall. He grunts, his eyes wide. Her hand scrabbles at his crotch and my mouth drops open. In one blink, she's jangling a bunch of keys and skipping down the stairs.

"We do not have time for this shit, *queridas*," she says.

Nate shoves away from the wall and thunders after her, bright spots of colour in his cheeks. "Sofia! Don't you dare—"

The lock clicks. I launch away from the door as it swings open. Sofia heads straight for Julian, Nate storming behind her and trailed by the others. She selects a small, silver key from the bunch, no shaking in her fingers despite Nate looming over her, her expression serene and perfect.

"Sofia, if you let him go, so help me—"

"Shut up, Nate." She keeps talking over his sharp inhale. "We can figure out what to do when we do not have three

Drakul bearing down on us."

The first chain clanks against the floor, curling like a dead snake. Julian tentatively hugs his freed arm to his chest, the skin of his wrist bright red where it touched the dragon's-bane. Anger crackles from my feet to the fillings in my teeth at the sight of it. Sofia takes a step towards Julian's other wrist. Nate clamps a hand on her upper arm. A blade flashes under the light and stops an inch short of Nate's jugular.

Where the hell did she pull it from? Her dress leaves little to the imagination, and even less for hiding weapons.

"Let go of me," she says, her words soft, her accent thick.

Nate drops her arm, scowling hard. "Fine. No time to argue. But he's getting his hands cuffed."

Sofia's knife disappears to wherever she magicked it from. She unlocks the second manacle and Julian rubs his wrists.

"Hands behind your back, asshole," Nate says.

A snarl vibrates in my chest. I swallow it and try to keep my tone reasonable.

"Cuff his hands in front or we won't be able to run fast enough." I sip a cautious gulp of air. "And call him asshole one more time, *I'll* stab you."

Whoops.

Julian holds his hands out, his wrists together. Nate scowls harder but pulls a pair of cuffs from his back pocket and snaps them on. More dragon's-bane. The skin tightens around Julian's eyes but he shows no other sign of discomfort. Sofia quickly frees his ankles. Nate gets in Julian's face, forced to look up to match his height. Julian meets his gaze. I slip around Sofia as she straightens and place my hand on Julian's elbow. Nate's jaw works but he marches up the stairs without a word. After a pause, Fabian, Dustan and Rick scuttle in his wake.

Sofia arches a brow. "I hope you are right about him, honey."

"I am."

"Good enough for me."

She trots after the men. I tug on the dirty sleeves of Julian's top and tuck the material under the cuffs, rolling it back to stop the metal touching his skin. His grateful smile warms me to my toes. I re-button his jeans, my fingertips lingering, and give him a smile of my own. We hustle out of the cell and meet the others waiting for us at the front door. We creep outside, our weapons drawn—blades only since we're too close to Edinburgh for a loud gun battle.

The night is hushed, humid, almost peaceful. There should be the whoosh of wings, roars, screams to indicate death aiming for us somewhere in the black sky but there's only the occasional hum of a vehicle from the City Bypass. Something winks amid the stars. We press our backs to the rough wall of the building.

"They're close," Julian whispers, his shoulders hunched, strain etching lines into his face. "It's too late to take a vehicle. They might see."

Nate motions us with his crossbow. "Into the trees—you know the drill. I'll distract them."

We've practised the evacuation procedure a thousand times to cover a thousand variables—night, day, on foot, in a car, in the rain. On and on until we can do it in our sleep.

"You can't fight them alone," Dustan says, his shoulder against Sofia's.

"I'm not going to fight them. I'll make them think we're still in the building so you can get away." He jerks his crossbow. "Now go before they land in the fucking car park."

"They'll hear that there's only one heartbeat," Julian says.

Nate's lip curls. "This isn't the first time I've hunted dragons."

Julian flinches.

I tense to punch Nate for touching him. "What is it?"

"Supersonic alarm attached to the building," Nate says, smug. "That's all the dragons will hear."

Nate stays against the wall. Our boots slap concrete, Sofia's heels discarded for slip-on pumps. Two shapes drop from the sky between us and the trees. We all skid to a halt in an ungainly huddle. The silver dragons are the size of Clydesdale horses, their dark, narrowed eyes focused on Julian. He shivers under my hand. Two objects twirl towards the Drakul. Glass smashes and the sharp stench of petrol fills the air. The dragons snort and shake their heads, their eyes squeezed shut against the stinging liquid dripping from their scales. A third beast thumps behind us before we can take a step. It bares its teeth and spreads its bronze wings. Nate shouts and dances away from the wall. The dragon turns its head. Nate's crossbow twangs but the monster ducks.

"Go!" Nate yells.

The sides of the bronze dragon heave. Nate sprints for the corner of the building and dives around it as flames streak across the car park. The bronze dragon gallops after him. The two silver dragons claw at their eyes, still blinded but not for long. We part around them and throw ourselves into the trees. Earth and leaves muffle our steps, branches whipping against our clothes. We run until we almost reach the bypass then hunker in the bushes—five people breathing hard, vibrating with adrenaline; one dragon hardly breathing.

How good is Julian's night vision? I have a feeling it's miles better than the amorphous shapes I see when I squint into the blackness.

"Do you have those things in your pockets ready to go?" Sofia says, her voice floating from the dark.

Dustan's grin flashes white. "Why do you think I wear such baggy clothes?"

After his ill-fated burglary of a Drakul house in Alicante and witnessing his hooligan friends being torn apart for their sins, Dustan managed to escape by throwing a Molotov cocktail. The fire doesn't hurt the Drakul but it confuses and distracts enough for someone to escape or attack. It's why he's our weapons development expert. The dragon's-bane canisters were his idea—the Vanatori version of pepper spray.

We catch our breath. A lorry rumbles by on the bypass, its lights sweeping the trees. No sounds come from the direction of our headquarters.

"We should go back and help him," Dustan says.

Fabian nods his bald head, his skin glowing in the dark.

"He told us to go, so we go," Rick says. "We rendezvous at Sofia's house."

Undergrowth rustles as the others slither away. I help Julian to his feet and we walk parallel to the bypass. Now we're no longer hurtling through the undergrowth, thorny bushes tug at my clothes. My sword catches in the bark of every tree.

Julian halts me, his cuffed hands on my arm. "Get on my back. It'll be quicker."

I hesitate but not for long. I sheath the sword and jump, wrapping my legs around his waist.

Damn, he smells good.

Maybe the Drakul don't sweat that much. If I'd experienced the stress of his evening, I'd be a mess. Hell, I *am* a mess.

Julian lopes easily through the forest with me bouncing on his back. I guess he can see a lot better. I cuddle tighter to him, my arms around his neck, legs gripping his waist since he can't hold me himself.

I love the way he moves—confident, strong, sensual. Sensual? Christ, I'm an animal.

"Uh, Raine?"

"Mmm?" I mumble, cosy against the heat of him, his muscles bunching underneath me.

"That is very distracting."

I freeze, caught in the act of nuzzling his throat, my lips on the flutter of his pulse.

"Sorry."

"I didn't say stop. Just thought I'd warn you in case I fall over."

"And what's the risk of that?" I trail kisses to below his ear and gently bite.

His breath catches. "Pretty high."

Somehow, we're on the ground, rolling in the leaves. I come out on top, straddling him, his body a pale shape in the dark. I wriggle under the loop of his cuffed arms and capture his mouth. His hands hug me tight, splayed on my butt. My fingers steal under the hem of his t-shirt to caress his flat stomach, the dip of his chest.

The need doesn't care that only a block of woodland separates us from a fury of dragons. I need Julian naked and trembling to prove he's still the same person despite tonight's revelations. I need him to touch me with the same gentleness, watch me with the same awe.

"Raine, where are you?" Sofia whispers from off to the left.

Crap. Maybe I should be worrying about whether Nate's

been eaten instead of getting into Julian's pants.

Though I really want to get in his pants.

"Raine?"

I sigh into Julian's mouth and his lips curve against mine. It takes me a few swallows to form words.

"We're here," I say, squirming out from Julian's arms and pulling him to his feet.

The others are clustered in a clearing where the trees thin beside the Union Canal, a slice of the stars and sky above. Their eyes shine in the lights from a nearby residential street.

I feel transparent, like my transgressions are written clear on my face—easily waylaid by a pretty boy who happens to be a Drakul and who I will definitely shag as soon as we're alone.

Some Vanatori I am.

Without a word, my fellow hunters disappear into the night.

24

Sofia's cottage nestles in a shrub-filled garden on the edge of Roslin, hidden from neighbouring properties by trees and a hedge of rhododendron. Gravel crunches under our tyres, the vehicle one of many we keep in garages scattered around headquarters for emergencies. Sofia yanks the handbrake and the engine putters to silence. I jump out of the rear of the Land Rover Defender, Julian landing next to me. The jeep blends into the dark except for the rack on the roof and mounted lights at the front, the spare wheel fixed to the bonnet.

The thing is as bulky as a tank.

Sofia's front door shuts behind us and we all stand awkwardly in her square-tiled hallway. Four Vanatori, whatever I am, and Julian. The absence of Nate and George's hulking figures is painfully obvious and one of them is never coming back.

What did they do with his body?

"I think we all need a drink," Sofia says after a couple more minutes of shuffling.

We trail her into the kitchen and take a seat at the heavy pine table in the centre. Darkness presses against the glass of three casement windows. Sofia draws the floral curtains across, sealing us into the room lit by a buttery-yellow bulb.

She bustles around, switching on the kettle, clattering cups onto the matching pine counters. We stare at our hands, the three men facing Julian and me, Julian's cuffs clunking on the wood. Sofia places a tray of filled cups on the table and hands them out, the rich smell of coffee warming the kitchen.

She splashes a generous dollop of cognac in each and sits in the chair beside me. "Decaf. We are all jittery enough. Help yourselves to cream and sugar."

I stir two sugars and a swirl of cream into Julian's cup, one sugar and way more cream in mine.

I glance up, aware of Dustan's eyes on me. "What?"

"You know how he takes his coffee."

"So?"

"He's not human, Raine." Rick cradles his mug, steam curling under his unassuming chin. "I mean, shit, he's already healing."

The bruises on Julian's face look days old rather than hours, blue morphing into green and yellow. The split on his eyebrow has a healthy scab, the swelling gone from his lip.

"You can address him directly. He's sitting right there."

Everyone stares at Julian. He ducks his head and takes a careful sip of coffee. The only sound is a big clock ticking over the pale green AGA oven.

I sigh. "Julian, this is Fabian, Dustan, Rick and Sofia."

"Hello," he says, nodding at them.

More silence.

Julian peeks at me and straightens his shoulders. "I'm sorry about your… About George. I didn't mean to kill him. I forgot I'm stronger than most humans."

"How much stronger?" Sofia says, interested rather than accusatory, her body twisted to look past me.

He flashes her a sad, half-mouth smile. "Stronger."

She bites her lip and looks at me. "Damn, honey. He has a sorrowful, sexy thing going on."

Rick huffs into his coffee. "It doesn't matter if he's good-looking. He's a Drakul."

"Give it a rest, Rick." I roll my eyes. "You sound like Nate."

"Well, someone needs to remind you of your training."

"Oh, don't give me that—"

"What's it like being a dragon?"

Fabian's nasal voice cuts through our bickering. We gape at him. He keeps his gaze fixed on Julian, his smooth head shining under the lights.

"Flying is cool. But we can only do it at night or underground or if it's foggy."

Fabian rests his chin on his steepled fingers. "You don't give off much of a heat signature except if you're breathing fire but how does no one see you on radar?"

We all lean forward, breaths held.

It's hard to study something that will eat you when it's alive or dissolve to ash when it's dead. And in terms of time, we've only known of their existence in the last hundred years.

I don't envy the poor souls who first discovered that monsters were real. It happened in Romania, which became the birthplace of the Vanatori. It's still the base of our ruling body.

"It's our scales," Julian says. "They absorb radar."

Fabian smiles. "Like a biological stealth bomber."

"Something like that."

"Does it hurt to change?"

"Not usually." Julian's handcuffs clink on his cup. "Unless a powerful Drakul forces you. Then it really hurts."

His mother. The goddamn bitch. I bet she forced him and enjoyed his pain. How could she torture her own son?

I place my palm on his thigh under the table. His expression softens and he shifts closer, the line of his leg hot against mine. I struggle not to climb into his lap.

The tension fades from the room. Fabian, Dustan and Sofia pepper Julian with questions. Could he change into a dragon when he was a baby? How heightened are his senses? What injuries can he heal? Has he ever made any Lessers? Why do dragons disintegrate into ash when they die? I sip my coffee, happy to watch him, the liquid burning pleasantly down my throat and heating my stomach. Rick mashes his lips together and frowns at his cup, refusing to join question time.

We rarely get this close to a Drakul, especially in their human form. The heads of the powerful families are not so secretive—Evelyn Romanov, Jackson Della Valle—since we're completely beneath their zone of concern. It's not like we've ever had a conversation with one.

"Sorry to ask this but I am curious—did you have any Drakul girlfriends?" Sofia flicks a glance at me. "Before Raine came along, of course."

I will myself not to blush. Fail miserably. Julian squirms a little in his chair.

"Um, no. No girlfriends. The Drakul mate for power."

I squeeze his leg and can't resist walking my fingers higher. My pinkie brushes the crotch of his jeans and he does the whole catching his breath, holding really still thing I love.

"No girlfriends at all? Does that mean you were a…?" Sofia smiles slowly and raises her brows at me. "Oh, my."

Yup, I'm definitely blushing.

"I think—" I clear my throat, my voice husky. "I think that's enough interrogation for one evening. Or morning. I could do with some sleep."

Sofia winks at me and clears the dishes away. "I know I am beat. You and Julian can take the spare room upstairs. Fabian, Dustan and Rick can spread out down here. Nate should be back in a couple of hours."

"We can't leave them alone together," Rick blurts, shoving up from his seat. "One cosy chat does not negate the fact he's a Drakul."

Sofia levels a cold stare at him. "My house, my rules."

"But Nate wouldn't—"

Fabian slaps him on the shoulder. "He's done nothing tonight to indicate he's dangerous."

"Of course he's dangerous! He killed—"

"We attacked him. He's been pretty darned polite to us despite that."

This is the most I've heard Fabian talk in one sitting. He steers Rick towards the living room, his hand still clamped on his shoulder. The thick stone walls muffle Rick's protests. Sofia washes the cups and stacks them neatly on the drainer. Dustan sidles around the table and Julian and I stand to face him.

He holds out his hand. "It's not exactly been nice but it's been interesting to meet you, Julian."

Julian's expression does crazy stuff to my stomach. He swallows a couple of times and shakes Dustan's hand.

"Likewise," he says.

Dustan nods to me and leaves the room. Sofia pats her hands dry on a dishtowel covered in images of cats.

"Sorry about the cuffs. Nate took his keys back." She pulls a pin from her hair. "You should be able to pick them with this."

I accept the pin and fist my hand around it. "Thanks, Sofia. For everything."

"No problem, honey. I like him." She grins and it's full of wickedness. "In case you were wondering—noise does not travel far in this house."

Oh, Christ. Does everyone know I'm going to sleep with him? Nerves jitter in my stomach. It'll be almost like our first time. The first time since finding out what he is but wanting him, anyway. Freely and eagerly.

Maybe a bit too eagerly.

25

The spare room is at the front of the cottage overlooking the driveway. It's small but clean, the double bed neatly made, a narrow, free-standing cupboard opposite the foot. Julian watches me close the door, his cuffed hands clasped below his waist.

"Are they hurting you?" I say.

He shakes his head. I drop the pin on the glass-topped dressing table at the side of the room.

"Lie on the bed." Good lord, my voice is right back to husky.

The knowledge he's about to get lucky darkens his beautiful eyes. There's softness, too. Tenderness. A crap-load of hunger.

The nerves zip out from my stomach to tighten my throat and speed my pulse.

This is ridiculous. Why am I nervous? We've had sex multiple times. I've seen every naked and glorious inch of him.

But I thought he was human.

He kicks off his trainers and lowers himself onto the bed, his gaze never leaving mine. He wriggles on his elbows and settles into the centre of the mattress, his head below the mound of pillows. He tents his fingers on his stomach and waits. I remove my sword and lay it on the dressing table. No sign of anxiety from Julian.

He knows I'll never use it on him.

Jesus, I'm going to make love to a dragon. *My dragon.* It changes everything and yet somehow nothing.

I strip down to my black underwear, slowly, letting Julian's eyes linger. I straddle him on the bed and pin his cuffed hands above his head. The move arches his spine, thrusting his hips into mine. My heart kicks hard and leaps into my mouth.

Man, he's hot. Pinned and helpless and looking at me like I'm the most amazing thing he's ever seen.

"So you can hear my heartbeat?" I say.

He licks his lips and whispers, "Yes."

"That's how you knew when to slow down our first time. When to speed up. Seems like cheating."

His smirk arrows fire between my legs. "You hold your breath when you're close. Your heart races. I just follow the cues."

"And how does my heart sound now?"

"Fast," he says. "Swollen."

"And yours?"

"Pretty fast."

"Only pretty fast? Guess I'll have to do something about that."

I shove his t-shirt and long-sleeved top up and over his head to bunch around his wrists but keep his hands free, tangling my fingers in his. I stretch myself across him, skin to skin, and thoroughly explore his mouth with lips, tongue, teeth. God, I love his tongue. I sizzle when it touches mine.

"How about now?" I lever myself up, panting a little.

"Definitely faster."

I laugh and nibble his neck, his collarbone, sucking on his nipple and grazing it with my teeth.

"Shit," he gasps and writhes underneath me.

I place my ear on his chest. His heart thunders in tandem to mine.

"Very fast, now," I say, and swirl a fingertip around his nipple, damp from my mouth.

His heart skips and it's delightful. No wonder he enjoys hearing mine, aware of the effect of every caress, every stroke. Knowing what his touch does to me.

I wish I could listen to his heart beat all day.

Moving lower, I kiss the warm skin below his ribs. His dazed eyes watch me. There's no mark where the Lesser tried to remove his liver. Or where Julian did it to himself, desperately wanting to appear human.

How unhappy was he before I met him?

I push myself up, kneeling between his legs, and just stare at him for a few minutes. The slide of his ribs as he breathes, the pulse fluttering in the hollow of his throat, the tantalising jut of his hip bones. I let what I feel for him fill my face. Every overwhelming bit of it.

"I love you, Julian."

His chest hitches. "I love you, too."

I kiss him and he's shaking and I fall in love with him all over again. I only stop to undress the rest of him, the rest of me. We fit together perfectly—hands, mouths, hips. Every pleasure sound is swallowed and reciprocated. He matches my pace, strong and hard underneath me. I'm bathed in his vanilla scent. I don't last long but neither does he. I collapse onto him and bury my face in his neck, every muscle limp, glorious aftershocks zinging inside me.

"Racing," I manage to say past the canter of my pulse and his.

His hands drop to my back and hug me tight, the metal of his cuffs digging in. "Definitely racing."

I recover enough to wobble to the dressing table and scoop up the hair pin. Julian sits on the edge of the mattress, the cuffs held out. I unlock them and they thud to the carpet. I kiss the reddened bands at his wrists. He stands, wrapping me in his arms, and just holds me, exactly like I wanted him to. Or maybe not exactly. The nakedness makes it better.

"Your heart rate is slowing," I say.

He smiles against my hair. "Yours, too. Can't have that."

He kisses my forehead, my eyelids, nose, cheeks, finally my lips.

"Do you want to know how much stronger I am?" he whispers, his mouth trailing to my ear.

Oh boy.

I swallow hard but nod. His grin weakens my knees. He picks me up, his hands on my hips. I curl my arms around his shoulders and wrap my legs around his waist.

"I can do it like this," he says, no strain in his voice. "Probably for hours but I think you might go insane if I tease you that long."

He must have been so careful with me before—careful not to hurt, careful not to show his true strength.

I sob his name and his grin widens.

"I'm so glad you came to Tantallon that night," he says.

He kisses me but that's okay since I can't speak. He shifts his grip, cradling the backs of my thighs and my butt. I cross my ankles and rest my heels against him. He eases inside me, the friction rocketing my heart rate. He flashes a smile before he returns to snogging me senseless. He starts to move, a slow, gliding rhythm with me balanced easily in his arms. My hips meet his, the effort trembling in my abdominal muscles and heightening the sensation, everything tight and swollen and *oh holy crap,* I'm going to come already.

But, of course, he doesn't let me.

He eases off, leaving me begging. The dance of his body proves he has muscles in places no human male ever will. The stamina of a Drakul.

I may yet go insane.

He guides me to the threshold again and twirls me away, expertly coaxing me down so he can drive me back up. My fingers clutch his shoulders hard enough to bruise but if I relax my grip I may burst apart. I lose track of how many times I quiver on the maddening edge of orgasm. All I can hear is my heartbeat. I could be screaming the house down. I moan his name and whisper, "I love you," over and over and over.

Somewhere, during the ten-millionth repetition, he takes pity on me.

26

There's someone in the room. I blink awake, tangled in the sheets and Julian, who seems to have more arms and legs than when we finally collapsed onto the mattress. It's still dark but getting grey, enough light to see the shadow at the end of the bed. My heart thuds against my ribs. Julian tenses beside me and I know he's awake, ready, but he keeps still.

"Nate?" I say.

"Is this how it's going to be, Raine—you defying me at every turn?"

I sit up slowly, the covers pressed to my chest, very aware of the fact I'm naked underneath them. I angle my body to protect the vital parts of Julian, figuring he can probably survive a crossbow bolt to the leg if Nate snaps. I'm much more fragile but I'd throw myself in front of him, no hesitation.

"It's not defiance," I say in a calm voice. "We're not drones. We follow you because you're a good leader. We have a common purpose."

"You seem to have forgotten that purpose."

"I haven't forgotten."

His gaze burns where I clutch the sheet to my chest.

"You fucked a Drakul in the full knowledge of what he is. No hiding behind your wide-eyed ignorance now—you're sleeping with the enemy."

"Julian isn't your enemy. Neither am I."

Nate snorts. "How can you do this to us? To me?"

"I'm not doing anything to you," I say mildly.

"Really? It's nice to see how worried you were while I was out hunting alone."

I swallow a retort. He seems happy to forget our intel-only orders direct from Principal Cozma when it suits him.

"You can take care of yourself." I force my muscles to relax. "Did you kill any of them?"

Silence stretches as the darkness fades and I think he's not going to answer. Julian strokes my leg under the covers, a delicate brush of his thumb, back and forth.

Does he feel any grief towards his brothers? I vow to talk to him about it once Nate says whatever he's here to say and buggers off.

"No, I didn't kill any of your precious Romanov brothers."

"Don't be an ass, Nate. I don't care about the Romanov brothers. Only Julian. He's not like them."

The dark bulk of Nate shifts. He's shaking his head.

"How can you stand him touching you? His kind slaughtered your parents. Thousands of others. Our lives are short and brutal because of *them*."

"So what are you saying—every Drakul is evil? The world isn't that black and white."

"Our world is, Raine." He sounds sad, like a father disappointed by their once favourite child. "You believed that before."

"How can you not see he's different? If he were like any other dragon, I'd be long dead. He'd have infiltrated our group as soon as he got the opportunity. We'd all be dead. But we're not."

"Tell that to George," Nate says softly.

Julian flinches against me. I slide my hand over his where it rests on my thigh and squeeze his fingers. After a pause, he squeezes back and cuddles tighter around me.

"He defended himself against an unprovoked attack," I say, keeping my voice level.

"We attack the Drakul. It's what we do. They're born to eat us and we're trained to stop them."

"Julian had done nothing to you—"

"You are *mine!*" Nate's shout batters the pre-dawn hush. "You're one of mine and he was corrupting you."

The angry words ring long after they leave his mouth. His shadow is hunched, his breath rasping, the bunch of his fists bulging from his sides. Tension sings from Julian's body to mine.

I force myself to speak past my heartbeat, my voice even quieter than before. "I know why you thought he was deceiving me. I would've believed the same a few hours ago but I don't need saving. Not from him."

Nate's heavy gasps dominate the room, his aggression thickening the air and clenching my throat. I glance towards my sword still on the dressing table.

It's too damn far to reach and would I even use it? If Nate tries to hurt Julian, will I raise my weapon against him? Cut down the man who taught me all I know? The growl in my chest says yes, my hackles rising to match the threat of violence.

I guess we all turn into monsters to protect the ones we love.

"What the hell changed?" Nate says, his voice so deep it's

almost painful to hear. "In the space of a few hours, you've gone from hating the Drakul to sacrificing everything you've learned for this one. Is he really that good a lay?"

Seriously, the guy needs to quit obsessing about my sex life. His misplaced possessiveness is affecting his judgement because the evidence is clear—Julian is no danger to us. I've not been fooled by a pretty face and become too emotionally involved to see the beast beneath the mask. He's not tricking me or using me, biding his time to strike. He is as innocent and gentle as he appears.

I sit up straighter, one hand clutching the sheet to my chest, the other gripping Julian's. The grey of first light carves darkness into Nate's face, his eyes nothing but pits. I lick my lips. Suck in a breath. My pulse pounds in my fingers.

"I love him," I say, the steady words at odds with the rigidness of my muscles, my gaze fixed on the centre of Nate.

If he throws himself at us, I'm going for my sword.

Silence drowns the room. How does my heartbeat sound to Julian? It's slapping against my ribs like it's desperate to get out. And what about Nate's? He seems to have frozen. I'm tempted to ask Julian if Nate still has a pulse.

A laugh as sharp as fractured glass bursts from Nate's mouth, making me jump.

"Humans not good enough for you, Raine? Just some pretty-boy monster who acts the victim." Another slicing laugh bleeds through the space separating us. "You haven't seen him change. You going to love his dragon, too? Will you fuck it as enthusiastically as his human form?"

"I don't think that's physically possible, Nate," I say.

Oh god, what is my heart doing now? Can Julian tell anxiety from uncertainty? Is it obvious I dodged the real question?

So, I'll admit I'm a little nervous about seeing his dragon form. The whirlwind events of the evening helped gloss over that teeny-tiny factoid. I know he's a dragon—he's a Romanov, ergo, he was born one—but to me, he's just Julian. He looks human, feels human. Smells heavenly. I love him.

But what if I freak out? Faint, run screaming, vomit. What if I can't take it? Love conquers all is the crap peddled by movies, not real life. I don't think I can live with myself if I break his heart and make him feel like the monster he's tried so hard not to become.

Maybe I don't need to see it.

Sure, and doom our relationship from the beginning by choosing ignorance and lies. Christ, the thought of hurting him because I'm not strong enough films my eyes with tears. My cramped stomach jets bile into my throat.

"When this is done," Nate says, his voice empty, "when we've decided what to do with him and the rest of the Romanovs, you're out of the group, Raine. I can't trust you anymore."

I swallow a couple of times and hope Julian thinks it's because I'm upset at the threat of being forced out, not because I'm having heart palpitations at the reality of him turning scaly and distinctly smoky.

"You can't—" It comes out a croak and I clear my throat. "You can't do that. The others won't let you."

"The others will do what I tell them."

"They talked to Julian while you were gone. They're coming around to accepting him."

Nate drifts towards the door, his bulk merging with the shadows clinging to the corners of the room. "I don't care. When this is done, you're done with us."

"You don't have the authority to banish me," I say with more confidence than I feel, greedily dropping the issue of Julian's fire-breathing side in favour of this more human problem.

Nate can't force me to leave. The group is the closest thing I have to family. Losing them would be like losing my parents all over again.

"Principal Cozma does so don't turn this into a battle you can't win, Raine," he says, pulling the door open to a warm, yellow glow from a light somewhere down the hall. He stands silhouetted in the doorway, one hand on the handle, as cool as you please. "There is one way you can stay with us. With me—the person who took you in, protected you, trained you. Cared for you."

He starts to pull the door closed. The wedge of light dwindles. My pulse thuds dully in my temple, my mouth dry. He pauses when only a sliver of light remains.

"Kill the fucking dragon," he says, and seals me into the darkness.

27

"He really doesn't like me, does he?" Julian says in a quiet voice, the mattress bouncing as he rolls out from behind me.

I drag my gaze from the black outline of the door. Julian props himself on his elbows, the murky grey light shining in his eyes and tracing the smooth path of his collarbone. I command my heart to quit thrashing around but it pays me no mind.

The foundations of my life are sinking and taking me with them.

"I wouldn't take it personally," I say, the words tinny and distant to my ear. "If you were human, he still wouldn't like you."

But he's not human, is he Raine?

Shut up. It doesn't matter. I didn't stop loving him after I learned he was a Drakul. Why should I stop loving him once I see the proof of what I already know?

Because maybe I'm fooling myself, like a child hiding under the bed. If I can't see the monster, it's not real.

A sob slips out. I swallow the next one and it hurts. I duck my head, an awful clawing sensation tearing at my gut.

"Raine," Julian whispers, anguished.

His arms slide around me and cradle me to his chest, my

head tucked under his chin. His heart thumps against my cheek and, dammit, it's comforting. He's solid and warm. I want to cuddle closer and forget about everything.

Why couldn't he be human? Then he'd be perfect.

"Nate can't force you to go, can he? Your friends won't let him."

I shrug in his hold. "Sofia would threaten to leave or leave with me if it comes to that. Dustan and Fabian might argue but they'd stay. Rick is clearly going to be on Nate's side. And Nate's right—if the Vanatori ruling body expel me, it doesn't matter what anyone else says."

Part of me is relieved Julian thinks I'm only unhappy at the potential banishment and destitution. The other part snarls at my cowardice but it's too much to worry about right now. First, there's the problem of keeping Julian alive and unharmed in the same building as Nate, not to mention the danger posed by Julian's family.

Evelyn Romanov is an issue for all of us.

Julian sighs into my hair and hugs me harder, tight enough to squash my ribs. He releases me before I get woozy and slips out of the bed. His pale shape stoops to gather his scattered clothes.

"What are you doing?" I say.

He pauses, his back to me, the sweep of his spine and the curve of his butt not enough to distract me. The silence lengthens. The tearing in my gut spreads to each organ, leaving me hollow.

"I'm—" He clears his throat. "I'm going to go."

I blink. My mouth drops open.

"But I don't want you to go."

Christ. I could've said, "Where?" or, "Why?"

"The people in this house are your family. They love you." Another heavy sigh. "Family is the only thing I've ever wanted. I can't take it from you."

I toss the sheets aside and plant myself in front of him, my back to the window. His gaze drops, reminding me we're both naked and he sees better in the dark than I do.

"I love you," I say.

His eyes meet mine. "I love you, too. But tell them you changed your mind. We argued and I ran away."

"There's nowhere for you to go. You said you ran away once and you were tortured. I'm betting your mother is a better hunter than the lot of us."

He says nothing. It's confirmation enough.

"If you leave, she'll find you." My throat closes, making each word an effort. A scalding tear trickles down my cheek. "She'll kill you."

His mouth tilts in his sad half-smile. "I'm not human, Raine. It's selfish of me to stay and ruin your life."

It's one thing arguing with myself, it's a whole other thing to have my words repeated in his resigned voice. Like he doesn't deserve happiness.

"There's nothing you can possibly do to ruin my life," I growl at him, "except leave."

"Raine…" His voice wobbles. The stubborn lines of his face crumble.

He's scared. He doesn't want to go. But he will. He'll sacrifice himself and his tiny slice of joy if it means Nate accepts me back into the group.

How can I not love every piece of him?

I step closer and raise my chin. "You're not going anywhere, Julian."

"Are you sure you can stop me?" He sniffs and attempts a smile. "You humans are so fragile."

I stand an inch away, not touching. The heat of him tingles along my skin and dries my tears, his breath brushing my lips. Fast but soft.

"I can stop you because you're not leaving this room unless you hurt me. And you'll never hurt me."

He licks his lips and ducks his head but I've already seen the glitter of unshed tears in the morning's half-light.

"I don't want to go," he whispers.

"I don't want you to go, either."

He smiles a proper smile and peeks at me. "We're so screwed."

"Yup," I say, and kiss him.

Julian wraps his arms around me, his hands pressing me to him.

And what do you know—I forget about everything else.

* * *

Despite snatching only a few hours of sleep, we lie awake afterwards, snuggled in the bed, sweaty and satisfied. Well, I'm the sweaty one. Julian doesn't seem to sweat, except in extreme circumstances, and his body runs warmer than mine, which doesn't help my sweating situation. It's like cuddling a hot water bottle after an intense twenty-minute workout.

When our heart rates and breathing return to normal, I ask him about his childhood, his brothers, his mother. He tells me everything. No more, "It's complicated," for fear of letting something slip and revealing his identity. He talks about the large cruelties—his sick bitch of a mother threatening to remove his private parts on his fifteenth birthday, torturing and forcing him to eat a person, his brothers encouraging the girl of his dreams to pretend she wanted him.

How was a guy starved of contact and affection supposed to resist?

Other cruelties—physical and emotional abuse, keeping him isolated, treating him like a burden, convincing him he was ugly and worthless. His dragon form, his resistance to dragon's-bane and his different-coloured eyes—one of his most beautiful features—mark him as weak.

So, in answer to my question, no, he won't miss his brothers if we kill them all tomorrow.

Killing Lukas removed one of the biggest tormentors from his life, excluding his mother. I'll gladly slaughter her and her other sons if I ever meet them. I want to leap to my feet and hunt the bastards down but Julian hugs me close, his hand tracing the cleft of my spine.

Protective lioness to purring kitty in one stroke of his fingers.

He talks about the night we met on the cliff at Tantallon Castle and my tears pool on his chest. He thought about throwing himself to the mercy of the sea, if jagged rocks and frothing surf can be merciful. He sat and worked on his courage, unsure whether the fall would kill him and afraid of floating around in agony in the freezing dark, every bone shattered. He planned the best way—head first.

Even he couldn't survive a caved-in skull.

Then my voice surprised him since he was too preoccupied to hear my approach or my heartbeat. He says I smelled like coconut. Probably my shampoo. He tells me every little thing he couldn't before—how he seemed stiff when we met in

Portobello because his mother beat him for daring to be alive when her eldest was dead; how the Lessers who attacked us knew him and he was terrified they were going to give away his secret. He didn't contact me in the week following our kiss because his mother ordered him and his brothers out every night to search for the spot where Lukas died. During the day, he hid, lest the mere sight of him send his mother into a rage. The house was filled with people as she questioned them about her son's murder. Julian couldn't risk phoning me in case he was overheard.

I scrub my cheeks and push myself up to look at him. The grey first light has changed to burnished gold, tinting his hair, his eyes. My fingertips trace his cheekbone, nose, jaw and the curve of his lips. He tries not to wriggle but he's so adorably ticklish.

How can anyone hurt him?

My mouth follows the path of my fingers and he opens his lips to the slide of my tongue. His arms pull me on top of him, one hand cupping my butt and pressing me to the part of him that tells me he's quite happy with how things are going. It pulls a moan from my throat, heat arrowing to the place we fit so perfectly together. I stop kissing him before I get too distracted but the way he's moving his hips doesn't help.

"Julian, I—"

He tilts his pelvis and his erection rubs across swollen flesh.

"Oh, fuck me," I gasp, my eyes rolling back in my head.

He pauses only long enough to grin. "Okay."

"No, wait."

"Wait?"

"I have to tell you something but I can't if you keep doing that. I'll forget my own name."

He flashes me a delighted smile. "You always remember mine. You say it a lot."

It's true. Like a hundred times during sex. I can't help it. I love the sound, the taste, of his name in my mouth. Among other things…

Crap, now I'm distracting myself.

He rolls over, his weight on his elbows, the lower half of his body lifted off me. I pout at him and he chuckles, his hair flopping over his forehead.

"What do you want to tell me?" he says.

My cheeks heat under his steady gaze. I drop my eyes, suddenly shy.

"Raine?"

"You deserve every day to be your best day from now on," I whisper to his collarbone, "and I will do everything I can to make it that way."

He goes very still. I risk a peek. His face is as raw as I've ever seen it, more naked than the rest of him.

"You promise?"

"I promise," I say.

His expression softens into something so tender, tears prick my eyes and clog my throat. He lowers himself, his lips barely touching mine. I arch upwards, demanding more, and he collapses on top of me. I moan his name, again and again. The second before I forget my own, I pray.

Please, god, don't let me break my promise.

28

I keep my other promise to Julian before we fall asleep—I tell him about how I became an orphan in the desert of another country. The Burning Man festival. My parents travelled from Scotland every year to showcase their sculptures and participate in the community. They took me for the first time as my fifteenth birthday present.

I'd begged to go since I was ten.

It was more amazing than I imagined—the shocking heat, the dust storms that made everyone dress like they were extras from *Mad Max*, the beautifully free community of artists and hippies and everyone in between. I loved it. Especially the Saturday they burned the Man.

The first part of it, anyway.

I watched the burning in all its splendour, wide-eyed, mouth agape, my parents on either side of me, enjoying my reaction. Mum gripped my hand in her excitement, her rings digging into my fingers. She always smelled like incense, mostly jasmine, and wore enough bracelets to punctuate every movement with a musical jangle. Dad had his arm around us both. No one was taller than my dad and he had the deepest laugh. I easily picked him out of a crowd.

"Beautiful, isn't it, Rainey?" he said, his warm eyes alight with the reflection of the flames.

I could only nod.

My parents took me out of Black Rock City using a pass and circled the huge playa. Dad parked the car off the road, dust and brush scraping the sides. We climbed a hill in the dark and looked down on the City. The view was spectacular, the familiar C-shape lit up for the night around the burning effigy, tiny from that distance. Music and the murmur of thousands of voices thudded across the flattened landscape below us. The sky was midnight-blue velvet, cold and clear and lovely. I'd never seen so many stars.

When the ground vibrated beneath my hiking boots, I thought it was an earthquake. But earthquakes don't bring a wave of prickling warmth and wind. Earthquakes don't growl. We turned as a unit, my brain unable to process what my eyes told it because monsters weren't real, therefore two dragons couldn't possibly have joined us on the hill. They watched us. We watched them. I forgot to blink and breathe. The distant fire glowed on the scales of the huge gold. I'll never forget the circle of black horns like a crown and the crimson eyes. The hide of the other dragon rivalled the darkness of the sky and swallowed the starlight.

I almost convinced myself I was hallucinating—a side effect of the second-hand weed smoke I'd huffed that day—until the gold stretched its neck out and sniffed at my dad, the air from its nostrils ruffling his jacket.

Delicately—casually—it plucked off his arm.

Dad made no sound. Liquid pattered on rock. For a glorious, frozen moment, I thought it was a dream. I willed myself to wake up. Dad raised his hand, slowly, as if the air had thickened. He touched his fingertips to his ravaged shoulder.

They came away dripping and black in the darkness. Mum sucked in a breath and whispered his name. The gold dragon tilted its head. Lunged. It tossed my dad into the air and he hit the ground hard, the snap of bone loud against the dull throb of the festival continuing oblivious on the playa behind us.

Dad was no longer silent.

Mum rushed towards him. The gold picked him up by the leg and threw him to the black. It caught him in its mouth and shook him, then dropped him like a dog bored of its toy.

His foot was gone.

Mum reached him, her face a pale oval, her mouth opened wide. I couldn't hear her bangles or her screaming or my screaming, only a roaring in my ears. The dragons never let her touch him. They lobbed my dad back and forth, taking a nibble each time until there was nothing left but splashes of gore on the rocks.

Then they did the same to my mum.

She tried to run, her eyes on me, her arms stretched out as if she would scoop me up and spirit me away.

But soon, she couldn't run anymore.

The smell hit me, sweet and metallic, dense enough to choke on. The dragons stank of burning paper and something like wax. They loomed over me where I cowered on my knees, my hands pressed to my face, shrieking and whimpering as fast as I could draw breath.

Not a big tough dragon hunter but a terrified child.

The night closed in, the stars sparkling wherever I looked. I wavered on the edge of fainting, grateful for the mercy. Maybe I wouldn't feel them eating me alive.

The clatter of automatic fire seemed out of place in that

alien planet of dragons and blood. The black roared and its claws slashed the sky. A mess of pink flesh bloomed on its shoulder. The gold dodged and a shotgun blast scoured its flank. Whoops and yells followed but I couldn't turn my head. The dragons fled in a blast of sand. A twenty-two-year-old Nate cradled me in his arms, young and dark and intense. Less bulky.

"You're safe with us," he said.

He bundled me into the back seat of a Chevrolet pick-up truck, the soft light from the front console brushing his dark face. He used to be gentle, patient, almost like a brother. He taught me how to fight and how to be brave when fear sucked the breath from my body and clenched my stomach tight.

But then I turned sixteen and discovered his thoughts weren't brotherly. I wanted a comrade in arms, not a boyfriend, not yet. As white knight to my damsel in distress, he assumed I'd fall madly in love with him. Nine years later, his own group transported an ocean away from his home country, and he's still hoping.

I guess I should be flattered.

29

Gentle hands shake me awake to someone leaning over me, a spill of chestnut hair hiding one eye.

"Are you okay, Raine?" Julian says, his hands still now that I'm blinking at him. "You were whimpering in your sleep."

Bright sunlight blazes on the closed curtains and spears through a gap to stripe the rumpled covers of the bed. The sheets pool in Julian's lap, protecting his modesty but leaving his chest bare. My eyes follow the long, lean line of him to the flatness of his stomach. I reach out to trace all that smooth, warm skin but hesitate.

A few hours after recounting the murder of my mum and dad and all I can think of is sex. With a dragon.

I bunch the covers in my fists and pull them up to my chin. "I'm fine. Must have been a nightmare. I don't even remember it."

"Was it your parents?"

I flinch. "Why do you ask?"

"Because before you looked like you wanted to touch me." He moves away, lifting his hands carefully from where he placed them to shake me awake. "And now you don't."

I frown at him. The spurt of anger isn't fair. It's the guilt, giving me an excuse to push him away, to blame him for my

180

parents' death and every terrible thing the Drakul have ever done.

Like Nate.

Christ, only a few hours ago I promised to make Julian happy and here I am being unreasonable.

I sit up slowly, keeping the sheet in place. "You're the first person I've ever told about how my parents died, outside of the Vanatori. It's like reliving their deaths but all I wanted to do when I woke up was touch you. It made me feel guilty. Like I should be more upset. I'm sorry—it's stupid."

He plays with his fingers in his lap, the weight of his clasped hands shifting the covers to reveal his hipbones.

Man, those hipbones. How can a bony protuberance be so sexy?

"So you've not changed your mind?"

I drag my gaze to his face. He stares at his hands in his lap. "About what?"

"About me." He peeks at me, a sad smile dimming his eyes. "Maybe things look different in the daylight."

Was it only last night I learned who and what he is? It seems longer. Part of me wants to stay angry for thinking I'd turn on him so quickly but how can I fault him? His own family tortured him for years. He's had no one to trust. The thought of his loneliness burns a hole in my gut. Of course he needs a little reassurance. This morning is like waking up next to a stranger after a one-night stand. Will there be awkwardness and shame and regret or will they cuddle you and want to play some more?

I lower the sheet and roll onto my knees in front of him, one finger tilting his chin until he meets my gaze.

"I've not changed my mind. You are as glorious now as you

were last night and all the days before." I place a light kiss on his lips and the surprise on his face both saddens and thrills me.

He swallows a couple of times, struggling with his expression. "You think I'm glorious?"

"I know you are."

He smiles the shy, joyful smile only I get to see.

I kiss him, guiding him down to lie on top of me, the weight of him enough to speed my pulse. Somehow, the covers stay wrapped around his hips, separating us, and I moan my disappointment into his mouth. My hands slide towards the offending material. He pins them to the bed, his lips curving against mine. His hips start to move, gliding his body over mine, heavy between my legs. Even though we're not skin to skin, the pressure builds.

There's going to be a wet patch on the sheets if he's not careful.

"Julian, please." My word, I sound breathy.

He grins at me, a beautiful mix of cheeky confidence and awe, as if he still can't believe he's allowed to be here, doing this.

"I'm glorious, remember?" He circles his hips and I buck on the mattress, needing him closer. "Tell me again."

"You're glorious," I gasp, unable to keep from squirming. "Julian, *please*."

He stops and I almost weep.

"It's not just the sex, right?" he says, the cockiness replaced by his disarming vulnerability.

I force my eyes open, though can't remember closing them.

"I loved you before the sex," I say. "I loved you when I thought you were only a lost and wounded boy."

It feels good to admit how quickly I fell for him. Stupid-quick.

His arms tremble where he props himself up. "And now that you know who I am? What I am?"

I hold his gaze. "I know who you are. What you are. And I love you, Julian Romanov."

His smile softens his face, making him more beautiful, though it doesn't seem possible or fair. He lowers himself in a push up to nibble at my mouth. I fling my legs around his waist and shatter his careful control. He kisses me hard, deep, his hips resuming their dance.

"God, but the sex helps," I whimper.

He laughs and it turns into a groan when the sheet slips, my slickness pressed to his. He shifts his weight, angling his hips. I hold my breath.

I want him so badly, it's like a craving. My body aches for him, aches for release, aches—

"Raine, get your ass down here!" Nate hollers up the stairs. "Don't make me drag you out."

Julian freezes, the tip of him cradled by the most intimate part of me and I think seriously about ignoring the demand and shagging my dragon as the biggest, "Screw you," I could possibly give Nate. But the bastard probably would burst in on us and I don't want to risk Julian getting into a fight if Nate catches us in the act. He knows we're having sex but the human mind is all about delusion.

Julian keeps himself very still. "Would he?"

"Drag me out? Oh, yeah."

I breathe slowly, trying to calm my heartbeat and not move at the same time. If I move, even a little, I may forget why sex is a bad idea. Best not to start the day with Nate hating Julian more than he already does.

Especially since I need to convince him it's better for everyone if Julian stays alive.

30

A knock on the door disturbs us in the middle of dressing but it's too polite to be Nate. Wincing, I pull my crumpled, low-cut top on from yesterday and open the door to Sofia, looking fresh in a crisp pair of black jeans, a wide colourful belt and a deep-purple halter top with long, floaty sleeves. I usually feel dowdy next to her no matter what I'm wearing. She has that South American exoticness going on.

A petty little voice wonders if she would be with Julian had he met her at Tantallon that night. She's a classic beauty—curvy, sultry, lips to die for. Is he only with me because I'm the first woman who was nice to him?

I tell myself to shut up.

Sofia wouldn't have been nice to him, anyway. She wouldn't have accepted his silences and evasions. She's not as trusting as me.

She holds out a navy duffel bag, a neat pile of clothes balanced in her other hand. "Here is your emergency stuff. Dustan picked out some spares from his. He and Julian are about the same size since Dustan likes baggy clothes that showcase his skinny butt."

"What're the boxers today?"

She rolls her eyes but smiles. "Paul Smith."

We all have supplies at each others' houses, headquarters and various locations close to home. Our version of a bug-out bag, though probably with more knives than a normal person's. We used them once on a year-long mission to Brussels, hunting a diplomat who also happened to be a Drakul emissary. Mikala, who looked like a stocky Scarlett Johansson, seduced one of the diplomat's Lessers, hoping to gain information. Nate was against the idea but Mikala ignored him. She didn't plan on falling in love with the Lesser. He played her, sweet-talking her to betray her secrets. It cost her her life and the lives of four of our group, scattering the rest of us. Principal Cozma mandated our mourning and recuperation time to retrain and think on past mistakes.

So Nate has valid reasons for distrusting my relationship with Julian and for being a grumpy bastard in general. I just never held it against him until now.

"Thanks, Sofia," I say. "Is everyone waiting for us downstairs?"

"Yes, but I am distracting them with pancakes and coffee." She peers around my shoulder to Julian in his torn, dirty clothes. "You can use the shower in my en-suite. Both doors lock."

"I doubt Nate has the patience to wait for us to shower."

Sofia's black, sparkling eyes fix on me. "Showering together would save time *and* water."

A shower would feel pretty good… but no sex. Still a bad idea. There's no need to test Nate that much.

Sofia's room is decorated in autumnal tones, the king-size bed taking up most of the space. A burnished orange throw bordered by a triangle pattern dangles on the edge of the bed and matches a thick rug on the polished wood floor. I lock the door and hand Julian his pile of clothes—a black hoodie with a red, diagonal zipper and hood lining, and a pair of dark jeans. No t-shirt for underneath.

"You go first but be quick."

He disappears into the bathroom, leaving the door open a crack. Water hisses on. I inch closer then throw myself on the bed, my fingers tapping my knees while I examine everywhere but the bathroom doorway. A curl of steam licks out of the opening. Dammit, I'm watching the door. I frown at a vase of pink roses on the windowsill.

What is wrong with me? How can I crave sex more now than when I wasn't getting any at all? Maybe it's because I know how tasty Julian looks in the shower. Water slicking his shoulders and beading in his eyelashes. Rivulets trickling down that lean, muscled body...

Okay, not helping. If I frown any harder at the roses, I'll hurt myself.

"Raine?"

I jump and hope he can't hear my heartbeat over the rush of water. "Yeah?"

"Any towels out there?"

I shove to my feet and search a short wicker cabinet beside the bathroom, a blue glass bowl of lemon-scented potpourri sitting on top. Fluffy towels are crammed inside. I hover at the doorway, two bundles hugged to my chest. Warm, humid air caresses my arms. The sound of splashing water tempts me to throw the door wide. Or I could toss the towels in without looking.

Coward. Do I really have no self-control?

I square my shoulders and enter the bathroom. I glimpse golden tiles, marble and chrome. My confidence lasts until

I focus on the glass shower cubicle, barely fogged. Julian's head is tilted back, his eyes closed. Bubbles slither down pale, perfect skin. Down and down and down…

Oh, crap.

I must make a sound, a gasp, a moan—hell, my pulse is doing a tango—because he opens his eyes, his wet hair clinging to his cheekbones. I drop the towels on the floor. Somehow, my t-shirt joins them. Julian's slow smile tingles to my stomach.

"I thought we had to be quick," he says.

My fingers unbutton my jeans and shimmy them off. "I'm having trouble remembering why that is."

His smile widens. Anything that puts such happiness on his face can't possibly be bad.

I slide the lock on the bathroom door and step into the shower, engulfed by vanilla-scented heat. Julian's gaze falls all the way to my toes and back to my face, lingering. Hungry. I place a palm on the slick tile to steady myself.

"I think we can still be quick," he says.

I swallow hard. "You're getting cocky."

"Is it cocky if it's true?"

He holds out his hand and draws me towards him. Water mists my skin, splashing off his head and shoulders.

"Time to get you wet."

"Oh, I'm already wet," I say.

He chuckles and I love the sound. I slide my hands over his chest, drink the water from his lips. He kisses me with the same franticness I feel around him. His hands grip my hips and lift me up. My legs wrap around his waist. He feels, smells, tastes so damn good.

Turns out he's right about the quickie.

31

"Where the fuck are his cuffs?" Nate growls as soon as we enter the living room.

This would probably have been his response even if we'd skipped the shower and scrambled to his order, though I'm sure the twenty minutes it took us to appear haven't helped his mood.

The living room continues the autumnal theme of Sofia's bedroom—red brick fireplace, brown throws on the couch and chairs, burnt orange pillows. Nate has a pancake halfway to his mouth, a syrup-slicked plate balanced on his lap.

"He doesn't need them," I say.

The pancake splats into the puddle of syrup. Nate twists in the chair, catapulting the crockery, and straightens with his crossbow pointed at Julian. Sunlight through the bay window twinkles on the wicked tip of the bolt. The plate shatters on the floor. I jump in front of Julian, bumping my shoulder against Fabian, who leaps from the couch at the same time, his empty plate still in his hand. Sofia freezes in the doorway, holding a full cafetière.

Dustan, also on his feet but at the far end of the couch, makes a calming motion towards Nate. "She might be right, Nate. We shouldn't condemn him just for what he is."

"I don't believe this." Nate's black gaze slides between Dustan and Fabian, his frown deep enough to have its own shadow. "Just how cosy did you all get while I risked my life to protect us from *his brothers?* Do none of you remember Cian?"

We share a flinch. Dustan and Fabian shift their feet, their eyes anywhere but on Nate.

"We remember," Sofia says, placing the cafetière on the coffee table next to a stack of pancakes, clean plates and mugs. "This is not the same."

"How is it not? Cian tricked Mikala into betraying our confidence because he was a charming monster. The only difference is he was a fucking Lesser, not a Drakul. This is worse."

"Cian never met any of us beforehand," I say, aiming for authoritative, which is difficult when balancing on one's tiptoes to act as a human shield. "He would have tried to hurt us if he did. He slaughtered Mikala as soon as he knew she was Vanatori."

We found her body in the house she rented one town over from mine. Unless we're on a hunt or dealing with an emergency, we keep ourselves spread out, make it harder to destroy the whole group. I remember the blood, her glazed eyes. The marks of Cian's claws. He carved out her heart and we never found it. I imagine he took it to his master as a gift, along with the knowledge of where she could find more pesky hunters.

"Your beast-toy has simply lacked opportunity," Nate says. "He's been cuffed most of the time."

Beast-toy? What a fun play on boy-toy, except Julian is a year older than me.

"He hasn't been cuffed since last night."

A muscle bunches in Nate's jaw, his knuckles white where they grip the crossbow. "Was he cuffed when I was in the room?"

Sofia casts me a puzzled glance from where she's crouched by the coffee table and mouths, "In your room?"

I fix my gaze on Nate. "No, he wasn't."

"You stupid bitch." His voice is low, cold, almost unrecognisable. "Do you not like to fuck your little dragon when he's all tied up?"

I speak before my brain tells me it's a bad idea. "Oh, I already had, I just wanted some variety."

Nate's eyes narrow, the darkness spiralling down into a bottomless pit. I throw myself backwards, colliding with Julian. We slam to the ground in the hall but instead of it being a tangle of limbs and huffing breath and me giving him a reverse headbutt, he wraps an arm around to steady me against him, his other arm slapping the floor to keep his skull from connecting too hard.

Bloody fast reflexes. How did I not notice? I throw myself at him *a lot*.

The bolt thunks into the wall opposite the doorway. A trickle of bluish-white fluid leaks from where the metal pierces the plaster and paints a thick line towards the floor. Yelling spills from the living room. I roll out of Julian's grip and yank him to his feet, jiggling the front door handle. Damn thing is locked. I back him into the corner, my sword in my hand. The wide spread of Fabian's shoulders blocks the way into the living room. Rick slithers into the kitchen doorway at the opposite end of the hall, a knife in each hand. He must have sneaked through the dining room, though I can't recall where he was before the shit hit the fan.

The guy is invisible.

"I have eyes on him, Nate," he says. "Just give me the word."

My grip tightens on the hilt of my sword, the blade jerking to the heavy thud of my pulse. "He's not fighting back. He's not attacking us."

Rick places a careful foot into the hall, his brown eyes focused over my shoulder. Fabian throws me an apologetic look from the living room doorway, unable to help since his body is keeping Nate from taking more pot-shots with his crossbow.

I'll have blades over projectiles any day.

Rick claims another step. "He could shift and bury us in rubble in a second."

"It takes at least ten. And does he look like he's shifting?"

"No, but he could."

The dragon's-bane solution inches over the skirting board and forms a tiny pool on the floor. Dustan and Nate argue in harsh tones from the living room. The words 'stupid naive cow' are being used frequently by one party.

"And I could stab you with my sword before you get close to cutting Julian," I say to Rick. "So how about you stand nice and still?"

A blade like a sharpened chopstick appears at Rick's throat. His eyes widen and his foot freezes mid-step.

"*Sí*, Rick darling," Sofia says, her accent thick, "why do we not all calm down. *Mi casa, mis reglas*. And I say no one gets slaughtered today."

"You won't hurt—"

Rick winces. A bead of blood slithers down the groove of his neck and stains the collar of his white shirt.

"Do not push me, *querido*. I am tired of the posturing and the testosterone. The dick-waving. You will sit and behave or I will paint my walls red."

Man, she'll make an excellent mother someday—apart from the threat of exsanguination. Her kids will be too terrified to rebel.

"Nate?" Rick squeaks.

Sofia puts her lip close to his ear. "Do not seek permission from him. I am the one with the knife to your throat. Put up your weapons and sit in the living room."

Rick's blades disappear into the folds of his awful suit. He slinks back the way he came, his fingers pressed to his neck.

Sofia slips her knife into her perfectly pinned-up hair. "I am afraid if we are to reach any decisions today, Julian will have to be cuffed. I am sorry, Julian."

He nods. "I understand."

"Raine?" Sofia says.

I realise I'm scowling and puff out a breath. "Fine, if his pain will make everyone else feel better."

Fabian sheepishly dangles a pair of cuffs from the living room doorway. I stop myself from snatching them in a huff. Julian holds out his wrists, his mouth curved in a half-smile. I balance my sword against the wall and fasten the cuffs over the sleeves of his hoodie, loose enough so he can get free if he struggles but not too loose that they'll fall off when he lowers his arms. I pick up my sword and lead him into the living room. Fabian reclaims his seat on the couch. Nate frowns from the chair opposite, his crossbow in his lap but not pointed at us. Rick sidles over to stand behind him.

Sofia enters via the dining room and claps her hands. "Now, let us sheath our weapons and see if we can get through a conversation without bloodshed, like normal adults."

Nate glares at me from across the room. I usher Julian towards the chairs in the bay window but stay standing.

"Not all of the adults here are normal," Nate says, his lip curled.

I roll my eyes. "Yeah, some are more sociopathic than the average male."

"At least I'm not fucking the monsters, you—"

"*Nate!*" Sofia's voice cracks through the room before I decide to rearrange his anatomy with my sword. "Crossbow. Down. *Now.*"

After a pause, he places the crossbow on the floor at his feet.

"Your knives, Rick," Sofia says.

The weapons thunk on the carpet behind Nate's chair. Sofia raises an eyebrow at me.

I sigh. "Only if they promise to stop trying to stick sharp objects in my boyfriend from now on, not just this goddamn morning."

Oh, crap. I called him my boyfriend.

Nate throws up his hands. "Your dragon *boyfriend?* This is fucking ridiculous."

"Does that mean you're my girlfriend?"

Julian's soft voice drags my attention away from Nate and his dramatic gestures. Julian sits with his cuffed hands in his lap, the diagonal zipper of his hoodie open enough to show a flash of collarbone and the hollow of his throat. The fact he has no t-shirt on underneath is unbearably distracting. As is his tender smile. Joy glows in his face and glitters in his eyes.

He's so beautiful, I can't breathe. He's perfect and fragile and, oh god, I don't want to break him by accident. How can I be responsible for his happiness?

The light fades a little. "Raine?"

"I guess it does," I mumble, my cheeks hot. I give myself a mental slap and straighten my spine. "I mean, I am—I'm your girlfriend."

His smile brightens. I make googly eyes at him in front of everyone but can't seem to stop.

Sweet lord, my boyfriend's a dragon. There's no support group for this stuff.

Sofia serves Julian and me a cup of coffee and a stack of pancakes. I wolf them down. Thick, fluffy and soaked in syrup. I can't remember when I last ate. Yesterday? Was it really the Mexican takeaway with Julian?

It feels like years ago.

Sofia flits into the kitchen and returns with a dustpan, sweeping up the remains of Nate's breakfast and scrubbing a damp cloth into the splodges of syrup.

"What happened last night, Nate?" she says.

Nate leans back in his chair. Julian's cuffs clink against his plate, sawing his pancakes made awkward by the bonds. Nate's black eyes flick to Julian, his face twisting before it smooths and he focuses on Sofia.

"I ran back inside. The two Dustan tagged with the petrol didn't even bother searching for you. They tried to burn the building, presumably waiting for me to run out screaming. Instant barbecue."

I fork seconds onto my plate and split it with Julian. Nate's heavy gaze tracks me until I reclaim my seat. There's nothing familiar in his face, his expression predatory and calculating, sending a shiver down my spine. I pretend to be fascinated by my breakfast.

"So what did you do?" Dustan pours himself another coffee,

the fragrant steam wisping upwards.

"I shot the bronze one from a window. Aimed for the heart but the bastard moved at the last minute and my bolt hit its shoulder." Nate's smile is wicked. "He squealed and bled and the silvers swooped in and carted him away. I expected more of a fight from the mighty Romanovs but maybe all the sons are weak."

He directs his smile at Julian. I consider drowning it in my scalding coffee. Julian gives him nothing but a pleasant, blank face, no doubt perfected after years of abuse at the hands of his family.

Weak, my butt. He's the strongest person I know.

"Believe me, they're not weak," he says.

"Maybe they are when they come up against someone who fights back."

I bristle in my seat, my muscles tensed to leap to Julian's defence. He shakes his head at me.

"If I'd fought back, they would've hurt me worse."

"Or maybe they would've respected you."

Julian's mouth curls in a half-smile. "They'd never respect me, no matter what I did."

"No wonder," Nate says, throwing up his hands again. "Look at you! Every other Drakul would be trying to gouge out my liver for a mantelpiece decoration. You cower behind Raine every chance you get like a kicked fucking puppy. What pathetic excuse for a dragon are you?"

Julian laughs but there's nothing happy in it. "You sound like my mother."

"Jesus Christ, Nate, listen to yourself," I say, setting my plate on the carpet to remove the temptation of Frisbeeing it into his mouth. "You finally admit he's different but you're disappointed he's not a violent, bloodthirsty monster. What exactly do you want from him?"

"I want him to quit the fucking act."

"You just said he's not acting like any other Drakul."

"Exactly! He's faking it. No Drakul from a family as powerful as his has ever been anything but vicious. I've heard the stories. I've seen the bodies."

"So let me get this straight," I say, and scowl at Nate. "When he's sweet and gentle you mistrust him because he's not vicious but were he to be vicious, you'd kill him. Is there any way he can behave that would be acceptable to you?"

"No, and that's my point—he's a Drakul, it doesn't matter how he behaves. This"—Nate waves his hand at Julian—"wimpy, battered little victim act hides the real monster."

"Wow," Sofia says, crossing her arms. "This is what indoctrination is, yes? Sticking to beliefs no matter the facts?"

Nate scoffs. "It's called experience."

I lean closer to Julian and slide my hand between his cuffs to wrap my fingers in his. Metal bites my wrist but I don't care. He's warm and sweet and mine. No one gets to ridicule him for being any of those things.

Red spots flare on Nate's cheeks and his dark brows crash together. Rick hovers over his chair like a brown scarecrow.

"Why don't we get back to the real issue?" Dustan places his cup on the coffee table and waits until we all look at him. "What are we going to do about the Romanovs? Excluding Julian, of course."

Nate's head swivels back. "Oh, no, I very much want to decide what we're going to do with the reptile."

"His name is Julian," I say.

"Only humans deserve names."

"Coming from a guy who called his dog Horatio."

"Fine, Raine—humans and animals. He is nothing."

Julian's fingers tighten around mine. "Now you sound like my brothers."

"Oh, boo-fucking-hoo. If you're trying to be pitiful, you've succeeded."

"Raine!" Sofia shouts. "I said no bloodshed."

I'm on my feet, sword in one hand, Julian's hand in the other. My blood fizzes, my ragged breath roaring in my ears. Nate's eyes widen slightly but he schools his face. I swallow the anger and it burns all the way down.

"You don't know a damn thing about him," I say in a voice quite unlike my own. "Until you do, keep your mouth shut or I'll shut it for you."

I stare at him, my face rigid. My eyes feel empty, dead. I hope Nate is scared because I'm scaring myself. He finally looks away. I sheath my sword and sit down. My blood pounds in my temples.

"This is why women make bad warriors," Nate mumbles at his shoes. "Too fucking emotional."

Dustan drops his face into his palm. "For god's sake, Nate."

Emotional? I'll give him emotional. I'll emotionally skewer him like a shish kebab.

"You are the one being petty and hostile," Sofia says, perching on the end of the couch beside Dustan, her arms tightly folded. I suspect it's so she doesn't belt Nate. "What we need right now is calm and sensible discussion. Julian could be a real asset if you let yourself see him without prejudice."

"Prejudice? Well excuse me if the Drakul turned my brother into a Lesser slave and worked him to death. Or murdered Raine's parents. Fabian's entire family…"

"But none of them were Julian. He has not tried to cruelly or deliberately kill any of us."

"George—"

"Was neither cruel nor deliberate."

The flush fades from Nate's cheeks. He shifts in his chair, apparently at a loss. Perhaps it's Sofia's soothing voice or everyone bar Rick looking at him with expressions of disapproval.

The funny thing is, I understand Nate's anger and frustration—I used to feel the same. But now I have new information. I can see that Julian is different to anything we've encountered before. Sofia's right—the fact Nate won't consider the possibility speaks of a level of indoctrination that scares me. He's been in the Vanatori longer than any of us. Except Rick. I always forget Rick.

"Okay, Sofia, explain to me how he could be an asset," Nate says.

"Oh, goodness, no"—she tips her head towards him—"I bow to your tactical experience."

His black gaze fixes on Julian. "I know what I want to do with him but since most of you are inexplicably against it, we can go with my second choice—he leads us right into the Romanov compound and we destroy them."

Julian goes very still, his grip crushing my fingers. "Don't make me go back there. Please."

No wonder he doesn't want to go back to the place where they made his life a misery and where they'll kill him slowly if they capture him. He resigned himself to never escaping when I first met him but now he has an option he never dreamed of—we will protect him.

I will protect him.

"Don't get me wrong," I say, keeping my voice mild, "I'd love to storm the Romanov castle but we'd be massively outnumbered and trapped in their territory. If we managed to get in."

"Come on, Raine, it would be minted!" Dustan says, the hem of his baggy jeans practically obscuring his feet. "Taking them out at home where they feel safest."

Fabian nods. Even Sofia seems to be considering the idea.

But I don't want to shove Julian into danger. He's suffered enough. We're the Vanatori. We're the ones who leap into battle against evil.

"That's just it, though, they *are* safe. It'll be fortified. Despite Julian's insider knowledge, they'll have the advantage. We need to draw them out. Draw them away from their defences."

"You just don't want to put your boyfriend in harm's way," Nate says.

I keep my expression as unemotional as possible. "I think your first suggestion in the basement was stronger and more likely to succeed."

"What suggestion?"

I take a deep breath. "We use me as bait and lure Evelyn Romanov to us."

32

What the holy freaking hell was I thinking? Volunteering to lure the top dragon lady, especially after I killed her eldest son, is a short road to a long and horrible death. She's terrifying enough when viewed remotely on a VC screen. I'll pee my pants if I see her in the flesh. What will I do if she catches me? She'll nibble little pieces off until I die insane from agony or blood loss, whichever comes first.

"Are you all right, Raine?"

I jump at Julian's voice, his body twisted beside me in the back seat of Sofia's jeep so his fingertips can touch my hand clenched in my lap. Rick tilts his head but keeps his eyes on the road, his hands on the wheel.

"You don't have to do this," Julian continues. "I'll do what Nate wants."

I shake my head and tug the sleeves of his hoodie more firmly underneath his cuffs. "It's better this way. I'm a good teacher but one self-defence class doesn't mean you're ready for battle. And that's what it will be if we try to infiltrate your house."

More like a massacre.

"But what if you get hurt or…?" He frowns through his window at the buildings scattered between the trees, the car slowing as we approach Peebles. "You're the only happiness I've found in twenty-six years. I don't want to lose you already."

Thank god Nate isn't in our car. He went ahead of us in a black BMW with Dustan and Fabian to scope out the area around my house.

Sofia sighs softly from the passenger seat. Rick hunches closer to the wheel, the back of his suit ridged like a newly ploughed field. I squeeze Julian's hand until he looks at me.

"This is what I do—lure, hunt, fight."

Weaker dragons, screams my wimpy internal voice, *not the most powerful monster in the country!* And, even then, we hardly ever come face to snout. We mess up their food supply, Lessers and cash flow. Goading Evelyn Romanov is way out of my comfort zone.

"I'll be careful," I say. "Knowing you're safe will help me do that. I don't want to lose you, either."

Tears catch at the back of my throat.

Christ.

I feign interest in the kids skipping to school out my window, laden with book-filled backpacks. Such a normal activity in a nice border town. The adults inside, drinking their first coffee of the day. The usual worries of life—work, money, bringing your kids up right. Not whether you'll get burned to a crisp by a scaly, sharp-toothed, fire-breathing monster who happens to be your boyfriend's mother.

"We're almost to your street," Sofia says, peeking at me around the headrest.

Julian and I hunker down in the back seat.

"Park a few houses away," I say. "We don't want to be obvious."

Nate and Dustan will be scoping on foot to check if anyone's watching my house. Evelyn Romanov doesn't know what they look like so they should be able to blend in as residents going about their business. But we have Julian in the car and he can sense things we can't.

Rick steers left and the vehicle climbs uphill. Trees crowd in on either side as the road narrows to a single lane. I stare at a slice of blue sky from my cramped position, my knees against the rear of Sofia's seat. Julian folds himself into the footwell, his arms straight out and resting on his knees.

His head comes up, his hair flopping over one eye. "Dominic's here."

"As a dragon? In broad daylight?"

He nods. "I can hear him."

"Guess that answers the question on whether Evelyn Romanov knows who you are," Rick says dryly.

I shiver. "I thought the Drakul could select who they project their thoughts to—why would Dominic let you hear him?"

"Maybe he thinks I won't be with you." Julian shrugs. "The Vanatori don't tend to treat us nicely if they catch us in our human form, no matter what you said to my mother."

"So he's watching my house to let her know when I'm here?"

Julian nods. "He could be anywhere in the trees. He's the bronze but he can shift his colour to blend in. He'll look like a grassy mound. Or a rock."

Rick glances over his shoulder but he probably can't see more of Julian than his legs.

"You got any fancy tricks?" he says.

"No."

"Figures."

Julian cocks his mouth. "You and Nate would get on really

well with my family."

Sofia talks into her sleeve, passing the information to Nate. Rick drives further up the road and turns around. All seems quiet, Julian not sensing anyone else in dragon form. His mother, two brothers and an army of Lessers could be camped in my bedroom and we wouldn't know a damn thing.

But, as the bait, I get to find out.

Rick stops the car on a street to the south that runs parallel to mine. Fabian, Nate and Dustan pull their BMW in close behind ten minutes later. A man walking a massive fluffy dog strolls past and into the woods, the road another dead end. For vehicles, anyway. I open my door, the scent of hot concrete and greenery wafting in.

I don't want to get out. I have blades strapped to every part of my body but they're not enough. Evelyn Romanov can crush my throat in her human form without breaking a sweat.

Julian reaches for me but is brought up short, his body wedged in the footwell. He wriggles, trying to shove himself up on his bound hands. His growing consternation gives me the giggles. Somewhat hysterical but I'll take it.

"I'm stuck," he says, his lopsided grin setting my heart to flip-flopping.

"You're adorable."

"I'm not adorable, I'm a goddamn man. Nah, who am I kidding"—his grin widens—"I'm a kicked fucking puppy."

I tumble across the seat and capture his mouth, my fists bunched in his hoodie. I kiss him as if I want to climb inside. Eager, breathless, tongues everywhere. I slip my fingers in his open zip and play along his collarbone. He still smells of vanilla despite Sofia's citrus shower gel. He shivers and I immediately want to get in his pants.

Rick clears his throat. "Jesus, Raine. Even if he were human, this would be unseemly."

"Oh, quiet, you big prude," Sofia says. "It is sweet."

Rick snorts in a perfect imitation of Nate. "Tell me how sweet it is when we all find ourselves in chains after he betrays us to his family."

Sofia and Rick snap at each other. I drag Julian out of the footwell as Nate arrives at my open door, leaning his elbow against the rim.

"There's no signs of forced entry and no one we can see watching your house without making our presence obvious so we'll monitor the outside," he says. "Go in, see if anyone's there. If not, act normal. Make tea. Put the TV on. The bronze may be in his dragon form but that bitch will have to walk up to your door as a human."

"If she's not already in there," I mutter.

I push the earpiece into my ear and fiddle with the microphone in my sleeve. I pretend my fingers aren't shaking. Julian shimmies himself next to me, his hip pressed to mine.

"Be careful," he whispers, all the humour gone from his face.

"Did you hear that?" Nate barks into his mic, his voice echoing in my ear.

Dustan replies, "Loud and clear."

I ignore them all and kiss Julian. Slower this time, lingering, but no less amazing. It tingles to my toes.

I don't want to leave. I want to bundle him somewhere safe and forget everything else.

But Evelyn Romanov will never stop hunting us.

Reluctantly, I pull away. Nate's glower bakes my spine. I cup Julian's face and my thumb strokes over his cheekbone.

"I'll be careful, I promise," I say, and turn my attention to Sofia. "You'll look after him, right?"

"He will not be hurt on my watch, honey. I will make sure of it."

I slide out of the car and shut the door after a slight hesitation. Julian raises his bound hands in farewell. I muster a brave smile and wave as the jeep swings a U-turn and pulls away, disappearing around a corner and carving my stomach hollow.

Nate doesn't trust Julian not to signal to his family somehow so he's heading back to Sofia's. Rick is also tagging along since Nate doesn't trust Sofia not to uncuff Julian and treat him like a person instead of a prisoner. It takes two of our fighters out of commission but Nate refused to budge no matter how much I argued.

He is far too gleeful at me being the bait, in my opinion.

"We'll be watching," he says, heading for the BMW. "Good luck. Maybe we'll all have a Romanov kill by the end of the day."

Yeah, or maybe we'll all be dragon food.

33

Opening my front door is the most terrifying thing I've ever done.

The wood bangs softly against my novelty owl doorstop. The hallway stretches empty to the coat cupboard and spare bathroom under the stairs. I shut the door behind me like I'm locking myself in a cell. My fingers hover over the knives in my wrist sheaths.

At least no one attacked me on the brief but also terrifying walk to my house. If any Romanovs are hiding under my bed, they'll hear my pounding heart, my rasping breaths. They'll know I'm expecting them. What other reason do I have for entering my house mid-panic attack?

I pretend I've returned from a jog.

Now, I sound like I'm hyperventilating.

My shoes clomp on the polished floor. Nothing throws itself at me from the coat cupboard. No monster is hiding in my bathtub. I lope up the stairs, trip and slap my hands on the wood, my palms stinging. Clearing my throat, I direct my wobbling legs into my bedroom.

Everything is as I left it—crumpled sheets on the bed, damp towels on the floor of the en-suite. No strangers fondling my panties or leering at me from a corner.

Downstairs, I check the automatic feeder on my fish tank even though I've only been gone a day. My betta, named Adam-in-Chains after another Billy Idol song (Adam for short), expresses his disgust by wiggling his blue- and crimson-streaked fins at me before disappearing into his rock cave. There are no Lessers under my coffee table or eating breakfast in my dining room. My kitchen is shining and free of murderous beasts, the hint of Mexican takeout flavouring the air.

"No one in here except me," I whisper into my sleeve.

I argued for someone to come in the house with me but there's not enough of us with Sofia babysitting Julian and Rick babysitting Sofia. Nate didn't want to take a man off the outside.

"Check in every ten minutes," Nate says.

I fill the kettle and flick the switch.

Make tea and put the telly on. I can do this.

I find myself staring into the trees for the sheen of scales and the wink of an elliptically pupilled eye. Tearing my gaze away, I slam cupboards to get my favourite rainbow mug, almost smashing it against the marble counter. I force my muscles to relax. The teabag misses my cup on the first and second—hell, third—try.

Since my lungs have yet to be ripped from my body, Evelyn Romanov isn't here yet. I have some time. Has Dominic mind-whispered to his mummy that I'm home? She won't be able to fly, not on this wonderfully clear, blue-skied day. It took Julian thirty minutes to reach my house but he would've been careful sneaking out so I maybe have twenty minutes of safety until the monsters arrive.

I can do this.

Steam billows to the ceiling and the kettle clicks off. I pour water into my cup, my hand steady. I clear away the remains of our Mexican takeout while the tea steeps, filling my kitchen with the scent of mint. I avoid looking out the window. The teabag launches into the sink from the end of my spoon with a satisfying splat. I curl my hands around my mug and cradle it to my chest, perching on a stool at the breakfast bar. Silence stretches, no ticking clock to mark the seconds. My pulse does a little rabbit hop.

Background noise. That's what I need. Sounds normal and should cover my traitorous heartbeat. I don't want the Drakul to know how scared I am, slurping tea and watching TV in my own home.

The legs of the stool scrape on the tile floor. I grip the handle of my mug and head into the dining room, hoping if I inhale hard enough, the calming effects of the tea will start to work.

"I have movement at the back," Nate says in my ear.

I jump and slop tea on my boots.

My voice is somewhat harsh when I say, "What do you mean, *movement?*"

"Might be the queen bitch herself. I'm circling around."

"Nate, wait—"

"Movement at the front, too." Dustan curses. Fabric rustles. "It's Lessers. Shit—they're attacking."

"Engaged," Fabian grunts, sounding out of breath.

What the hell is going on out there? How could they be expecting us?

Again, our weapons are limited by the proximity of other houses. The men will have to rely on their knives and their fists unless the fight spills deeper into the trees. Fabian and

Dustan have their shotguns just in case. I grab a handle in my wrist sheath.

"Stay in the house, Raine," Nate barks.

I pant into my sleeve. "But—"

Glass shatters. A rock the size of a watermelon takes a chunk out of my dining table, splinters the back of a chair and thuds onto the floor, narrowly missing my toes.

My first random thought is vandals. Stupid kids. My second thought is *duh, don't be an idiot.*

Evelyn Romanov steps through the tinkling waterfall of what remains of my sliding door, her angular frame show-cased by a fitted teal pantsuit and a woven belt the same colour as her hair. My mug slips from numb fingers and goes the way of the rock, hitting the carpet and showering my boots in hot minty-freshness.

My third thought is along the lines of *oh, fuckity shit-fuck.*

34

This is the whole point of me acting as bait—to lure Evelyn Romanov to where we can take her out. The plan is a massive success. I should feel happy.

I'm two seconds away from peeing myself.

My feet freeze to the carpet, steeped in hot tea. My heart has quit beating altogether.

Drakul in their human form should feel warm but the air around Evelyn Romanov shivers as if it's trying to crawl away. Spindly fingers long enough to need an extra knuckle reach for me.

"You think you can threaten my family, you foolish girl?" she says in her growling voice. "Trap a grieving mother?"

Before I can respond—I like to think I would've said something witty—her hand clamps my throat and hoists me upwards, my dripping boots kicking at nothing. Her straight arm holds me aloft without a quiver of effort, high enough to stare down into hate-filled, amber eyes.

"You will die for what you did to Lukas." Her smile stretches impossibly wide for her narrow face. "But not for a while."

Delicate cartilage crackles under her grip. I tug weakly at her fingers, my tongue swelling, blackness flaring in my eyeballs with each thump of my heart.

Huh, look at that. I guess my heart is beating after all.

I need to resist, *attack!* Remember my training. She's an arm's length away. My hands are free. Okay, the crushing pain and the urge to breathe are a bit distracting but they can be remedied if I shove a knife brain-deep in her eye socket. Or I can draw my sword and bury it in her forehead.

Adiós, scary dragon lady.

My muscles lock. I dangle at the end of Evelyn Romanov's arm like a snotty handkerchief. Sweat slicks my face as it reddens from the pressure of blood with nowhere to go. My bladder burns, my cramping stomach jigging on top of it. My tongue slaps uselessly around my mouth. I scrabble at Evelyn Romanov's hand but she's made of steel, whereas I'm soft and puny and human, too petrified to defend myself.

Just like when I was fifteen.

A tear leaks from the corner of my eye.

Evelyn Romanov sneers. "Where is your fighting talk now, girl? You humans are all the same—posturing like peacocks at a distance but bring the beast to your door and you offer your neck."

Sobs collect in my chest, trapped by her hand at my throat. Soon, I'll burst in a splatter of blood and flesh.

Becoming a smear on the wall would be less humiliating than peeing my pants.

A crash from the hall filters through the buzzing in my ears. Boots thunder towards us.

Oh thank god. *Help.*

Evelyn Romanov bends her arm to bring my face close to hers. Her breath should smell like carrion and old blood but it reminds me of lilacs. My bladder twitches dangerously, a cold numbness sweeping up my legs.

At least I won't feel it when I piss myself.

"Did you think I wouldn't know?" Her expression twists. Bared teeth flow in her mouth, lengthening and sharpening to nightmare proportions. "You humans think you're so clever."

She tosses me over the dining table. I hit the vase in the centre and crumple to the floor in a blur of water and broken ceramic, sunflowers squashed beneath me, too bright for the horror surrounding Evelyn Romanov. My skin crawls where she touched me. My ribs struggle to suck air but it hurts to breathe. It hurts not to breathe. I roll on the floor, the carpet squishing under my back, my hands wrapped around my neck, my fingers ice-cold.

Nate, Dustan and Fabian clatter into the dining room, their weapons drawn. I wave my hand at the fractured shell of the sliding door, not wanting them to see what I've been reduced to by one visit from the dragon lady. Nate and Dustan crunch outside, the thud of their footsteps on grass fading as they run for the trees. Fabian hunkers next to me, his hand hovering over my shoulder.

"Are you all right, Raine? Is there anything I can do?"

I shake my head in answer to both questions. A sinking, desolate feeling says I may not be all right for a while.

"Go," I wheeze, the word scalding my throat. "Help them."

After a pause, he nods and takes a step towards the door. "Stay here. I'll be right back."

He disappears into the garden. I lie in the stale water and weep. Shame burns hotter than my crushed throat.

I'm not a big tough dragon hunter but a blubbering little girl. Killing Lukas Romanov was a fluke, just like Nate said. At the first hint of real battle, I collapse and show my belly to the monster. I could have killed Evelyn Romanov and saved us all. She was arrogant enough to appear alone and without weapons, not that she needs any. But all I did was tremble. Lucky I had no breath or I would have whimpered. Begged her not to hurt me.

I'm such a coward.

And what am I doing now while three of my friends risk their lives chasing after her and her Lessers? Crying in a puddle of dead flowers.

My cheeks heat, my scorching sobs petering to hiccups akin to sipping acid. My neck throbs, the area tender under my questing fingertips. I sit up. Shards of ceramic clink together. I lever myself upright using the table and a wash of dizziness shudders from my head to my stomach. Dread pools in my feet but I force myself to take a step. Another. I shuffle for the sliding door, stumbling across the grass and into the trees. It takes two tries to wrap my hand around the hilt of my sword and pull it free from the sheath. It weighs a hundred pounds, the point stabbing into the ground and almost tripping me. Growling, I yank it free. Shouts echo through the woods, lost in the foliage.

I can't tell if we're winning or losing. If Evelyn Romanov brought her army, probably losing.

The ground slopes uphill. I usher my legs into a shambling trot that makes me woozy, not enough oxygen getting past the swelling in my abused tissues. Leaves slap my thighs and tickle my face. Beams of sunlight dance on the undergrowth and chase each other up the tree trunks, the day far too cheerful for hunting monsters.

How can I feel this terrible with the sun warming my tears and snot and the birds twittering in the canopy?

Maybe because I'm not as strong as I thought I was. I'm not

strong at all. Nate was right—women can't be warriors. Or this woman can't. Sofia would have spat in Evelyn Romanov's face and lopped off her head.

I stumble over a rise, fall down a hill and burst from a tangle of rhododendron. I stutter to a stop, my blade scraping a furrow in the dirt. Nate is mid-dive, a crossbow bolt zinging towards a dragon of bronze scales and slashing claws—Dominic, Julian's brother. Blood oozes from two knives sticking out of its neck, too high to hit the major vessels. The stink of petrol brings tears to my eyes, shards of glass glittering in the undergrowth. Fabian and Dustan take cover behind the scorched remnants of pine trees. Two shotguns lie at the dragon's feet. My stomach lurches as my eyes scan the vegetation but there's no sign of Evelyn Romanov, which is a relief so soon after my humiliation.

Where are the Lessers that attacked Dustan and Fabian? Were they simply a distraction to draw them away from the house and let Evelyn reach the real prize—me, the soft, gooey centre?

The dragon dodges Nate's bolt in a graceful swoop, the point thunking into bark. Nostrils flare, its orange-gold eyes fixed on Nate thrashing free from a clump of raspberry. I taste ash on the air. Heat pulses from the earth and the rearing shape of the beast.

My battle cry is more choked whisper. I raise my sword and charge the dragon, stealing its attention before it can loose a plume of flame on Nate faster than you can say, "Crispy fritters." It twirls, leathery wings tucked tight to its flanks, and a heavy copper tail slams into my ribs, catapulting me sideways in a blur of green and brown. My shoulder slams into a tree, my breath blasting out and tearing my throat. The pain is so hot, I'm surprised a curl of fire doesn't lick from my mouth. I hit the ground on my belly in a huff of mulch and mushrooms, my sword lost, my brain rattled. I may not be able to breathe for a millennium. My shoulder aches in tandem to my neck.

"Raine!" Fabian shouts.

I raise a groggy head at his voice. He sprints towards me, the sunlight blinding on his bald pate. His t-shirt is ripped across his stomach, both knees of his khaki combats stained with mud. His left hand holds a fan of throwing knives.

The dragon's sides heave, its slim head tracking Fabian. I open my mouth to yell—wheeze—a warning. The Drakul's maw widens, the depths of its throat bathed in flickering orange.

Fabian has his back to it. He's twenty metres from me. Ten.

The dragon breathes out as softly as a sigh.

Fabian, haloed by flame, vanishes in a wisp of smoke.

<h1 style="text-align:center">35</h1>

Fire crackles all around me, singeing my hair and nibbling at my clothes. My eyes sting, my skin stings, the delicate lining of my nose stings. The snap and pop of burning wood smothers every other noise. The charred lump that used to be Fabian smokes gently on the ground.

He told me to stay. He said he'd be back. If I'd stayed, he would have come back.

Despite the heat, tears flow down my cheeks and drip from my chin in murky droplets of swirling grey. I press my forehead to the mud and squeeze my eyes shut. Hands tug at my shirt. I shrug them off.

"Raine, get your ass up or we're all dead." Nate's hiss is almost lost in the roar of the fire.

Or maybe it's the Drakul.

Nate and Dustan hoist me to my feet, my weakly kicking legs doing little to help. Nate releases me only long enough to swing his crossbow to his shoulder and loose a bolt at the monster rearing over us in the boiling smoke and flames. The arrow passes through the membrane of its wing, leaving a perfect circle. The dragon's bellow batters my ears. Nate and Dustan run through the woods, dragging me between them, my boots barely touching the ground. I twist my head to look behind me and my hair flutters across my face.

The dragon licks at its damaged wing, crouched in the centre of blackened earth and trees, thick clouds purling into the sky and staining the blue. It swings its head to watch our escape, its jaw dropping open and tongue flopping out as if it's laughing. It nudges what's left of Fabian with its snout. In one flick, it scoops him into its mouth. Scorched flesh cracks to show flashes of pink. The Drakul's throat bobs and it swallows Fabian down. The dragon snorts and thrashes after us, wood splintering against its shoulders, its maw wide but dark, flecks of black caught in its teeth.

It'll take a few minutes to build up another burst of flame.

I yank my gaze forward, my head jerking as Nate and Dustan leap hunks of deadwood and weave past bramble thickets. Their fingers crush my arms but I have no breath or will to complain. I have no energy. I'm a passenger in my own body.

Pity I still feel every ache, scrape and bruise.

We stumble down the hill. Slivers of sunlight pierce the trees. We burst out of the forest into my back garden, a carpet of glass surrounding my broken screen door. There's a whoosh and a wave of blistering heat. I find myself on my face with a mouthful of grass. A fireball slams into my house. Dustan and Nate nearly dislocate my arms pulling me upright, bundling me down the driveway and through the gate to the street. My neighbours cluster in front of their houses, talking in excited voices and glancing towards the hill and the woods and my merrily burning home. Their eyes widen on seeing us stumble onto the road, smudged in soot and trailing smoke. Sirens wail in the distance.

My neighbour, Mrs Abernathy, clutches her cat to her chest.

"Raine! What happened?"

There's too much ash in my mouth to answer.

How much of it is Fabian?

I tumble into the rear seat of the BMW. Doors thunk, tyres squeal on tarmac. The car lurches. I sprawl across the leather, staring at the back of the driver's seat. I should sit up and put on my seat belt. A kid in my school died in a car accident from not wearing a seat belt. The force tossed her forwards and broke her neck.

A time when death could be tragic but normal and not involve the inside of a dragon's gullet.

The BMW swerves, horns blaring, and I rock with it, flopping onto my back to blink at the ceiling. The journey passes in a blur.

Does Evelyn Romanov or her army of Lessers try to follow us, Dominic left in the woods to shift to human? Given the sudden jerks, the screech of rubber, the heavy silence when Nate cuts the engine, I think they do.

The engine purrs. Nate and Dustan talk but I'm too tired to focus on the words. The rest of the drive is smooth. We've escaped. We're safe.

But I don't feel safe.

Gravel crunches under the wheels. Doors slam. I memorise the shape of the light on the roof in the peace that follows. A warm breeze caresses my face and stirs my hair. My skin is flushed from the brush of flames but it's not enough to thaw the chill inside me. I'm cold all the way through.

"Come on, Raine," Dustan says, coaxing me from the car.

His skinny arm guides me into Sofia's house. Nate starts yelling before the door has even closed.

"This is your fault!" he screams at Julian, who sits on the

couch beside Sofia, empty coffee cups on the table. "Fabian is dead. *Ash!* Because of your fucking family!"

Sofia's hand flies to her mouth. Her gaze fastens on me and Dustan on the edge of the room and some of the tension leaks from her face. Rick shoves away from the wall he's leaning on and scowls at Julian.

"Then let's take what we're owed—an eye for an eye." He slides a knife from the sleeve of his suit. "Except you owe us two eyes."

A hysterical giggle gets lost somewhere in my chest. I open my mouth, fully expecting a wash of bile to splatter the carpet.

"It's my fault." A whisper is all I can manage past the throbbing in my throat. "Fabian is dead because of me."

Julian jumps to his feet despite the cuffs and Sofia's ridiculously squishy sofa cushions. He slips past Nate and Rick so quickly, my brain struggles to process the movement. And then I'm in his arms, my head tucked under his chin, his heartbeat steady in my ear.

"How badly are you hurt?" he says.

"Not badly. On the outside."

Nothing compared to Fabian.

My eyes are dry, somehow, my tears evaporated by the heat of dragon fire. My chest hitches and pain flares from my bruised ribs.

"It's not your fault, Raine," Dustan says, stepping further into the room. "You distracted the Drakul or it would've been Nate. Or me. Maybe even both. The bastard swiped our guns before we could take a shot."

Sofia appears at Dustan's side and wraps him in a hug. He stiffens for a second then his arms come around her, his cheek on the top of her head. Her fingertips play with the waistband of his boxers beneath his ripped t-shirt. Nate and Rick stand awkwardly, Rick's knife at his side, the frustrated anger fading to sadness and loss.

I cough and taste blood, unable to stop a cry even though it burns. Julian unloops his arms from around me.

"Raine, your throat…"

I wince at the soft press of his fingers.

"Let's get you all patched up," Sofia says, disentangling herself from Dustan.

"Raine was also hit by the dragon's tail," Dustan says. "It slammed her into a tree. I think she got hurt the worst out of the lot of us."

"Not the worst," I wheeze.

"Let me see," Julian says.

I raise the hem of my top and he sucks in a breath. It aches too much to crane my neck. His warm fingers are tentative over my ribs.

"Nothing's broken."

"How can you tell?"

He gives me a sad smile. "I know what broken ribs feel like."

"Honey, head upstairs and lie down while I make a poultice. Julian go with her. The rest of you, into the kitchen."

Nate opens his mouth but Sofia's glare shuts him up. The men troop into the kitchen. She tosses a small key to Julian and the cuffs hit the carpet. He guides me up to our bedroom and helps me pull off my top, peeling the microphone from my sleeve and placing it plus the earpiece on the dressing table. He lowers me onto the bed and fluffs up the pillow, tracing a fingertip across my throat.

"You met my mother," he says softly.

"Is it obvious?"

"Only she can inspire that look on your face."

"What look?"

"Shame and fear and self-loathing."

My eyes burn. What do you know—my tear ducts are full again. I don't want to cry as it's going to hurt but it hurts to hold it in. I cover my face with my hands.

The bed dips. Julian peels my fingers away to see his stricken expression.

"Julian," I choke, "I'm no Vanatori. Not strong or brave. I can't defend you from her. I can't even defend myself."

"How much did she make you want to pee yourself?"

My laugh is watery and rips my throat. "So much."

"But you didn't, which means you're stronger than most people who've met her. Including me."

I cup his cheek, my thumb stroking the curve of his lips. "I'm sorry you had to live with that monster."

"I'm sorry about Fabian. I liked him."

"Me too," I say on a sigh. "I think your brother also killed my fish."

The thought of my poor little betta boiled in his tank releases the floodgates. Julian gathers me in his arms and rocks me until the sobbing peters out, my throat filled with glass.

I'm not really crying for the fish. I'm crying for all of us. For Fabian and George, for my cowardice, for how puny we are against even one Drakul and for Julian, who knew nothing but abuse.

How are we ever going to be free of the tyranny of Evelyn Romanov?

I calm myself by the time Sofia knocks and enters the room, cradling a towel of steaming leaves, the scent of sage and vinegar preceding her. Julian eases away from where he's cuddled into my side to give her space to work. Soot smears the covers wherever I've touched them.

"I'm getting your sheets all filthy."

"I am pretty sure they were already filthy, honey," Sofia says.

I manage a weak smile, though the blush on Julian's face soothes the ache in my bruised flesh.

He's so adorable.

Yet I couldn't save him from his mother.

I clench my fists while Sofia carefully smooths the leaves around my neck and on my chest, holding them in place with hot towels. The heat sinks deep. Sofia slips out and Julian carefully curls himself around me, the warmth of him finally melting the rest of the chill.

Next time. The next time I see Evelyn Romanov, I'll picture every terrible thing she's done to Julian. I'll use my sword to slice the cruel smile right off her face.

Though, like Fabian, my sword is lost to the blackened nightmare of the woods behind my house.

36

The VC screen covers the space in front of the bay window, casting the living room in twilight. Sofia prods at the unit while the rest of us rearrange the furniture. Julian is cuffed to a chair in the kitchen with a book and a cup of coffee to keep him occupied, the adjoining doors closed. Nate doesn't want him to see the faces of the people we're about to call. I picked my battle and let it slide.

Maybe Julian can still hear us through the thick walls from the kitchen.

Sofia perches on the couch next to me, her hand on Dustan's thigh. Rick and Nate flank us, their backs ramrod straight.

I caught Sofia tugging Dustan into her bedroom three days ago when I slipped out to refresh my poultice, Julian napping, the sage leaves cool and crinkled.

"Raine," Dustan grinned, glancing through the doorway behind him. "This is totally what it looks like."

Sofia's arm snaked out and yanked him inside, the door clicking shut, giggles following not long after.

Funny how death and destruction makes for horny survivors. What a way to celebrate life.

The blue VC screen splits into six, our own image shrunk into the bottom right corner. Five people wink online, one after the other, five variations of a study at their backs—bookshelves with titles I can't read, a window onto a rain-streaked night, a painting of abstract shapes.

A woman leans forward, her long fingers clasped on a glass-topped desk, her brown hair styled and swept over the left side of her face. "Nathanial Reed of the Titan Group and the rest of the Titan Group, I see. To what do I owe the pleasure?"

"Greetings Principal Cozma," Nate says, his hands gripping his knees, "we are in an emergency situation. Our headquarters and the home of one of my members, Raine Waller, have been compromised."

Cool, grey eyes shift to me. I stop myself from waving like a nervous idiot and nod professionally, pain flaring in my necklace of bruises.

It's the first time I've seen the Principal and the heads of the four largest groups on the planet. The Vanatori ruling body are almost as secretive as the Drakul. Only leaders are invited on conference calls and get to vote for the new Principal when the latest one dies in battle. It happens a lot. At eight years, Principal Cozma is the longest incumbent we've had.

"We also have two members to remove from the records," Nate continues. "George MacAllister and Fabian Ward."

"I didn't know gathering intel was so dangerous, Mr Reed. It seems your group can't keep themselves away from the action."

Nate glances at me but his expression stays blank. "As we discussed after our Dunbar raid, ma'am, the Drakul presence in Scotland is beyond anything we could have imagined."

"Then my condolences to you all. Is there anything else?"
Man, she could use some warmth.
"We need help," Nate says.

A man who looks like Tarzan in a suit flicks his fingers at the screen. "I believe we will need the full details, Nathanial."

The Romanovs are a world-renowned family of evil so there's not much explaining to do on who they are. Five pairs of eyes fasten on me at the news of Lukas Romanov's demise.

Are they wondering how a slight girl with such frizzy hair managed to execute the eldest Romanov heir, with a sword no less? I wonder it myself.

Where was that girl when Evelyn Romanov was a blade's length away?

"We've captured the youngest son," Nate says, unable to mask a smug smile. "We want to use him to infiltrate the Romanov household, where we will kill them all."

There's a little too much emphasis on the 'all' for my liking.

"Then it is confirmed—the Romanovs have a residence in Scotland?" Principal Cozma says.

"They've been here for years, apparently, though Evelyn Romanov travels frequently to Nevada."

"This is wonderful news," says a woman in a sari the colour of blood. It really brings out the bronze of her eyes. "If it's manpower you need, we of the Vijayasara Group are happy to assist."

The others pledge their hunters and Nate's smile widens to a grin as we swell from a pathetic group of five to an army of over a hundred.

"Are you able to hold your position for the two or three days it will take them to mobilise?" Principal Cozma says. "Is the prisoner secure?"

"Yes, we should be safe here for a few days and the prisoner is—"

"He's not a prisoner," I say, my voice still croakier than usual.

"Shut *up*, Raine," Nate hisses out the corner of his mouth.

"I'm not going through this again, Nate. They need to know he's not to be harmed."

Maybe that's part of Nate's plan—invite the rest of the Vanatori to our party, drowning my protests in numbers. And Julian in his own blood.

"What are you talking about, Miss Waller?" Principal Cozma dusts a piece of lint off the sleeve of her silk shirt, which is buttoned to the collar. "Standard procedure is to execute any prisoners once we have extracted the information we need. We're not cruel."

I raise my chin. "Julian Romanov is not a prisoner."

"Mr Reed made it quite clear—"

"Mr Reed has not been entirely forthright." Holy crap, I just interrupted our top dragon hunter. By the deepening frown on her face, it's not something she finds endearing. "Nate captured him but he's not a prisoner. He's… here voluntarily."

Probably best not to tell them he's my boyfriend.

"This is most irregular—"

"Who is this girl—"

"Sounds like a trap—"

"Is he there with you?" Principal Cozma says through the chatter of the other Vanatori.

Nate's jaw clamps tight, his arms crossed over his chest. His eyes meet mine and they're as hot as smouldering coals. "He's in the next room."

"Bring him to me. Blindfolded, of course."

I jump to my feet before Nate can lever himself from his chair. Silence sweeps me through the dining room and into the kitchen. Julian's face lights up when I enter. He's twisted in a seat at the table, his wrist cuffed to a strut of the seat back. He could easily break the wood and free himself but he's been reading his book and drinking his coffee like a good boy.

I sit on his lap like a good girl and claim his mouth.

My god, how can the smell of vanilla be so erotic? Or maybe it's the glide of his lips, so eager against mine. Metal scrapes on wood, the fingers of his cuffed hand curling around my leg. I open them without any command from my brain and he walks his fingers higher along the sensitive curve of my inner thigh.

Yes, perhaps we should dampen the addictiveness of his touch with a little foreplay so I don't embarrass myself in the presence of my peers. Great idea.

His hand stops short and I whimper into his mouth. He grins and wiggles the chain of his cuffs.

"Can't quite reach. Are you finished already?"

Finished? I've barely even started.

I manage to shake my head. "No, um, they want to talk to you."

"Oh. Is that good or bad?"

"Could go either way." I slide off his lap and free the band from around his wrist, leaving the cuffs to dangle on the chair. "Maybe don't mention anything about us being together."

He quirks his mouth. "At least I'm used to people not liking me."

"I like you." I cup his face and kiss him lightly, just the once. Okay, twice. For two minutes. "But I think finding out I love you—a Drakul and a Romanov—might be a bit much for them to process."

"It's still a lot for me to process," he says.

And what do you know—I'm kissing him again. The

thought of Nate's increasing impatience forces me away.

"If there's even the slightest chance of you getting hurt, I won't let any of them near you," I say.

"Don't we need their help?"

"We do but not at the expense of your safety."

He pulls me into a tight hug and I listen to the frantic thud of his heart.

I don't want to parade him in front of the Vanatori and their cold, calculating eyes. Will they see past the Romanov name to who he really is? Or will they tell me what I want to hear then use him, abuse him and kill him when he's outlived his usefulness?

How can I protect him from hundreds of gun-wielding hunters and his brothers *and* his mother? Yet the danger increases if we don't have back-up.

It's just a shame the back-up might shoot him in the chest.

37

I lead Julian into the living room, Sofia's cat-patterned dishtowel wrapped around his eyes. It gives me an excuse to hold his hand. I watch the expressions of the five people on the screen. Four curl into similar reflections of disgust, although Principal Cozma's features are carefully blank.

Would I have reacted the same way if this was the first time I saw him? Would I see nothing but a Drakul and one of the hated Romanovs?

I peek at Julian through my lashes while everyone's attention is on him. The light from the screen paints his face and the blindfold in a kaleidoscope of colour. Shadows play along the vulnerable line of his collarbone and I fist my hand to keep from stroking it.

His hotness is distracting, even with a third of his face covered. Most men would use their looks to their advantage. A Drakul? Well, they'd ensnare the hearts of gullible females and laugh while they ripped them out, still beating.

But there's no cruelty in Julian.

Are there others like him? Drakul who try to live a decent life the same as any other person? It was easy to scoff at Nate that the world isn't black and white but, before Julian, I believed it. I believed in good vs evil. Before Julian, I would have looked at him and thought only of burying my blade in his soft throat and removing one more monster from the world.

Before Julian, I was a Vanatori. Now, I don't know what I am.

"You are Julian Romanov?" Principal Cozma says, her tone as empty as her face. "Youngest son of Evelyn Romanov?"

Julian's head tilts towards her voice. "I am."

We stop at the back of the couch. I force myself to let go of him. Nate's gaze drops to Julian's uncuffed hands but he turns his scowl to the screen.

"Why have you agreed to help the Vanatori when it will inevitably lead to the death of your family?"

Inevitably? Her faith in us is touching.

"They've abused me since I was born." Julian shifts his feet. "They're family in name only."

A man at the bottom of the screen scoffs, peering into the camera, his headscarf a blinding white over a simple blue and beige tunic. "Clearly, he is lying. Evelyn Romanov may be many things but she is also pragmatic. Why would she abuse one of her beloved sons?"

"Because I'm the weakest in the line for over five hundred years."

You're not weak. I clamp my lips on the words, even though they're true. Show me anyone else capable of surviving what he suffered at the hands of the people who should love him.

"What colour are you?" This from a striking blonde woman with a square jaw.

The question feels too intimate, like asking him to strip in front of strangers, though part of me is curious. I don't know the answer. I still can't picture him as anything other than the boy who touches me as if he can't believe he's allowed.

His throat bobs once. "I'm not any colour."

"How needlessly cryptic," the second man sneers. "If you are as weak as you say, you'll be one of the pretty colours— violet, sapphire. Or are you saying you're transparent, like a diamond?"

"He's risking his life to help us, what does it matter if he's fluorescent-bloody-pink?"

The man gapes. Julian flashes me a grin and it makes my outburst worthwhile. Though I need to be careful. I don't want them to treat him with the same contempt his family does, he deserves better than that. He deserves for everyone to love him.

But I can't show them I already do.

"A valid point, Miss Waller," Cozma says, her lips lifted in a smile that doesn't reach her eyes. "How exactly did he come to be in this oh-so-helpful situation? Mr Reed said he was captured."

"He was my informant."

"Did you know what he was?"

Crap. A tricky question. The truth may make them dismiss me as an idiot but I'm not a very good liar.

"Not at first," I say. "He was understandably cautious. He told me later, after we'd built a degree of trust."

Nate and Rick frown at me. I ignore them. It's practically true, except he told me when he was already in chains.

"And how did you come to capture him, Mr Reed?"

I send Nate a pleading look. The muscles in his jaw bulge.

The truth paints him as an ineffectual leader with no control over the members of his group. He has to lie, unless he wants validation from Cozma that he's right and I'm wrong.

I have no doubt the other Vanatori would side with him.

"Raine was secretive about the identity of her new informant," Nate says and a prickle of sweat trails down my spine. "I learned the identity of Julian Romanov from separate intel and caught him, not knowing he was also her informant. I thought he could provide valuable information on the rest of his family."

The last is said through gritted teeth.

Frosty eyes settle on Julian. "And can you?"

"I can show you how to get past the fence and the cameras and the guards, right into the mansion."

"And right into a trap," the second man says. "How can we possibly trust a Drakul? He lures us with a sob story, hoping to slaughter us all."

"Do you trust him, Mr Reed?" Cozma says, her hands clasped so tight it mottles her skin. "Would you stake your reputation on Julian Romanov's honour?"

Uh-oh…

"No, I would not," Nate says without hesitation.

"Nate—"

"No, Raine. I'm not damaging my reputation for *him*."

"He won't damage your goddamn reputation because he'll do exactly what he says." I turn to Cozma and slap a hand to my chest. "I vouch for him. I'll stake my reputation on his honour."

Cozma's gaze flits between the three of us, an emotion I can't read sparking in her grey eyes. "How are you so certain he will keep his word, Miss Waller?"

"He knew I was Vanatori the second we met but he's never hurt me. He had the opportunity to kill the whole group and he didn't take it."

"Ah, yes, but perhaps he has his sights set on something bigger than your small group. Something such as wiping out two thirds of the global Vanatori population."

"I don't want to hurt you," Julian says quietly. "I don't want to hurt anyone."

"And yet we are to believe you will let us execute your family in their home?"

"As long as they're alive, they will never stop hunting Raine for killing Lukas."

"Why is Miss Waller important to you?"

Okay, ouch.

My heart skips at Julian's tender smile. It's too much—*too obvious*—but I don't want it to fade. My fingers itch to rip off his blindfold so I can see his eyes.

"She saved me from my family," he says.

"Saved you how?"

I'm really starting to dislike Principal Cozma. Why can't my word and his actions be enough?

"By showing me I'm not weak in the ways that matter. By treating me like a person."

Man, I want to hug him. My fingers twitch, aching to take his hand, but I press them to my thigh.

"But you're not a person, are you?" Cozma says sweetly. "You're a Romanov."

"My mother would beg to differ."

"He is telling the truth." Sofia sits up straighter on the couch. "We all saw it. His *madre* disowned him in front of us."

"And do you trust him, Miss Castenada?"

"Raine trusts him. That is good enough for me."

"This is all very touching," the second man says, straightening his headscarf, "but it doesn't explain how *we* can trust him."

"So you're not going to help us?"

"We didn't say that, Miss Waller. But there will be conditions."

"What conditions?"

Cozma glances at Julian. Her lip twitches. "First, I want to see his face."

The other Vanatori protest but she dismisses them with a flutter of her fingers. Their screens switch to grey as they turn their cameras off, leaving Cozma staring out alone. I pick the knot from the blindfold and it flops loose in my hand. Julian's gaze finds mine and I give him an encouraging smile. He runs a hand through his hair and a stray beam of sunlight blazes in the part he flicks over one eye.

He always hides one eye when he's nervous.

Cozma examines his face as if she'll be tested on it later. Julian stands perfectly still and watches her.

"I see a lot of your mother in you," she says.

He flinches. "I hope that's not true."

She sweeps her hand at him. "Thank you, Mr Romanov. You can go back where you came from."

"You can gag me, chain me up, whatever. I just want to help."

"I'll keep that in mind," Cozma says.

Julian leaves the room and shuts the door behind him, the click of the second door obvious in the silence. I reclaim my seat on the couch and fiddle with the dishtowel in my lap. The four cameras of the Vanatori group leaders wink back on.

"For someone you don't trust, Mr Reed, the Drakul is surprisingly free to move around."

Nate slides a quick frown my way. "He was chained to the chair and has been cuffed for most of his time here."

"Though he doesn't need it," I say.

"You mentioned some other conditions, Principal Cozma?" Dustan chimes in, and Nate turns his attention to the screen instead of glowering at me.

"Yes, in order to proceed, we must get every scrap of information out of the Drakul prior to the operation. I want to know every detail about the Romanovs and their territory before we engage. Use whatever means are necessary."

I cross my arms. "He will tell us if we ask him."

"Third," Cozma says, her teeth clenched, "he takes point during the operation to guide us into and through the Romanov compound for a surprise attack. A lot can happen during a mission. It would be hard to keep track of everyone in the chaos. Perhaps a certain Drakul will get caught in crossfire or be killed by a member of his own family." Her thin lips curve. "So tragic."

Nate and Rick nod enthusiastically. My nails bite into my palms.

"A masterful stroke," the second man says. "He knows too much."

I seem to be having trouble breathing. There's a fire in my chest, clogging my throat with smoke and filming my vision. The same feeling I got when I placed myself in front of Julian and called his mother a bony old bag. But this is Principal Cozma, the head of the Vanatori. She's highly respected, experienced. She protects people.

Maybe I've misunderstood.

"Perhaps it would be safer to kill him once we have the information, rather than take him on the operation?" says the woman in the sari.

Words burn my throat. I try to swallow them. I should play along, get them to commit, and sneak Julian away in the confusion as soon as we breach the Romanov compound.

Cozma taps her chin. "Perhaps but think how useful he would be as a martyr. An honourable Drakul, fighting alongside the Vanatori. We could trick other weak and abused Drakul into doing the same, use their brutal society against them. It's almost poetic."

I shouldn't say anything, I should just walk out. If I want to stay a Vanatori I certainly shouldn't say—

"You traitorous witch."

Whoops.

My words fall into a pool of silence and ripple outward. Nate flinches as if I've slapped him. Sofia sits very still next to me. Rick slowly shakes his head and stares at his lap. Principal Cozma shows no emotion while the rest of the Vanatori splutter and glare.

"What a strange reaction to a plan that could shatter the Drakul and save thousands of lives," Cozma says.

I surge to my feet. "You're talking about stabbing Julian in the back!"

"Yes. Back, heart, neck—all would be acceptable."

I'm so incensed, I can't speak. I don't know any other curses to throw at her. None are despicable enough for what she's suggesting.

Julian has done nothing to them except be born a Drakul, something he had no control over. He's been attacked, chained, berated, threatened and suffered it uncomplaining. He would lead all of us into the heart of the Romanov's territory if I asked him to. Right into the place he was tortured and hoped to never see again.

And Principal Cozma would look into his lovely, different-coloured eyes and slit his throat.

"Tell me, Miss Waller," she says, cocking her head, "how

long have you been fucking the dragon?"

So much for keeping it a secret.

I speak past the drum of my pulse. "Long enough to know he's not the monster here."

Nate drops his face into his hands with a sound between a snarl and a sigh. The four Vanatori on the screen around Cozma turn disgusted expressions on me, a caricature of revulsion worse than what they directed at Julian.

"How can you let that thing touch you?" the blonde woman says, her lip curled so high it almost bypasses her nostril.

Tarzan jerks forward in his office chair, the material of his suit straining at his shoulders. "You stupid girl! You've jeopardised all of us with this betrayal."

"I haven't betrayed anyone."

"Clearly, you've been comprised," the second man says, his dark eyes glaring into the camera. "How else can you be swayed by a beast in a pretty mask? Have you forgotten your training so easily?"

Cozma's cold gaze settles on Nate hunched in his seat. "This behaviour is becoming an alarming regularity in your group, Mr Reed. Are you not disciplining your members properly? Must I remove you as leader before someone else, quite literally, loses their heart?"

Discipline? What the hell is she talking about? We work together. We follow Nate's orders but we have some autonomy. He doesn't smack us when we're bad.

Nate straightens in his seat, the rigid line of his jaw stark in the light from the screen. Rick slides from his chair to cross in front of where I stand and places himself beside Nate. He stops short of putting his hand on Nate's shoulder but his position is clear.

"You do not need to remove me as leader," Nate says, the words as stiff as his posture. "I can handle this."

"You seem to *not* be handling it, Mr Reed, particularly since a Drakul—a *Romanov*—has infiltrated your group and brainwashed at least one of your members." Her attention shifts to Sofia and Dustan. "Perhaps two. You said you trusted him, Miss Castenada."

Sofia slowly rises to stand beside me, tugging Dustan to his feet and eliciting a severe eyebrow arch from Cozma.

"Raine is not stupid," Sofia says. "Julian has had several opportunities to kill us or lead us into a trap. He has done neither."

"Do not confuse the fact he hasn't eaten you yet for evidence of his good intentions, Miss Castenada. The Drakul are masters of treachery."

The snort slips out before I can clamp my teeth on it. Cozma's eyes brand my skin like frozen metal. My shaking legs want me to collapse onto the couch but I'm tired of being bullied.

"You're the one talking about stringing him along then murdering him."

"Murder? He is not human, Miss Waller, he cannot be murdered. He can be slain, executed. Hunted to extinction."

Tarzan slumps in his chair and the seat back screeches from the weight. "How did he convince you to turn against your own kind? Did he hold you in his arms and whisper how special you are, how you're the only one who makes him feel this way, how he loves you—"

"He does love me."

"Oh, sweet Durga," the woman in the sari says, rolling her eyes to the ceiling.

I slice a glare at her. "And I love him."

Principal Cozma barks a laugh as brittle as ice. "Love? You think that creature knows anything about love? Feels anything beyond greed and hate and bloodlust?"

Julian has never felt any of those ugly things, except maybe hate towards his family for tormenting him. I can't blame him for that. I hate his family, too.

"You are really quite deluded, Miss Waller. The Drakul do not love." She sweeps the hair away from the left side of her face. "This is what they do."

Scars unfurl in ridges and whorls from her collar, feathering up her throat and head, a stump of tissue surrounding a hole where her ear should have been. A shiny bald patch shows where a graft was applied to her skull before reaching the healthy, untouched area of her scalp.

Her hair falls to hide her scars with one regal flip of her head. "I was thirteen. My father was the Principal, although I didn't understand that yet. A new boy befriended me at school. He swept me off my feet with tender words breathed in my ear. When I still had two ears. He was everything my little heart dreamed of."

We all stare at the screen, riveted by Cozma's voice despite knowing the story won't have a happy ending.

"He told me he loved me and I told him anything he wanted—how my father held meetings in his study when he thought I was asleep, how my parents collected weapons in the basement, how people on the phone called my father 'Principal'. I was a good little sneak back then." She tucks her hair behind her non-existent ear and it swishes forward to brush her cheek. "One night, my gentle, perfect boyfriend led his family to my house and they set it on fire while we slept inside. I was the only one who made it out. I saw him before he disappeared into the dark when the fire trucks screamed around the corner. I saw his true face beneath the mask and it was twisted and cruel and inhuman. That is what Julian Romanov is, Miss Waller. That is what he will do to you if you let him."

I'm shaking my head before she finishes speaking. "Julian isn't like that."

"There's no point talking to her," Rick cuts in but he's too far away for me to slap. "Nate has tried. Both Raine and Sofia have shown a blatant disregard for his orders. Raine has consorted with the dragon and Sofia has enabled it."

Consorted? What year does Rick think this is?

Sofia bristles beside me, her hoop earrings jingling.

"Ah, Mr Smith," Cozma says, "I was most impressed by your manipulation of the Lesser family and the invaluable information it provided for our Morgenstern operation. I'm interested to hear what you think our next steps should be in the case we have here."

Rick puffs out his chest, his suit the colour of dirt. He must be loving the attention. The drawback of being invisible is one tends to be overlooked. I always wondered if he was happy being Nate's yes-man when he's experienced enough to lead his own group. Does it rankle to take orders from someone fourteen years your junior?

"Thank you, ma'am," Rick says. "There's only one solution: Raine and Sofia should be punished and retrained—if not banished—and the Drakul should be killed. The safety of the Vanatori is paramount."

I take a step towards Rick, the brown-nosing little weasel, but Sofia curls her fingers around my wrist and holds me in place. She gives a tiny shake of her head when I frown at her.

"And you, Mr Reed? Do you agree?"

Nate puts his hands on his knees and shoves to his feet. "The Drakul needs to die. Sofia needs to be reminded who the enemy is. And I've already told Raine she's out of the group once this is over."

Sofia gasps. "Nate, you cannot be serious—"

"Of course I'm serious! I've been serious the whole time but neither of you listened. You're standing in front of the head of our organisation and you're still arguing with me. Jesus Christ, listen to her if you're too damn stubborn to listen to me."

"Eloquently put, Mr Reed," Cozma says with a small smile.

"It's not that we're ignoring you, Nate," Dustan says and we all look at him. "We're not stupid or arguing to be stubborn. We really believe Julian is different."

Cozma strokes her chin. "While I appreciate your contribution, Mr Wassel, it is a moot point."

"What do you mean?"

"Let's say Mr Romanov is this elusive and mystical beast known as a 'good dragon'," she says, making air quotes with her fingers. "He has seen my face. That is a security breach I cannot tolerate."

"You asked me to remove his blindfold." My words fall from numb lips. "You wanted to see his face and you kept your camera on."

Her smile flashes her teeth. "So I did. But as there is no such thing as a good dragon, that is also a moot point."

"But think how useful he could be," Dustan persists. "He could infiltrate Drakul society as one of us. We put a camera on him and suddenly we know the faces and names of everyone he meets and where they gather, where they *live*. We could finally be a force to be reckoned with rather than an annoyance."

I don't want any of that for Julian. I don't want to send him out, again and again, to mingle with the monsters. What if his cover is blown? I want to take him somewhere safe. Play video games, eat ice cream, introduce him to other fun stuff he's never done and watch the delight on his face at each new discovery.

"I'm afraid you're forgetting the obvious, Mr Wassel," Cozma says, not bothering to disguise her smug expression. "If Mr Romanov is as weak as he claims then he is all but useless for infiltration. The upper echelons of Drakul society will not tolerate his presence if his mother does not tolerate it. If his weakness is a ploy and we release him back into their care, he will betray us."

"Are you so arrogant to assume that every Drakul will react the way you expect?"

"Why, yes, Miss Waller, I am," she says with the same cold smile. "Everything I and my peers have experienced confirms it."

"Then what do you suggest?" Dustan says through his teeth, and it gladdens my heart.

The pig-headedness is frustrating the crap out of me, too.

"I believe I made myself clear earlier, Mr Wassel. Get all the information you can out of the dragon, although I will change one condition. The Drakul will no longer accompany us on the Romanov operation since his presence has corrupted three members. No, if you want our assistance"—she fixes her gaze on me and it's like staring into the eye of a storm—"first bring me his ash."

"Let me do it," Rick says to Nate, his voice echoing inside my skull. "I'll have the information we need in less than an hour then we can get rid of him. For George and Fabian."

He'll last longer than an hour. It's not the first time he's been tortured and I imagine his mother was inventive. He'll fight and struggle and scream. No matter where I go, I'll hear him screaming. He'll look at me, his eyes bright with pain—pain from the slice of Rick's knives, pain from my betrayal—but deep within his disbelief, there'll be a glimmer of resignation.

Of course I hurt him. Everyone else does.

I twist around, Cozma's self-satisfied smirk branded into my mind, and vault the couch in a single bound.

"Stop her!" Cozma yells.

I crash through the dining room into the kitchen. Julian is already on his feet, hands raised but not quite clenched into fists. The cuffs dangle empty on the chair.

I wrap my cold fingers around the delicate bones of his wrist and say, *"Run."*

39

Each step, each breath, throbs in my bruised ribs and claws at my throat, like the sunshiny air is filled with splintered glass. A branch whips my cheek in a stinging line. Brambles snag my trousers and steal tufts of material on the tips of their thorns. Julian jogs a few paces ahead, a bunch of spruce needles bristling from the sleeve of his black hoodie where he brushed against a tree.

When we burst from Sofia's house and reached the surrounding woods, he made me hide then ran off in the opposite direction, crashing and crunching through undergrowth to lure Nate and Rick away. He circled back and popped up next to me, silent and barely out of breath. It gave us a good head start while Nate and Rick chased shadows.

Julian glances behind him. He keeps turning to check on me, which explains why he's not moving as gracefully as usual. I focus my gaze on the slide of his shoulder blades and try to mirror his easy gait. My boot catches something and I land on my face, a clump of moss tickling my eyeball. I pant and tell myself it's not blood I taste in my mouth.

"Are you okay, Raine?" Julian kneels next to me, his eyes flicking to the trees around us.

His skin is pale, perfect. I'm a sweaty tangle of hair.

I shove myself up on my hands. "I'm finding it a little hard to breathe and run at the same time. I wish I could heal as fast as you."

"I could"—he stares at his lap—"I could shift and carry you."

My heart skips and then leaps into the whispering leaves above us. I can't control it. The stupid thing always gives me away.

"It's daylight," I say, my voice two decibels higher. "You can't be seen. Though I wouldn't say no to another piggyback."

He smiles and helps me to my feet, patting the mud from my clothes. I hoist myself onto him while a little voice in my head snarls *you cow. You ungrateful, deceitful, horrible cow.* The heat of his palms brands the back of my thighs. I curl tighter into him and risk a peek behind us.

The forest is a splash of dazzling green and gold, too picturesque to also hide Nate and Rick and their bloody intentions. Have they realised they're going in the wrong direction? Are they back on our tail? No sounds reach me beyond the sighing wind and the trill of a wren. Are Sofia and Dustan trailing after them, shocked and unhappy? What happened to the conference call or are they all still there, waiting on the screen for Nate to return, his fingers clenched around a pile of blood-soaked ash?

I swallow hard and bury my face in the warm skin beneath Julian's ear. He moves smoothly, throwing himself into the space between the trunks, dodging, jumping, holding me steady. The trees blur and I shut my eyes before I get dizzy.

Nate and Rick won't catch us now. Julian is too fast for humans.

His footsteps are quieter than the thud of his pulse against my cheek. He's like a deer slipping through the forest, shy and beautiful, all long legs and doe eyes and, Jesus Christ, I think the stress is getting to me. I sit up straighter, the breeze settling my stomach and burning less when I suck it down.

Julian picks his way into a valley, skirting shards of grey rock veined with pink. A river splashes through a series of steps, each small waterfall sparkling in the sun. The smell of mulch and wet stone reminds me of playing by a pond in Figgate Park near my house in Portobello. I loved to slap my chubby little hands against the surface to scare the minnows. My mum distracted me by naming every insect and plant and bird. She said names were important. Knowing where everything fit.

I used to know where I fit.

The river unfurls through the trees. On the other side, next to a wide pool, a family skims stones, the shrieks of the children echoing over the water.

They know nothing of death and the Drakul. The only monsters are the imaginary ones hiding under the bed.

Their voices fade as we join a dirt path leading to a road and a bridge across the river. I slide from Julian's back and we slow our pace to a brisk walk, his hand hot in mine.

Our only possessions are our wallets, two knives and my phones. I drop one in the river and keep the burner phone Julian first gave me, still with a single number saved under J, not that it's active anymore. Nate smashed Julian's phone to stop his mother from tracking him, before Julian could tell him it was impossible to hack.

What was the point in him sneaking out if his mother knew where he was the entire time?

Money, credit cards, knives and a phone. It's not a great haul for a pair of fugitives but it's better than nothing, though my spine feels naked without the weight of my sword.

We cross the bridge and follow a dog-walking path along the river. For the next three hours, we cut across fields, sprint down empty roads and sneak under the Edinburgh City Bypass. I finally lead Julian into Gilmerton past a martial arts studio that reminds me of Gytes Leisure Centre, where I found it ridiculously difficult to concentrate on teaching him when all I wanted was to pin him to the floor and have my wicked way.

Hell, I still want that.

The buildings become a maze of houses. I pause at a battered row of metal-fronted garages and glance around.

"There's no one else here," Julian says. "Not close."

"Just our heartbeats?" He nods and I press my hand to his chest, feeling the throb against my palm. "Long may that continue."

He rewards me with the tender smile only I get to see. I hunch over the keyhole at the base of the door before the prickle behind my eyes can turn into tears.

I am a badass dragon hunt—nope. I am a badass good dragon protector. We do not weep when sad, lovely boys trust us with their lives.

We hope we deserve it.

My wallet contains a single master key for our garages and another for our many safe-houses. Standard Vanatori protocol even in a country where the Drakul population was considered to be low or non-existent. I heave the door open far enough for Julian and me to duck inside then close and lock it. The air is stale with dust and oil. Julian sneezes.

Even his sneezes are cute.

"Can you see me?" I say instead of grabbing him in the dark

and hugging him.

"A little." The chuckle in his voice weakens my knees. "Your eyes are really wide."

I try to stop blinking like an idiot. "Can you get the key? It should be stuck under the front passenger side wheel arch."

Metal scrapes. The bleep and flash of the orange hazard lights catapults my pulse into the roof of my mouth. The interior bulbs of the Ford Ranger flare on.

"Climb in the back," I say. "We'll stay here until dark."

It's far enough from Sofia's house in Roslin to not be the first place they'll check. I ignored the couple of other garages between here and there for that reason.

Julian hops onto the seat, offering a hand to pull me into the tall vehicle. The leather squeaks as I twist to shut the door behind us. My breathing fills the hushed space. Julian raises his arm and I tuck myself into his side. The interior light fades to blackness.

A few days ago, I was happy. I had a super-hot, amazing-in-bed, so-sweet-I-could-cry boyfriend and now everyone wants to kill him. Even if we escape, we'll always be on the run. From the Vanatori, from his family. From my adopted family. I'll never be a member of the Titan Group again. No giggling on the couch with Sofia at headquarters, no being surrounded by people who want to save the world, our collective grief only making us stronger.

No avenging my parents.

"Do you have somewhere we can go?" Julian says, soft enough so his voice doesn't startle me.

"A safe-house."

"Won't they look there?"

"We have a few scattered about the country. Maybe we can

get far enough away and move around so our paths never cross. It's the best I can think of for now."

My stomach gurgles. I try to ignore it and the dryness of my mouth but I'm tired and sore and worried about how to protect Julian from every person on the planet.

"A safe-house sounds fine to me," he says.

I rest my head in the crook of his shoulder. "What did you do when you ran away?"

"Jumped on a train to Edinburgh. Got on another to Stirling then Perth. Got off in Aviemore and walked into the hills. Slept beside a loch. Lucky I don't feel the cold." His fingers draw a swirling pattern on my bicep. "I thought I could live off the land until the initial hunting frenzy died down but I'm pretty rubbish at catching my own food. Someone connected to my mother must have spotted me in the supermarket. My brothers caught me the next day."

If he travelled to Aviemore via Edinburgh then the Romanov compound isn't in the Highlands. It must be somewhere in East Lothian or the Borders given his presence at Tantallon Castle and how long it took him to get to my house when I demanded he come round for sex. I still haven't asked him where he lives—or lived. I no longer care. He can tell me if he wants to.

"How long did you last?" I say.

"Three days. I'm probably not the best at giving advice on running away."

I don't need to see him to know his mouth is quirked in his sad half-smile.

"Couldn't you have flown to another country under cover of darkness?"

"My mother has connections everywhere and I was scared

someone might see or hear me. Everyone flies at night, and higher if it's clear."

I shudder at the thought of the Drakul swooping unseen through the black sky. Its vastness would offer no hiding place, not from monsters with night vision and telepathy. I don't have the courage to ask Julian to shift, anyway, so it's not an option for us.

I sigh into his neck. "Between your mother and her spies, and the Vanatori, it's like we're just waiting to be captured."

"Hey, it's only been a few hours and already we have shelter and a vehicle and somewhere to go. We're not doing too bad."

He gives me a squeeze and I curl my legs across his lap, cuddling into him, his cheek pressed to my forehead. His hand strokes my hair and my muscles gradually relax. The warmth of him makes the interior of the car cosy and intimate. Silence grows between us but it's comfortable. I scooch a little lower until I can listen to his heart, mine slowing to match it. I close my eyes and drift.

"Raine?"

"Hmm?" I mumble, about two seconds from falling asleep and drooling on him.

"I'm…" He clears his throat. "Even if we are caught, the past three weeks with you have been more than I ever hoped for."

I whisper his name in the dark. His lashes tickle my fingertips and I trace his face from cheekbones to nose to lips.

"What if I want more than three weeks?" I say.

His mouth curves against my hand. "You can have me as long as you like."

If only that were true.

<h1 style="text-align:center">40</h1>

Two days later, we're in a safe-house near Llanspyddid, a place in Wales I can't pronounce, eating ice cream and playing *Mario Kart* on the Nintendo Switch. It's almost how I pictured it, minus the constant threat of capture and death. Oh, and the fact I'm alienated from everyone I've fought alongside for the past ten years.

Never thought that would happen.

Although the Cyhyraeth Group are based in Wales, I'm banking on them being called to Scotland to search for us. All our vehicles have tracker boxes fitted and I stuck the one from our Ford Ranger on a bus to Inverness before we left Edinburgh.

I've given my burner phone to Julian to keep me from calling Sofia, though I'm desperate to hear her voice, to know she's okay and not being punished for the trouble I caused. Dustan, too. I'm going to cave and ask for my phone back soon, anyway. Maybe after another hour of games.

I'm not real keen to remember I'm the one being hunted.

Julian is sprawled beside me on a bean bag, his long legs stretched towards the TV, his trainers on. We sleep in our shoes, just in case. He cradles the controller close to his chest, his eyes on the screen. He's biting his lip.

"Raine?"

I jump and realise he's looking at me. "What?"

"You're stuck on a wall." He flashes me a grin and I'm glad I'm sitting down. "I'm winning."

I glance at the TV. My kart is jammed in a corner going nowhere and I'm dead last. Stupid Rosalina. Julian's Shy Guy icon is way out in front with one lap to go. The bean bag shifts beneath me as I lurch forward and focus like a proper gamer instead of a besotted teenager. A bullet and a star get me to fifth place. I smirk at Julian when my next box contains a blue shell.

"You wouldn't hurt me with that, would you, Raine?" he says and peeks at me through the hair flopping over his forehead.

At his chuckle, I yank my gaze back to the screen. The giant Bowser statue has punched me to a complete stop.

"You did that on purpose!" I gasp but it's too late.

Julian crosses the finish line and I limp into a dismal eighth place. Serves me right for laughing at him when he was learning how to play. It was probably a bit mean to start him on Rainbow Road but he was all flustered and cute, elbows everywhere, groaning each time his character flew off the edge.

I drop my remote on the rug and crawl towards him, plucking his controller from his hands. I straddle his lap and tangle my fingers in his hair.

"Since when did you become a master manipulator?" I breathe against his mouth.

He swallows hard and it soothes my dignity no end. His hands fall lightly to cup my hips.

"Is that what I am?"

"You are when you use your gorgeousness to bedazzle me."

His slow smile rolls through my stomach. I kiss him and the glide of his lips still does crazy things to my pulse. He makes a noise low in his throat, his fingers tightening on my waist.

He knows exactly the effect he has on me. My heart sings for him. Not being able to hide it is worth the delight on his face, the soft surprise as each touch skips through my chest.

No one ever touched him. No one wanted to be touched by him.

Their loss.

I woke up on top of him in the back seat of the Ford Ranger, his arms cuddling me close. Night had fallen so we ransacked the nearest safe-house for food. I drove while Julian fed me forkfuls of cold macaroni cheese and beans and peaches. We travelled until the horizon flared pink and blue then parked well off the main road on a forestry track. Another night of driving brought us here, to a safe-house on stilts above a small lake. We slept to the gentle slap of water on wood.

It's a beautiful place but we'll move on in a day, two at the most. I want to put as much distance as possible between Nate's crossbow and Julian.

Julian tilts his hips, his hands pinning me against him and returning my attention to the present. The very hot, very hard-to-resist present. His black t-shirt is a tiny bit too small for him. It teases the top of his jeans and hints at the promise of smooth, warm skin.

I swear, all he has to do is stretch for something and it turns my brain to mush.

My fingers slip under the material to stroke the taut muscles of his belly. He shivers, his mouth hungry on mine. The mixture of innocence and eagerness is captivating.

I somehow drag myself away. "I can't believe I'm going to say this but we shouldn't... um, get naked, I mean."

We also sleep in our clothes. One person showers while the other stays fully dressed and on watch. We have to be ready to run. I'm hoping the sensation of being stalked will fade but I can't risk losing myself in Julian. Nate walked in on us naked once before. I have no doubt he'll kill us the next time, so no sex until we're safer.

Though I'm pretty sure I'll cave on that soon, too.

* * *

I sleep fitfully, which means Julian sleeps fitfully. He folds me in his arms and reads me a bedtime story by candlelight. Joe Abercrombie's *Before They Are Hanged*. Not exactly a happy tale considering one of the main protagonists is a torturer but I love the unapologetic grimness, the filth the characters have to wade through and the perfect portrayal of good and evil in everyone. The smell of the pages reminds me of the library in Peebles. I miss the reverent hush and the shelves of books.

What did my boss think when I failed to show for my shift yesterday? Will she get worried and phone the police? I'm not sure whether that would help or hinder us at the moment.

I rest my cheek on Julian's collarbone and just breathe him in, lulled by the rumble of his voice.

"'Strange, isn't it,' mused Glotka as he watched him struggle for air," Julian reads. "'Big men, small men, thin men, fat men, clever men, stupid men, they all respond the same to a fist in the guts. One minute you think you're the most powerful man in the world. The next, you can't even—'" Julian giggles and squirms underneath me. "Raine, that tickles."

My nose snuffles at the hollow of his throat. It's my favourite spot, followed closely by the soft skin below his ear. There's just something so vulnerable about it. I touch my tongue to the flutter of his pulse and the book thuds to the floor. He rolls, pinning me beneath him, and claims my mouth.

God, his forcefulness turns me on. I love it when he's confident enough to take charge without fear of betrayal or ridicule or being treated like he's ugly, weak, disgusting. And the fact he has to be careful with his strength just plain does it for me. He could do what he wants and I wouldn't be able to stop him. I know he won't but the thrill of it is amazing.

Dammit, I'm whimpering into his mouth.

"I'm sorry, that was my fault," I manage to say, my heartbeat thundering between us. "Man, I really want to but we shouldn't."

He pulls away and smirks at me. It's like a lightning bolt to the chest. Honeyed light sparkles in his amber eye.

"Who said anything about getting naked?" he says while I remind myself I need air to survive. "I'm only trying to help you sleep."

How is this helping when my body is so aware of him, it throbs in all my sensitive places?

He bends his head and nibbles at my lips. He shifts his hips so his lower half is tucked into my side. His hand caresses downward, the tips of his fingers grazing one extremely erect nipple and continuing south. He pops the button on my trousers and pushes himself up to look at me. When I offer no protest since I've forgotten what words are, he slips his hand into my pants.

"How come rain is so wet?" he says and grins at me.

I choke on a moan and a laugh. It becomes a full moan as he slides a finger inside me, his thumb stroking my clitoris to the same rhythm. He guides me expertly, no teasing, no long, slow burn, as if he understands what I need without me having to tell him. I shout his name and explode into a million pieces.

A number of minutes later, I regain my senses to Julian spooning me from behind, the candle out, my trousers refastened. My heart trips along in a body gone fluid.

"What about you?" I say.

"Don't worry about me."

"Impossible," I whisper.

41

"Raine, *gracias a Dios,*" Sofia says as soon as she hears my voice.

I'm standing in the living room of the safe-house on the lake near Llanspyddid, peeking through a sliver in the blinds at the serene water and still trees. Julian rustles about behind me, packing a couple of bags with food, clothes and weapons. I have a spare sword hidden in a cylindrical poster tube on a strap over my shoulder. It came with a spine sheath but the blade is too long for me to wear comfortably. It's also heavier than I'm used to, the grip alien unlike my own that seemed moulded to fit my hand, but it's better than being unarmed.

"Sorry I didn't call sooner," I say to Sofia, letting the blinds slip closed. "Is it safe to talk? Are you and Dustan okay?"

"Oh, honey, we are fine. It is you I am worried about. I cannot talk for long, the *pendejos* are watching us but they are still letting me go to the bathroom by myself." Her words are muffled as if she's whispering through her fingers. "How are you holding up?"

The toilet flushes and I wait for the swirl of water to fade.

"We're doing all right. We have shelter, food, transportation. Does Nate—"

Something thumps on Sofia's end.

"*Dios mío,* I will be out in a minute! Can a girl not get a little privacy?" I imagine her hunched over the phone, cupping it to her face as she hisses, "Nate's called in the cavalry. They arrived yesterday. Destroy this phone. Get as far away as you can. Do not—"

There's a crash and shouting and the line goes dead. I turn the phone off and remove the battery but can't bring myself to smash it, tucking both pieces into my pocket instead. For emergencies.

What was Sofia going to say? Don't go back to your house. Don't use your credit cards. Don't board a plane or a train. I could call her from a pay phone but I imagine her mobile privileges have been revoked.

I hope they're not hurting her for talking to me. If they are… What in actual hell can I do about it? I might never see her again.

I scrub my face and help Julian finish packing. I just need some time to think. It would be too easy to get depressed. What joy is there in the life of a fugitive? We need a base of operations where we're safe enough to plan. Maybe Sofia and Dustan can join us there. We could find other allies. Fight back. A band of misfits taking on Principal Cozma and Evelyn Romanov and their respective armies.

Sounds plausible.

I yank the zipper on my bag shut. Julian's hand settles on the white ridge of my knuckles.

"Sofia will be okay," he says.

"You could hear her side of the conversation?"

He quirks his mouth. "I can hear animals snuffling in the forest outside."

"Must be difficult for you to get any peace."

He smiles fully and squeezes my fingers. "There are

different kinds of peace."

***

Branches screech on metal and glass. I toss them to the side and brush mud off the windscreen of the Ford Ranger, hidden in bushes a mile from the house. I slide into the driver's side and unsheathe my sword from the poster tube, wedging it between my seat and the door for easy access. Hard to explain if the police stop us but I plan on driving very carefully at the speed limit. I guide the huge car onto the rutted track.

Julian can't drive. His brothers learned as soon as they turned seventeen but no one wanted to teach him. I guess they didn't care to be trapped in an enclosed space with someone they loathed.

That's why he thought he was the ugly one, compared to his brothers. Because everyone treated him like he was. How can they look at him and see ugliness? I look at Julian and want to curl in his lap. I could sit in his arms all day, breathing in the comforting vanilla smell of him, and be content.

I'll teach him how to drive at the next safe-house—a bunker hidden in an abandoned airfield near Penzance. There are loads of concrete roads and junctions and rusting hangars to manoeuvre around. He'll grin at me when he gets the hang of it. I'll tell my pulse to behave itself.

Normal couple stuff.

A light mist hugs the ground, hazing the sun and gathering in valleys. The road unwinds beneath us, the mist parting after two hours to reveal a beautiful blue sky.

"What do you think your mother is doing now?" I say into the hush.

"Apart from hunting us? She'll be waiting and hoping to feel when I die. Apparently, it's a lot like vertigo."

"*If* you die." My fingers tighten on the wheel. "And she won't feel it because she's going to die first."

Right around the time I ram my sword hilt-deep in her bony chest.

"I'm not immortal, Raine." Julian's soft smile squiggles through my stomach. "Even you can't make me live forever."

"Maybe not but you *are* going to die old and happy if I have anything to do with it."

I turn off the road after another two-and-a-half hours. Gravel crunches under the tyres, the small track leading into a block of trees. Flat fields stretch to more trees on the horizon, the wavering grass broken by low concrete buildings, metal sheds and a control tower, the roof collapsed. A ragged windsock flaps in the breeze.

The bunker could potentially be our secure base—no one can open it if the door is locked from the inside—but the thought of staying underground, no windows and no fresh air, clamps my chest in the 'cannot breathe without wheezing' position. I need sunlight and breezes not electric bulbs and concrete.

Plus, if Principal Cozma ever finds us, she'll bury us alive. Same for Evelyn Romanov.

I almost spin the car around but we're out of land, unless we want to travel east to Kent or back-track on ourselves.

The further we travel, the more it seems we'll have to risk Julian flying us out of the country. If I weren't such a wimp, we could be in the Caribbean on some tiny island where no one would find us, sipping from a coconut and enjoying the sunshine.

But I'm not sure I'm ready for the reality of Julian as a beast with claws and teeth.

I guide the Ranger into a hangar and shut off the engine. Silence settles in the car. Julian jerks against his seatbelt. His eyes snap to me.

"Heartbeats," he says. "Lots of them."

42

I twist the key in the ignition and slam the car into reverse. Four loud bangs echo in the shed and the vehicle judders like an animal in pain. The tyre pressure warning light goes haywire. A wall of black-clad people blocks our exit.

I could stomp on the accelerator pedal and mow them down, sparks flying from exposed wheel rims.

I turn the engine off.

"Well, we lasted a whole extra day compared to when I ran away." Julian stares at his fingers clenched in his lap. "Guess my mother has more spies than you."

I grab his hand. "I won't let them kill you."

"I doubt you'll have a choice."

Boots scrape on concrete, the crowd pressing closer to the back of the Ranger. I don't recognise a single face in the rear-view mirrors.

"Stay in the car," I say. "Hunker down in the footwell."

"What are you going to do?"

I ease my sword from the gap between my seat and the door. Words of bravado flit through my head: 'Encourage them to leave.' 'Tell them to get lost.'

"Haven't a clue," I say.

Julian's grin flickers and fades. He trails a fingertip across my cheek.

"Thank you."

"What for?"

"For fighting for me." His smile is as sad as I've ever seen it. "I'll never regret meeting you."

"This isn't goodbye," I squeak.

His expression says he doesn't agree. Loss wrenches my stomach, worse than when he left me on my doorstep, his secret hanging huge and unspoken between us. I want to kiss him, tell him I love him, but that will only confirm our parting. Instead, I let my gaze drink him in. His chestnut hair flops over his forehead but not enough to mask his amber and peridot eyes. I place my hand on his chest and his heart thumps against my palm.

He's not a monster. He could shift into a dragon right now and I bet he'd still look at me with tenderness. No monster could have such innocent joy or be so gentle.

"This isn't goodbye," I say in a firmer, less hysterical tone.

He nods once and I pop the handle, slipping outside. The air tastes of metal and exhaust fumes. The pulse in my mouth muffles the thunk of the door. I face the crowd, my movements careful, my hand squeezing the grip of my sword until it moulds to my skin. I crab-walk around the nose of the Ranger to Julian's side, risking a glance through the window. He's folded into the footwell, his knees around his ears.

"Drop the sword, Miss Waller or I'll tell my men to open fire until there's nothing left but shrapnel and blood."

The crowd parts to reveal Principal Cozma, deadly in her hunter leathers. Two pommels stick up from her shoulders like broken wings. Her brown hair is pinned back to bare the furrows of her scars.

"How do you have automatic weapons?" I manage to say with very little wobble despite the number of assault rifles aimed at me.

"Your laws can't stop me," she says. "I am the law."

"Not for everyone, you're not."

"For everyone who matters." Her cold smile shivers to my toes. "Tell me, Miss Waller, why is your dragon cowering in the car? Is he incapable of defending himself?"

"He's not cowering. I just don't trust you not to hurt him."

"Of course we're going to hurt him. But if he cooperates, I promise the pain will be brief."

"How about you leave us alone instead?"

She laughs and her teeth flash in a beam of light spearing through the roof. "Don't be ridiculous, Miss Waller. You sealed your fate and his as soon as you made the video call. I am here to ensure justice is done."

"Killing him is not justice."

"You're right. Removing the scourge of the Romanovs will transcend justice. It will be our greatest triumph."

Christ, there's no talking to this woman.

Sweat slicks my palm where it grasps my sword. The men and women ranged behind Cozma are utterly still, their features as blank as stone.

Is this what I look like when I'm hunting the Drakul? Too blinded by doctrine to see beyond prejudice?

"I want nothing more than to end the Romanovs but he's not like the rest of his family," I say.

"I didn't come here to argue with you, Miss Waller. Drop your sword and get your dragon out of the car or I say again— shrapnel and blood."

I pause with my fingers on the door handle, the tip of my

sword pointed at the concrete.

"His name is Julian."

"I don't much care what he calls himself." A muscle twitches in her jaw. "This is becoming tedious."

I open the door. Julian's eyes meet mine with a physical jolt. He gives me a brave smile and unfolds himself from the footwell. I plant my body in front of his.

Cozma clicks her fingers at a man to her right. "Washington, if Miss Waller does not drop her sword in the next five seconds, please shoot her in the kneecap."

Jeez, I'm really starting to hate this bitch.

Julian strokes his fingers across my shoulder blade where the hunters can't see. I sigh and let the sword fall. It clangs on the floor and imprints its shape in the dust.

Cozma's lips twist. "Wonderful. Now—Washington, Noble, secure our captive. I have no wish to be trapped in this pile of rust should he foolishly decide to shift."

Two men peel away from the line and step towards us. They halt at a safe distance.

Noble flicks the barrel of his rifle. "Move over there, Drakul whore."

Julian's hand tenses on my back. I lean into him.

I don't care what the stupid man thinks. His hateful words can't sully our relationship.

"There's no need for name-calling, Mr Noble," Cozma says, though she sounds amused.

"Sorry ma'am." The rifle flicks again. "Move over there *now.*"

Noble and his gun track me to where I stop a couple of strides from Julian, leaving him open. Vulnerable. Washington keeps his weapon on Julian while one hand unclips a pair of cuffs from his belt. Julian, pretty familiar with the routine, holds his arms out, wrists pressed together.

"Oh, no, Mr Romanov," Cozma says sweetly, "we'll have your hands behind your back, if you please."

Washington ratchets the cuffs and Julian winces. Anger simmers in my chest but has nowhere to go.

Noble waves his gun at me. "Hands on your head."

He pats me down, removing the knives from my wrists, waist and boots.

"How did you find us so quickly?" I direct at Cozma.

She hooks her thumbs in her belt loops. "I simply let it be known we had a traitor colluding with a Drakul. Obviously, they were disgusted by this abomination. So much so, I had to turn people away as it would be dangerous to gather in such numbers. We had enough teams to send to each garage and safe-house and Vanatori-owned property. It really wasn't difficult."

I imagine 'don't use the safe-houses' was what Sofia tried to tell me on the phone.

I'm such an idiot.

Noble wraps icy fingers around my wrist and yanks my arm behind my back, fastening one cuff then the other. Rifle barrels to the spine encourage Julian and me out of the shed, the rest of the hunters covering us from all angles while Cozma watches with a satisfied smirk. We're led at a trot to the other side of the airfield where a collection of vehicles are parked in a large hangar. Further prods guide us to some kind of modified minibus sporting tinted windows and black paint. We're shoved into the middle seats and the doors slide shut, sealing us into the gloom.

43

Julian's wrists start to bleed after an hour on the road. The cuffs slice into his skin, the metal painful enough without the dragon's-bane coating. I don't know how he stands it. My cuffs are loose but having my arms pinned behind me screams through my shoulders.

I kick at the panel separating us from the front of the minibus. A window slides open and Cozma's eyes appear, as cold and dead as ash.

"Julian's cuffs are too tight, they're cutting into him."

Her gaze shifts to Julian, who is twisted on the seat to relieve the pressure. Washington and Noble are just visible in the seats behind us.

"It's only a little blood," she says. "I doubt his hands will fall off."

"Why are you being cruel? He's cooperating."

"Ah, yes, Miss Waller. He's so very *cooperative*. Meekly accepting whatever is done to him."

She sounds like Nate.

"What would you do if I struggled?" Julian says, his jaw stiff.

"Why, shoot you, of course."

He raises an eyebrow as if to say, "Well, there you go."

The panel thumps shut.

The rest of the journey doesn't improve. We're cramped in the seats with no doors or windows in our compartment, the only light filtering from the glass beside Washington and Noble. Their seats recline, letting them stretch out and nap in turns. We drive for ten hours with few stops. Going to the bathroom is a humiliating experience of being uncuffed and watched then re-cuffed in patches of scrub with litter flapping in the branches. Julian's wrists are torn and bloody. He flinches when the cuffs are fastened but makes no sound.

The urge to sink my teeth into something, preferably Cozma's throat, builds at each casual mistreatment.

They toss food at us, not caring if it falls to the floor or even how we're going to eat it. At first, we scrabble for it but it becomes a game, a tiny bit of fun to soothe the pain. I hold a burger in my mouth while Julian bites his half. He steadies mine until there's nothing left but our lips, slippery with sauce and grease.

We quit it when Noble growls, "You make me fucking sick."

Julian lies with his head in my lap and my fingers itch to brush his hair from his face. I think about where we met and how little time we've had together. I remember his joy when he tasted a milkshake, ice cream, played an arcade game. His adorable nervousness when I took his virginity and how quickly that flipped to his complete mastery of me.

I love this man. This Drakul. I can't let them kill him. So what if I'm disowned as a Vanatori? They can banish us to Alaska for all I care. I just want Julian to live.

He deserves to be happy.

The minibus jerks to a halt. I attempt to roll the ache from my shoulders and bite my lip on a moan. Julian sits up without effort.

Man, his abs are amazing.

His hair is fluffed on one side, a line on his cheek marking where he slept on a ridge of my jeans. He manages a sleepy smile but it fades as his gaze cuts to Washington and Noble unclipping their seat belts and gathering their rifles.

Looks like we're here, wherever that is. Back at Sofia's? Another headquarters quickly fashioned to contain the many hunters raring to spit at the traitor and her dragon?

I dread to see the smugness on Nate's face.

"How are you doing?" I whisper to Julian while he stretches his neck.

The bones of his spine crack. I guess dragons get stiff, too.

"I'm okay. I've had worse."

The door of the minibus grinds open. Rough hands and prodding guns usher us out. Stone stables and metal sheds squat in a yard smelling of hay, casting long shadows as the sun sets. It's Sunday evening and the place seems deserted. A horse munches grass and watches us from the edge of a field. Cozma steps beside me, looking annoyingly refreshed. She's changed her clothes in the brief moments we stopped on the road. My yellow top is crumpled and my hair is a mess.

"Where are we?" I say instead of, "I hate you."

She sucks in a contented breath. "Near somewhere called Aberdour. Depressing little town but it has a nice beach. That's where most of us entered the country."

Washington and Noble shove us into the closest building at Cozma's signal. A large dryer rusts against the rear wall, the chequered linoleum badly scuffed and smeared with more rust. The room smells of bleach. At the back, we're encouraged down concrete stairs into the basement. Fresh powder dusts the floor where chains have been bolted to the wall.

Nate and Rick watch us enter. Nate's face is carefully blank but Rick treats me to a top-to-toe body scan and curls his lip. He's swapped his awful brown suit for beige hunting leathers.

It's not an improvement.

"Where are Sofia and Dustan?" I say, betrayed by a slight quaver.

Washington pushes Julian over to the chains, Nate and Rick easing away as if Julian might be contagious. Noble's bruising fingers hold me in place.

"They are being retrained." Cozma crowds into the room with two more gun-toting strangers. "They don't seem to be taking it to heart since they won't stop whining about how Julian is different and you're innocent and we should just work together. Frankly, Miss Waller, it's starting to piss me off."

"Have you considered they might be right?"

Rick tuts and shakes his head.

I want to kick him in the nuts.

Cozma gives me a rigid smile. "They're not right. *You're* not right. You're all delusional and caught in the spell of this creature."

She crosses to Julian, shadowed by the two guards. Washington uncuffs him and clamps the chains on the wall around his wrists and ankles. The manacles don't tighten so hopefully they're a reprieve, if he can ignore the sting of dragon's-bane. Maybe his torn skin will heal in the next few hours without the constant bite of metal.

If he has a few hours.

Noble's hand crushes my arm. Julian meets my gaze and I force myself to stand still.

"Let's see how cooperative you really are." Cozma's eyes trail over Julian spreadeagled against the wall. "Tell me where the Romanov compound is."

Julian watches her, his spine straight. No hunching like he did when Nate chained him in our basement. When he waited for me to punish him.

"I'm not telling you anything until you let Raine go. She gets to leave, unharmed, and you never bother her again."

"I can make you talk, Mr Romanov," Cozma says.

Julian raises his chin, his eyes hot. "I'm not unfamiliar with pain. You might be disappointed."

Her smile sinks claws into my stomach.

"It's not your pain I'm talking about, *dragon*."

She nods at Noble. He releases me and blood tingles to my fingertips. His grin warns me a second before he switches his grip, captures my wrist and pistons my arm upwards. My scream bursts out while he happily attempts to dislocate my shoulder.

Chains rattle. Julian shouts my name. I try to tell him not to give Cozma what she wants, that I can cope, but the pain slices up my arm and stabs at my brain until I can barely think of anything else.

Except how the holy fucking hell did Julian survive this kind of agony for the last two decades?

I hear him faintly through the fireball engulfing my shoulder and oh crap, I'm still screaming.

"I'll do it," he says. "I'll tell you anything you want just, please, stop hurting her."

The pain fades to a horrible throb. I'm on the floor, curled in a ball. Julian strains at his bonds, wobbling on his tip-toes with the rapid rise and fall of his chest, his face stricken.

No one is watching Cozma but she's watching me the way a snake watches a mouse.

And nothing good ever happens to the mouse.

44

Pine needles muffle our footsteps, the ancient trees towering over us and whispering in the dark. My night vision goggles turn cones and rocks into alien objects. Our soft shuffle halts when Julian holds up his hands.

He's cuffed again. I swear, he's spent more time in chains than he has free since I met him. I still can't believe him when he says I've made his life better.

I've only made it shorter.

Noble stops so close to me, his breath brushes my ear. I glare at him but it's probably lost behind the binoculars mounted to my face, the straps tight against my chin and forehead. He's been hovering around me since his little torture display, as if eager for another opportunity to hurt me. My shoulder continues to ache and it's been three days.

Washington stands next to Julian, the barrel of his SA80 rifle trained on his midsection. At seven hundred rounds a minute, it'll cut him in half, never mind the underslung grenade launcher.

I asked Cozma about the weapons. She smirked and informed me she has a contact in the British Army.

So why does the Cyhyraeth Group in Wales only fight with single-shot rifles and shotguns? Why weren't we given more firepower on our new assignment to Scotland? We might actually kill a Drakul if we had automatics.

She looked at me as if I were stupid and ignored the question.

"We're getting close to the fence," Julian says in a hushed voice, the eerie green of my goggles painting his eyes the same colour. He's the only one of us who has night vision without the aid of technology. "Follow me in single file or we'll never get past the cameras."

"How do we know this isn't a trick?" Noble's mouth twists below his goggles.

"You grilled me for two days. Has anything I've said been untrue?"

Noble's lips turn down at the corners. "No, but since you're an untrustworthy monster, it doesn't mean shit."

The man beside Noble snickers, dressed all in black like the rest of us.

Cozma hand-picked three of her elite hunters to join Noble and Washington, the rest of her army stationed nearby to assist if the Romanovs have an army of their own. She thought a subtle attack might be more successful. And she changed her mind on letting Julian come on the mission, with me along to make sure he behaves. She said she wants him to witness the fall of his family, to risk his life and prove he's on our side but I don't trust her for a second. With Rick and Nate, it means we're outnumbered seven to four and six of them have guns. Nate opted for his crossbow but Rick has been strutting through the forest holding a silenced pistol as if he's James Bond. He also has so many knives attached to his person, he clinks when he moves.

"Fine, do what you want," Julian says. "Step out of the blind spot and get us all killed."

"You'd like that wouldn't you, dragon? I don't care what your whore says, your sob story is an act. Your family will be waiting the second we're inside the fence."

"God, I hope not," Julian murmurs but Noble doesn't appear to hear as Sofia plants herself in front of him.

"Call her a whore again, *cabrón*," she bristles, her hand clenched on her axe.

Nate sighs. "For god's sake, Sofia. Principal Cozma allowed you and Dustan on this mission as a show of faith."

Noble leans down until he and Sofia are lens to lens.

He smiles and says, "Whore."

Dustan launches himself between them, all elbows and knees, before Sofia can bury her axe in Noble's head. She strains against Dustan's grip, her shiny hair quivering in its ponytail.

"Fighting among ourselves on the edge of Romanov territory is a very bad idea," Dustan says, sounding out of breath. He stares towards Noble. "As a so-called elite hunter, you should know that."

Noble opens his mouth, no doubt to continue the argument or call Dustan a name, but stops and puts a finger to his ear, whispering into his sleeve. "There's no problem, Principal. We're about to enter the blind spot of the cameras."

The elite hunters have earpieces so they can communicate with Cozma while the rest of us commoners are deaf to her commands. Personally, I'm glad I don't have her whispering in my ear but Rick got huffy when he realised he was excluded. He would have complained had Nate not sent him a look.

Noble flicks his rifle at Julian. "Lead on then, Romanov."

He says 'Romanov' the same as 'whore'.

Julian walks deeper into the woods. I try to be next in line but Washington barges in front. Rick flashes me a cold smile and skips ahead. I grit my teeth and focus on his back, copying his movements, my sword a comforting weight in its tube strapped tight across my back. Sofia, Dustan and Nate join the line, the rest of Cozma's elite taking up the rear. We weave a path around trunks and elder bushes. The space through the trees flares white the further we go, the goggles adapting so I'm not dazzled. We crouch on the edge of a forest ride and I tip my goggles up, blinking as my vision adjusts.

Security lights top a chain-link fence that must be at least twelve feet tall, barbed wire curling between. The pines end about twenty metres from it, replaced by stumps extending beyond the fence before the pines start again on the other side. A rusted sign says 'Danger: Quarry. Do Not Enter.' There was a similar fence a mile back, minus the lights and cameras.

The Romanovs are my neighbours. The dangerous quarry and collapsed cave system hide their compound in the heart of Glentress Forest, just north of Peebles. The place is an urban legend in my neighbourhood. Dogs and cats go missing all the time and people blame it on the quarry. They say it's haunted by the workers who died when they dug too deep into the rock. Anyone who goes there will be cursed or never seen again. It even shows as blurry on satellite pictures.

Julian says the workers weren't crushed when the ground collapsed into an unknown cave system. There are no caves. The Romanovs just wanted to move in.

Julian was fourteen and forced to watch.

He takes a deep breath and steps from the shelter of the trees, his perfect figure silhouetted by light. My pulse flutters in my mouth, waiting for shouts, gunfire, the triumphant roar of a she-bitch at the sight of her youngest. Julian kneels at the base of the fence and lifts a hatch completely indistinguishable from the ground, propping it open. He motions to us and slips into the uncovered hole.

The drop into the tunnel catches me by surprise. My boots finally hit mud and I steady my hand on the dirt wall. There's a not unpleasant earthy smell. Wooden joists recessed into the walls shore up the roof at the entrance and, hopefully, throughout the tunnel. I follow the soles of Rick's shoes onto some kind of synthetic sheet covering the floor, which explains why Julian wasn't filthy every time I met him. I crawl into total darkness until my head collides with what I pray is not Rick's butt.

I tell myself I'm not claustrophobic. Nope, not one little bit.

Rick inches forward. Grey light filters in and Julian hoists me out of the shaft at the other end. I grab the chance to hug him, his bound hands pressed to my hip, his heartbeat thudding in my ear. Rick grumbles something derogatory. The last person closes the hatch and we hustle into the trees in our conga line, flipping our goggles back on.

Julian pauses in a small clearing. "That's us past the cameras until we get to the house."

The others range themselves around him. I smile sweetly at Washington and insert myself next to Julian.

"How long did it take you to build the tunnel?" I say.

"A month." He quirks his mouth. "I had the motivation."

"Enough chit chat," Noble barks. "Remind us what's next."

The silence stretches long enough for a muscle in Noble's jaw to twitch.

"I lead you through the gardens and into the house," Julian finally says. "You disable the guards and the cameras in the security room. Then we search for my family."

"Very good," Noble says on a sneer, "but there's been a slight change. Rick?"

Rick grins wide and jumps into the centre of our loose huddle. I tense but huge arms wrap around me and drag me from Julian's side. Sofia and Dustan are similarly pinioned by two of the elite hunters, Sofia spitting and trying to slice her axe into her captor's leg.

"Sorry, Raine, but this has to happen," Rick says, his expression not sorry at all.

"Rick, don't—"

He points his silenced pistol at Julian and pulls the trigger.

45

Julian drops and my heart stops beating. Washington's hand clamps over my mouth, muffling my scream and mashing my lips against my teeth.

Where did Rick shoot Julian? If it's anywhere but the head or heart, he can still heal. I struggle to see past the blur of tears, like peering through a sea of watery green.

Rick falls over with an, "Oof!"

Julian shoves up on his bound hands. I blink. Rick is sprawled on his back, his legs swept out from under him.

Exactly as I did to Julian in Gytes Leisure Centre.

Washington's moist palm swallows my half-sob, half-whoop. Rick curses and jumps to his feet, the pistol clutched in his hand. I toss my head and bite Washington's thumb. His grip loosens. I jerk my hips to the side and hammer-fist him right in the crotch.

His turn to drop, huddled around his man-parts.

I dive in front of Julian, covering his beautiful head and heart with my body. He curls against my back and breathes into my hair.

I fling a hand up. "Please, Rick. Don't."

"You know, Raine," he says, shaking his head, "once that would have stopped me but now you have to go, too. Same with Sofia and Dustan. Cozma's orders."

"*Tu puta madre*," Sofia hisses, struggling in the arms of the hunter holding her, her axe on the ground.

Dustan gapes at Rick and his throat bobs. "We're family, man."

"Not by blood," Rick says and raises his gun.

I stare down the barrel. His features show no remorse or hesitation. I'm glad I can't see his eyes. The blind conviction would probably hurt more than the bullet.

Something tugs on my arm, breaking my balance and shoving me onto my face. Needles prickle my cheek and I huff the scent of pine. A weight rolls onto my back.

"Don't kill her," Julian says. "Kill me but not her."

"Oh, I'm definitely going to kill you both," Rick says, his smile as chilling as one of Cozma's.

"What the fuck, Rick?" Nate says. "Cozma never said anything to me about special orders. We were to remove Julian, not everyone."

It's the first time Nate has used Julian's name instead of 'dragon', 'beast' or 'lizard'. Okay, so he's talking about killing him but it's still an improvement. The subject matter is no surprise. I have few illusions about Cozma letting Julian live but I planned on sneaking him out in the chaos of battle.

Because running away is obviously so effective.

"She knew you wouldn't go through with it," Rick says, keeping his focus on Julian sprawled on top of me. "We can't have bleeding hearts but you're not strong enough to cut them out. It's why she promised me my own group once this is done. You can be a member but the Titan name will be struck from the records in disgrace."

Nate's fingers blanch on his crossbow. "So you schemed

behind my back?"

"She made me an offer I couldn't refuse."

Noble appears at Nate's shoulder.

"Ease up on the crossbow there, Reed," he says, his rifle steady. "We don't want any accidents."

Nate lets the weapon hang on its sling and his mouth sets in a grim line. He has the grace to shrug one shoulder at Sofia and Dustan.

Dustan flaps his mouth. "Nate, you can't seriously—"

"What am I supposed to do—die with you?"

"You spineless, weak-willed *pendejo*," Sofia says and wriggles furiously in the hunter's arms. "I hope the Romanovs eat you."

The final hunter presses his rifle to Sofia's temple. "Quiet down now, Castenada."

I'm finding it hard to breathe under Julian without inhaling pine needles. I suppose I should savour it since I'm about two puffs from stopping altogether. My sword sheath and goggles are digging into my skin but he's so warm curled around me, so solid, I'm dreading the second he goes limp.

Rick slides closer. "I'll kill you first, dragon, but know the rest of their deaths are on your head."

"I get to kill the bitch," Washington growls and heaves himself to his feet while massaging his gonads.

Note to self—punching a man in the privates is liable to make him dislike you.

"Smith, would you hurry up and pull the trigger?" Noble says. "We've lingered long enough."

Julian tenses. I can't see his face. I want to see his face, to hug him properly and have my last breath filled with the scent of vanilla.

"I love you, Raine," he whispers.

A sob catches in my throat.

"I love—"

Gunshots clatter over the rest of my words and I feel an impotent burst of anger. Can't Rick wait one fucking second for me to say my last I love you?

The thunder of bullets fades to leave a ringing in my ears. For a silenced pistol, it isn't particularly silent. And why am I still alive?

Julian shifts on top of me. "Raine—"

I slap my palms to the ground and shove hard, twisting until I'm kneeling over him. He lies on his back and blinks at me, his cuffed hands raised above him. I run my shaking fingers over him.

"You're not hit. Are you hit?"

"I'm not hit," he says softly.

"Then what…?"

I drag my eyes from him to the rest of the clearing. Sofia and Dustan huddle together. Nate stands with his crossbow notched to his shoulder and pointed into the trees, Noble in a heap at his feet. Rick's goggles aim at the night sky but the mess of his chest tells me he's not star-gazing. Four other black shapes are unmoving.

Is Cozma barking uselessly into their earpieces?

A single shot makes me jump. Nate cries out and collapses, his hands clutching his leg, his crossbow forgotten. Three men materialise from the forest, all bulging muscle and glowing green skin, though that's probably the night vision.

"Hello, little brother," one of them says.

46

The huge underground room extends for about five hundred metres, the roof supported by massive stone pillars. Flames dance in sconces, chasing shadows across the brick walls. Our steps echo on the rough-hewn floor, Nate supported by Sofia and Dustan and trailing droplets of red, a wet stain on his black trousers. Julian's brothers herd us confidently from behind, armed with handguns and dressed in identical grey suits.

Kester, Blane and Dominic. They haven't hurt Julian yet but they will. I can see it in their amber eyes. Julian was wrong, though—they aren't more beautiful than him.

Cruelty twists their features into ugliness.

I glance at Julian walking next to me, his hands still cuffed. His face is carefully blank, his hair flopping forward to hide his peridot eye. He's faring better than me. My whole body started sweating as soon as his brothers led us down the too-wide-for-human-feet stairs, anticipating my reunion with Evelyn Romanov. Then there's Cozma hovering somewhere on the perimeter. I doubt we'll be best friends if I somehow manage to defeat the Romanov matriarch. She's more likely to kill me and claim the victory as her own.

Funny how one psychotic witch looks much the same as

the other.

The far end of the room draws closer and my knees begin to wobble, a familiar burn in my bladder warning of the imminent risk of peeing myself. A figure reclines on a raised throne flanked by two dragon statues. Brown stains streak the marble and the steps below, chains dangling empty. Evelyn Romanov stands at our approach, her maroon dress sweeping the floor, a cape of black lace pinned to the shoulders.

"Did you really think I knew nothing of your little tunnel, runt?" she snarls with her slash of a mouth. "I allowed you those brief moments of escape, and do you know why?"

Julian meets her burning gaze. "No, Mother, I do not."

"Because that tiny bit of freedom gave you hope and hope is so much sweeter to crush than resignation." She flings out her bony arm and points towards a barred door inset into the wall behind the pillars. "Kester, leave me my worstborn and his human plaything. Oh, and the limping one. We don't want all that blood going to waste."

Kester has a chestnut ponytail and goatee. He jerks his handgun, motioning for Sofia and Dustan to precede him. They leave Nate balancing on his good leg. Sofia throws me a worried glance and grips Dustan's hand. Next to Kester, Dustan is a matchstick man. So easy to break.

The cell door clangs shut.

"I believe it's your turn, Kester," Evelyn says and aims an unpleasant smile at Nate.

Kester places his handgun on the dais steps and shrugs out of his suit jacket, folding it on top. He unbuttons his shirt, smoothing it onto the pile. The rest of his clothes follow while Nate and I gawp at him. The muscles of his arms bulge like he's wearing water wings, the groove of his hips a canyon of flesh.

Then he's not human anymore.

His skin ripples. Bones pop. Clear fluid splatters the floor. He grows and keeps growing to a dazzling silver dragon, his eyes gunmetal grey and split by an elliptical pupil. He flaps his wings, somehow dry, and lunges at Nate, his mouth wide. Nate throws up an arm as if that will help.

"No!" The yell echoes off cold stone.

Julian thrusts himself between Nate and his slavering brother, brandishing his cuffs. The dragon shrieks, the flesh smoking and blistering on its jaw. A leathery wing snaps out and bats Julian away, the beast hissing at the brief contact with the dragon's-bane. Its long neck tenses to strike. Instead of crumpling on the floor, Julian springs back and jams the chain of his cuffs into his brother's mouth. I clap my hands over my ears at the agonised wail. Claws scrabble on rock. Kester rears, strings of bloody saliva swinging from his teeth. He sucks in a breath and a lick of flame sparks in the darkness of his throat. Julian shields Nate with his body but it won't be enough.

"No fire, Kester," Evelyn says and Kester coughs, a curl of smoke escaping. "Not yet. Put him with the others—there'll be plenty of time to eat later."

Kester growls at Nate and the noise vibrates through the soles of my boots. Nate stumbles towards the barred door, his gaze on Julian, a jumble of emotions on his face.

It's probably not the right time to say, "I told you so."

Kester stalks back from the cell to loom over us, huffing hot dragon breath in my face.

"Blane, Dominic—remove the runt's cuffs before he gets an inflated sense of his own power," Evelyn says.

Blane has what can only be described as boy-band hair and a crooked nose. Dominic resembles Julian the most, if Julian sneered at everything.

"I may be weak, Mother, but at least I'm not debilitated by a tiny plant." Julian sidles to keep himself between me and his brothers as Blane circles behind one of the dragon statues.

"How different your life would have been if you were though, *Son*," Evelyn spits.

"Different doesn't mean better. I'd be a monster. Like you."

Evelyn laughs and drapes herself on her throne but hatred sparks in her amber eyes. "Yes, because not being a monster has worked out so well for you. Just like your father. Say hello, Hektor."

A head peeks from behind the throne—a glimpse of thinning, sandy hair and gentle, peridot eyes. Evelyn snaps her bony fingers and the figure retreats.

I can see where Julian got his looks, though he seems to have inherited his cheekbones and slim build from his mother.

"I have hope for him yet, if I can get him away from you," Julian says.

"Oh, how brave you are in front of your human friends but you will snivel as you always do. I warned you what would happen if you ever ran from me again." Evelyn's smile raises goosebumps on my arms and the urge to pee increases. "And that was before you were complicit in Lukas's murder. I doubt your little female will last but I plan on keeping you alive for a long, *long* time."

Julian swallows hard. I put my hand on his back and only then can I feel a fine tremble beneath my palm.

What abuse has he suffered in this medieval cavern? His pain treated as entertainment. He must have been so lonely.

So sad. His spirit slowly broken. No wonder he turned to thoughts of suicide.

And it's my fault he's here, at the mercy of his family and facing an agonising death. I'm sure mine won't be pleasant, either, but my fragile human body will give out way before his.

All because I froze instead of ramming my sword through Evelyn Romanov's chest.

Blane returns, wearing thick gloves to his elbow and carrying a pair of metal cutters. He passes the long-handled tool to Dominic.

"Hold out your arms, runt," Dominic sneers. "If I even think you're going to touch me with those cuffs, I'll break your woman's jaw."

Julian raises his arms. Blane grabs him above the cuffs. Two snips with the tool and the dragon's-bane-infused metal clinks on the floor. Julian's wrists are red and weeping. The sight clenches my stomach. Blane scoops up the cuffs and disappears briefly behind the statue with all the equipment. I slip my hand into Julian's and he squeezes my fingers.

"Isn't that sweet?" Evelyn strokes the material of her dress over her knee. "I'm surprised you could get a human besotted with you, my traitor son, and a Vanatori, no less. But does she know how weak you really are? His true form is quite pitiful."

"Shit." Julian lurches away from me. "Don't look, Raine. Don't—"

Evelyn flicks her fingers at him and his body explodes with a horrible sound between a scream and a roar.

47

Scalding fluid splatters my clothes, my skin, my hair. A howl builds in my throat at the thought of Julian torn apart, his bones and soft, pink tissue on the outside.

No one could survive the violence of that change.

But a dragon the size of a deer thrashes on the ground, all wings and elbows. He struggles to his feet, and shakes, raining more clear goop. His body is sleek and grey, his wings and spinal crest a swirl of rainbow colours that seem to shift under the dancing light of the sconces. Black, gazelle-like horns arch back from his head.

The flying rainbow-horse along the coast. It was him all along.

I meet his eyes and they're the same eyes I've been staring into for the past few weeks—amber and peridot and anxious. Exposed. Is he waiting for me to shy away, to flinch? Here he stands in the dragon form I dreaded because how could I love it like I love him?

"Look at him!" Evelyn says though I already am. "He's a pathetic excuse for a Drakul. I should have drowned him like the runt he is after his first change."

"Truly shameful," Blane says.

Dominic nods. "A fucking embarrassment."

Kester chuffs his agreement.

Julian stays very still on all fours, his wings tucked into his flanks, his slim tail curled around his rear foot.

"He's beautiful," I breathe, letting the truth fill my words and spill out my eyes. I swipe a tear from my cheek and glare at Evelyn. "Unlike you, you bony old bag."

Can dragons grin? Julian seems to be grinning at me.

Dominic and Blane's expressions darken, their huge fists bunching as they advance on me but Evelyn holds up her hand.

"Laugh it up, girl," she says. "Show her real Drakul, boys. Show her how terrifying her last hours will be."

Hours? She must think I'll break pretty quickly.

She's probably right.

I drag my stupefied gaze from Julian. Dominic and Blane don't bother undressing. Their clothes rip as they shift into the bronze that ate Fabian and another silver dragon, his eyes a midnight blue so dark, the pupils are lost. Guns clatter to the floor in wisps of cloth. The three dragons dwarf us, heat pulsing from their bodies.

"My glorious sons," Evelyn says, the maternal pride shining from her angular face. "And Lukas, oh, he was magnificent."

My fingers itch to touch Julian, to pet the slickness of scales over the solid bunch of his muscles and bury my nose in the warmth of his neck. I want to hug my dragon one more time.

I take a step towards him.

Evelyn snaps her fingers. "Cripple the runt but keep him alive. He will watch me torture his human, knowing the only way to end her suffering is if he eats her himself."

Julian bares an impressive set of teeth and a growl rumbles in his chest. His brothers roar and dive for him but he's gone in a flurry of wings and a flash of colour. Fireballs burst in all directions, scorching the walls in streaks of black. Julian dodges around the pillars, turning on a wingtip while his brothers lumber after him. Mouths snap on air, Julian's nimble body leaping, twisting, springing from floor to wall to ceiling.

He rakes claws down Dominic's side in furrows of red. Angry bellows batter the huge space. Julian pauses on the edge of the room, his ribs heaving, nostrils flared. Kester charges but Julian darts clear and Kester's skull cracks the rock in a puff of dust. While the silver beast is stunned, Julian shreds one of its wings and launches away before Dominic or Blane can touch him. He leads them to the far end near the stairs and I can see little beyond blurs of colour and the explosion of flame. Kester trundles after them, trailing his useless wing.

Evelyn doesn't know what the hell she's talking about. Julian is glorious. *Julian* is magnificent.

But he can't run forever. One wrong move, one exhausted stop for rest, and his brothers will catch him. Will they pull his lovely wings from his back like tearing the wings off a butterfly? Break his limbs or bite them off altogether?

I glance at the handguns discarded on the ground. I'm more likely to hit myself in the foot but I have to do something to help Julian. Something like shooting his mother in the face. Remove the queen and plunge the hive into chaos. Or is that bees rather than dragons? The thought of my boyfriend mauled half to death is affecting my recall.

A chill creeps up my spine and shivers through my shoulders. The scent of lilacs stirs my hair and my heart constricts to the size of a pea.

"Are you freezing up again, girl?" Evelyn whispers. "Perhaps you *are* a match for my son. You both quiver like little children."

I spin around but can't stop sliding backwards a step. Evelyn smiles wide and her bones shift under her skin, making her face more severe.

"So you're terrifying," I say with only a slight wobble. "Good for you."

"You have no idea how terrifying I can be." She stalks forward and I scramble a retreat. She sniffs the air. "Though perhaps you do."

The sounds of pursuit crash around us—claws screeching on stone, furious roars and the whoosh of fire. I ache to check on Julian but I can't take my eyes off the monster in front of me.

"What are you talking about?" I say through numb lips.

"It took me a while to place your scent since it's been, oh, ten years but I always remember the ones who get away."

She continues to advance until I'm almost running in reverse. My heels hit the dais steps and I sit hard on my butt. I scrabble upwards and my back meets cold marble, chains clinking as I brush against them.

"You know, I have a house in Nevada," she says, stopping at the base of the steps, her smile so wide, the top of her head is in danger of falling off. "That silly festival brings lots of fresh meat to the desert."

Her words burn inside me. The cavernous chamber blurs to be replaced by a parched mountainside, the throb of music and the screams of my mother. A black and a gold dragon tossing the scraps of my father between them.

Lukas and Evelyn Romanov.

I killed one of my parents' murderers and didn't even know it.

I blink myself to the present and Evelyn's smug expression. Shoving to my feet, I reach for my sword but my fingers grab nothing but air.

Julian's brothers stripped us of all weapons and equipment before they marched us out of the trees.

Evelyn laughs. "Your sudden courage comes too late, girl. You had your chance to cut me. Now, it's my turn. Now, you will squeal as I carve Lukas's name into your flesh."

She raises a spindly hand. Her fingers elongate to curved, black talons. She reaches for me with a reptilian grin. A blast of hot wind tumbles my hair across my face. I claw it free and find myself alone on the steps. Julian arrows away down the cavern and lobs his shrieking mother at Blane, who's flying at him head-on.

I've never seen a dragon look so surprised.

Blane flaps desperately and his claws skid on the floor. He juggles Evelyn in his arms, the lace of her cape tangled in his talons. Julian swoops over their heads and strikes at Blane with a clawed foot. Blane screeches louder than Evelyn but only briefly.

"Catch the little bastard!" she howls. "I want his regret painted in blood!"

Blane lowers her to the ground and rejoins the chase, one eye a weeping mess. Evelyn fixes me with a baleful stare, her chestnut hair in disarray. I dive for the weapon beneath Kester's neatly folded clothes. Gunfire erupts from the entrance of the chamber. My head snaps up. Julian weaves behind the pillars, his brothers' bulk blocking my view of the stairs.

People in black sweep into the room.

<h1 align="center">48</h1>

Evelyn Romanov doesn't seem to care that the Vanatori have breached her inner sanctum and are taking pot-shots at her sons. She snarls and strides towards me, both hands now tipped by claws. A flash of pale skin oozes red through a tear in her dress, her bare arms scored.

"I am going to decorate my throne with your entrails, girl," she hisses.

Julian is too busy dodging bullets to play another round of toss-your-mother. I point Kester's handgun at her.

I have no idea what model it is or how many shots it holds. It's heavy and black and cold in my fingers. Unfortunately, I need to shoot Evelyn Romanov in the head. I'm sure a round to the gut or chest would be a mild inconvenience but without dragon's-bane, it won't stop her from ripping my lungs out.

I suck in a breath and release it slowly. Evelyn raises her hand to swipe. I pull the trigger. The bullet puffs into a pillar way, *way* to the right.

She barks a laugh and her teeth are pointed. "You really are the worst Vanatori. Your parents would be ashamed."

"Don't you *dare* talk about my parents."

I squeeze the trigger again. Evelyn staggers and her mouth stretches in an awful howl.

Holy crap, I hit her. But where's the blood?

She whirls towards the far side of the room. I follow her gaze to a swirling cloud of ash sifting to coat the forms of two bellowing dragons, a silver and a bronze.

No more Kester Romanov.

Evelyn's howl becomes a ground-shuddering roar. Her angular frame explodes from human to dragon, drenching me in scalding fluid. A wall of expanding gold slams into me and catapults me backwards. Stone and flame and smoke blur into one but I glimpse an immense shape diving into the chaos. Then I thud to the ground and blink at the ceiling. A warm glob slides down my face. My head throbs, all the air pummelled from my chest.

A shadow looms over me in a scrape of claws and a flurry of wings. The gun stayed in my hand through my short flight but it weighs as much as the tonnes of earth above me. The beast lowers its head, its sharp teeth glistening in the firelight.

Julian licks my cheek and whines low in his throat. His tongue is surprisingly soft. He straddles me on all fours, shielding me with his body and outstretched wings. My shaking fingers brush the hard ridges of his face, my knuckles bloody.

"I'm okay," I wheeze.

He snuffles at my shirt, his hot breath tickling me through the damp material. I wrap my arms around his neck, forgetting the crest along his spine but it flattens under my touch instead of impaling me. He lifts me gently to my feet.

He's warm and solid and still smells like vanilla.

Screaming drives us apart. The cavern is a maelstrom of soot and charred bodies. Cozma's elite hunters scatter under the fiery onslaught of Evelyn Romanov and her two remaining sons.

Excuse me, her two remaining *evil* sons.

She towers over everyone in a blaze of gold, her head ringed by horns. That and her crimson eyes send a shiver down my spine. Her wings practically stretch from pillar to pillar. The air is thick with the sweetness of roasted meat and the coppery scent of blood. The corpses that aren't blackened beyond all recognition are crushed and twisted lumps of pink and red.

Julian nudges me with his snout and tips his head towards the cell. Three pale faces peer through the bars. He trots over, careful not to slap me with his wing on the way past. I tuck the gun into my waistband, hoping I don't shoot off a buttock, and scoop up the weapons dropped by Blane and Dominic. Julian wrenches the prison door off the wall with a screech of metal. Nate limps out first, a scrap of material tied around his injured thigh. Sofia and Dustan exit as one fused entity.

"That *bruja* is fucking crazy," Sofia says. "No offence, Julian."

Julian grins at her with his mouthful of fangs and she doesn't bat an eyelid.

"Here." I offer her one of the handguns. "No dragon's-bane but better than nothing."

She smiles her wicked smile and checks the safety. "At least it'll work on the humans."

I hesitate but hand the final weapon to Nate. He holds my serious eye contact for a couple of seconds then nods. I hope it means 'sure, Raine, I won't shoot your boyfriend.'

Julian chuffs for our attention. A group of Vanatori flee towards our part of the cavern, pursued by Blane. Principal Cozma gallops in their midst, her two pommels sticking up behind her shoulders. Julian, Nate and I duck behind one pillar, Sofia and Dustan at the next. Julian may be a slim dragon but he has to stretch upwards to hide himself, his wings tucked tight into his flanks, his grey belly arching over me.

"So, what's the plan, Nate?" Dustan says, peeking at the flash of gold and bronze and flames from the far end.

There's no animosity in his words. Maybe he's forgiven Nate for almost letting Rick shoot him and Sofia. Nothing like a common enemy—or enemies—to bring us back together.

Nate glances at me. "What was your exit strategy if everything went to plan?"

"I was going to sneak Julian out in the chaos," I say, and raise my chin.

"Then we get the hell out of here while they're busy fighting each other."

Footsteps slap stone. Two Vanatori career around the pillar, trailing smoke, and skid to a halt. Their eyes widen at Julian crouched above me and Nate. I fumble for the gun at my back but it catches on my shirt. The man and woman aim their rifles.

"Wait!" I shout. "He's a good—"

Two shots crack out. The hunters fall and I gape at Nate.

"He's a good dragon," Nate says quietly.

I swallow hard, my eyes prickling. Julian bows his head and he and Nate share a considering look. I try not to blubber over their male bonding experience.

Sofia passes her handgun to Dustan and scoops up a rifle. She cocks her eyebrow and holds the weapon out to me.

Nate raises a hand. "Bad idea to give Raine something that goes fully auto."

She gives the rifle to Nate and claims the second gun. We start a darting run down the line of pillars.

In other circumstances, the sight of Julian creeping along as a rainbow-coloured, deer-sized dragon may have been funny but my palms sweat at the bullets whining through the air and pocking the stone. The room is a furnace of dragon fire. Evelyn Romanov moves in a blur of claws and teeth, slashing, biting, burning. Her snout and scales are splattered red, blood oozing from wounds in her hide but she shows no signs of slowing beneath the agony of the dragon's-bane. Her eyes are solid crimson and glittering with fury.

Heading towards her seems like a stupid idea but her giant golden butt is blocking the only exit.

Nate, Sofia and Dustan dash to the next pillar. A wall of silver cuts Julian and me off. Blane fixes us with a midnight-blue eye and licks his lips. I squeeze the trigger of my gun. The shot gouges the ceiling. Blane treats me to a rumbling chuckle. He sucks in a breath. Julian and I scamper into the middle of the room, the floor shaking as Blane stomps after us.

We're too open. Figures in black run everywhere.

I sprint for the pillars on the other side of the room. Strong arms scoop me into the air, wicked talons tucked carefully away. Julian spoons his body around me and his wings create a warm cocoon of darkness. His heart thuds against my back. Fire crackles but no lick of flame sears my skin. Julian unfurls himself. His powerful legs bunch and he leaps across the space, his claws scrabbling on stone. He lowers me gently until my boots touch the floor, a pillar sheltering me from most of the room. He nuzzles my face, a soft sound in his throat, then he's gone in a flap of wings, rushing for Blane.

On the opposite side of the cavern, Nate, Sofia and Dustan are trapped in the middle of a group of Vanatori, and Dominic.

Evelyn Romanov is busy eating people.

A burst of gunfire yanks my focus to Julian harrying his brother. Blood splatters from the side of Blane's face, obliterating his other eye. Julian swoops clear as his brother rears, roaring and shaking his head. Principal Cozma advances, her eyes narrowed, soot smearing her cheekbones and gathered in the swirl of her scars. Another round of bullets patters into Blane, ragged flesh hanging from his splintered jaw. He crashes to the ground on his belly in a heap of flailing limbs. A final barrage from Cozma's rifle mangles the top of his skull. His body sizzles and erupts into ash.

Evelyn Romanov's scream shatters the cavern.

Cozma points her rifle at Julian. "Let's give her something else to screech about."

Her finger tightens on the trigger.

I'm too far, too slow, but I throw myself at Julian anyway.

Cozma's gun clicks empty and she tosses it aside in disgust.

"Looks like we'll have to do this the old-fashioned way, Mr Romanov." She draws her Romanian kilij swords, the blades curved.

Julian shelters me under his wing when I finally reach him. I point my weapon at Cozma and she smirks.

"Now, Miss Waller, you can't even hit a dragon at two paces. Do you really think you're going to hit me?"

I smirk back at her. "Something tells me I won't have to."

She frowns and glances over her shoulder. The colour leaches from her face. Evelyn Romanov thunders towards us, her mad eyes fixed on Cozma. Cozma squeaks and runs, her swords flashing silver as she pumps her arms. Julian sweeps us out of the path of his mother. She barrels through the ash of Blane and spits a fireball at Cozma, who ducks behind a pillar. Cozma dodges and rolls, metal sparking on rock, but Evelyn herds her into a corner.

Cozma meets my gaze past the bulk of Evelyn's shoulder. "Miss Waller! *Raine.* Help me!"

Evelyn stays out of reach of Cozma's swords. Her ribs heave as she prepares to roast a cowering Cozma. I aim my gun.

Evelyn probably won't even feel it. My bullets are like a midge bite to a cow without the aid of dragon's-bane. And if she does feel it, why do I want to attract her wrath to save a woman who won't stop trying to murder the man I love?

Evelyn Romanov opens her huge maw. Sweat drips into my eyes. I pull the trigger.

And shoot Principal Cozma right in the forehead.

49

Flames consume Cozma before her body hits the ground. Evelyn lunges and grips the burning carcass in her teeth, shaking hard. Cozma's swords fly in different directions, one skittering near my feet. Other lumps follow but I force myself not to look at them. I drop the gun and scoop up the sword while Evelyn crunches happily on what's left of Cozma.

Did I mean to shoot Cozma? I can't tell, though I'm not too cut up about it. It's hard to keep track of everyone in the chaos.

So tragic.

Evelyn finishes her meal and wheels to face us. Footsteps pound behind us. Nate and Sofia pant to a stop on either side of me. They aim their rifles at the monster licking flecks of Cozma from her teeth.

"This is for my friends, you fucking bitch," Nate says.

The guns clatter in unison. Dominic drops from the sky with a furious hiss to shield his mother. Nate and Sofia shred his wings then aim for his head. Bullets strafe his flesh into a mess of pink and bronze. Even a Drakul's thick skull is no match for concentrated automatic fire. I choke on the ash he leaves behind. Evelyn bellows, her monstrous shape rearing through the swirls of smoke.

"I'm out!" Nate shouts.

Sofia shakes her rifle in frustration. "Me too!"

"We're fucked."

Julian leaps over our heads as Evelyn charges. Even standing on two feet, his wings spread wide, he's delicate compared to the golden fury of his mother. He launches himself at her face. Ruby droplets splatter from his claws. He beats his wings, slashing at her as fast as he can but her huge, taloned hand swings out and smashes him to the ground, pinning him between her splayed fingers.

"Julian!" I jump forward, my sword raised.

Julian bites at Evelyn's hand. Her weight crushes him into the unyielding stone, forcing a horrible groan from his throat. I aim my blade for her wrist. A streak of burnished gold slams into Evelyn and tumbles her away. Julian rolls to his side and struggles to his feet, flakes of ash fluttering from his wings.

"Are you okay?" My hand hovers over him, my sword pointed at the ground.

He nods and gives himself a shake, more ash drifting down.

"Uh, Raine, you might want to see this," Dustan says.

Two massive dragons grapple in the centre of the room, one the black-horned bulk of Evelyn Romanov. The other is slightly smaller and red-gold.

"Your father?" I say to Julian, who nods, his head cocked.

The two beasts rip chunks out of each other, thrashing amid bursts of flame. Hunters huddle behind pillars or the charred bodies of their comrades.

"Then let's help him," I say.

Nate takes my dropped handgun. Sofia grabs Cozma's other sword. Together we storm towards the warring dragons. Our battle cry is weak compared to their bellows but it feels good tearing from my mouth. Julian roars and gallops beside me. He springs ahead, landing on his mother's back and digging his claws in. His father sinks his teeth in her neck while she's distracted. Nate circles around, peering down the sights of his weapon. Dustan hustles to the nearest rag-tag group of Vanatori.

"Shoot the gold!" he yells, gesturing with his gun. "Shoot Evelyn Romanov. Don't hit the red-gold or the rainbow— they're on our side."

Granted, it's hard to shoot the wrestling dragons and not hit Julian or his father. The hunters edge closer. Evelyn beats at Julian with her heavy wings and knocks him free. He scrabbles away from her slashing talons. She claws at Hektor and he loses his grip. Her tail lashes out, flooring the Vanatori. I throw myself flat and it whooshes past me. Julian dives, striking her with his back foot and powering himself out of reach. Evelyn shrieks and spins, the rest of us scattering to avoid her tail. With a great flap, she's airborne, chasing Julian, rivulets of red streaming from multiple wounds.

I can only imagine what she's screaming inside his head.

The dragons zoom off down the far side of the room. Julian weaves and zig-zags, bouncing from pillars and walls to change direction. Evelyn can barely flap her wings to their full extent, the tips brushing the ceiling.

She really is a humongous cow.

The Romanovs blast past us several times and we can do nothing but watch. Ineffectual, like always.

Julian easily avoids his mother but he's tiring, each twist less graceful, each leap shorter. Evelyn pursues him relentlessly and Hektor trails behind, his tongue lolling.

Julian's shoulder clips a pillar. He flaps but can't right

himself, his feet skidding on the floor, his legs crumpling beneath him. I'm running before he slides to a stop in a cloud of dust. Exhaustion dulls his eyes and his ribs heave beneath silken scales. His gasps swirl through the ash. Evelyn's landing shudders the ground and Julian rolls his eyes to look at her looming above him. His wings droop.

"Evelyn!" I shriek and fly towards her. "I told you I'd kill the rest of your sons, you bony old *bitch*."

She snarls and hoists Julian by his tail. His limbs paddle at the air but he can't reach her to do any damage. She opens her mouth. Strings of drool glisten between her fangs. Hektor tackles her from the side and drives her into the wall, fracturing the rock. Julian drops to the floor but wobbles to his feet. I sprint past him. Evelyn shrugs Hektor off and crouches against the wall, her great head swinging towards me. Her thick arm swats out. I roll beneath it, the hard floor bruising my spine. I leap to my feet and choke on the scent of sulphur and raw meat.

"For my parents," I say, and ram my sword into her chest.

50

Evelyn Romanov dies like her sons—in a cloud of ash. The powder rains onto me, somehow cold. It fills my mouth, my nose and blinds my eyes in sifts of grey. I hold my breath to keep from inhaling more Evelyn into my lungs. The dust must fill my ears because there's nothing but silence.

Something wet laps at my face. I drop the sword, my fingers cramped from gripping the pommel. Julian licks me until I can open my eyes. He tries to brush the ash from my clothes but his claws catch on the material. He makes an enquiring noise low in his throat.

"I'm okay," I say, and pat myself. Ash sifts down to pile on the toes of my boots.

Holy crap, I killed Evelyn, Queen of the Romanovs. Top dragon lady. Julian's mother. Murderer of my parents.

My hands start shaking. Julian nudges me with his snout. I wrap my arms around his neck, his head over my shoulder, his scales smooth beneath my fingertips.

But it's not the same.

"Julian," I mumble into the sinuous line of his neck, "I love your dragon form and all but I really need a proper cuddle."

He steps back and chuffs at me. I frown at him. He flicks his head. I finally get the message and turn away.

The survivors of the Romanov battle huddle in a loose group, some watching Julian and me, others slumped to the floor, hugging their knees to their chests. Nate, Sofia and Dustan stand together, their weapons still out, their gazes sweeping the small bunch of people. Not yet trusting the Vanatori will leave the last two Romanovs unharmed.

There's a sliding, ripping sound and the snap of bone. I very much want to peek, though maybe the change is an intimate process. Or a bit gross. A couple of hunters stir enough to gape but still I resist.

"Raine," Julian says and, *god*, I missed his voice.

I spin around a little too fast and there he is, standing in front of me with a shy smile. Scraped, bruised, filthy. Perfect.

Oh, and naked.

I launch myself at him and he laughs in surprise but catches me easily. I bury my face in the wonderful spot where neck meets shoulder. My hands glide up his back, his arms pressing me close. My mouth finds his. He tastes of soot and Julian and my legs go weak. Through no fault of my own, my fingers slide down to the lovely curve of his butt.

Purely for balance.

"For god's sake, Raine," Nate says on a sigh, "we can see you grabbing his ass."

"But it is a spectacular ass, honey," Sofia drawls.

Heat flares in my cheeks. I untangle myself from Julian and his tender smile tingles to my stomach. I can't help but trace his lips, his cheekbones and the arch of his brow. His eyelashes tickle my fingers.

"My son," a voice says behind us, cracking on the last word.

Julian goes very still. I kiss him lightly and try to give him some space but he turns us both towards the voice, his arm across my shoulders, hugging me tight.

"My beautiful, gentle son," Hektor Romanov says.

He cradles his arm to his chest. Angry red furrows rake him from shoulder to hip and, oh, yes, he's also nude. His body is losing muscle definition but he's still a good-looking man. I jerk my eyes to his face and my cheeks blaze brighter.

"The only one not poisoned by his mother. It killed me to watch her abuse you, to watch your own brothers torment you." Hektor limps nearer and halts an arm's length away. "She said if I ever intervened, she'd slaughter my whole family—sister, brother-in-law, niece and nephew, aunts, uncles, cousins twice-removed. And you last and worst of all."

Julian trembles against my side. I curl my arm around his waist, my fingers brushing his hip bone.

"I cut myself off to protect them. But I couldn't protect you." A single tear slides down Hektor's cheek. "I should have protected you, risked everything to save you. Can you ever forgive me?"

Julian swallows hard and shakes his head. Hektor's shoulders slump.

"I'm sorry. I'll go and never trouble you again."

He shambles for the stairs.

"Dad," Julian says and his voice breaks, "that's not what I meant. There's nothing to forgive. No one stood against her. She was terrifying."

"Utterly petrifying," I say on a nod.

Murmurs of agreement come from elsewhere in the room.

Hektor's sad smile is so like Julian's, I almost take a step towards him.

"You stood against her," Hektor says. "You and your friends."

"So did you, in the end."

Hektor's smile widens. "I guess I did. You finally made me brave, my son."

A sob catches in Julian's throat. Hektor holds his arms open and Julian falls into them, curling into his father's chest. Hektor strokes Julian's hair, his cheeks wet with tears. I stare at my boots to give them some privacy, biting my lip to keep from crying right along with them.

All Julian ever wanted was to be loved by his family. And now he is. Now, he can have a whole new family on his father's side who will love him as he deserves.

Drops of water plink onto my boots in little puffs of ash.

Dammit, I'm crying anyway. Maybe no one will notice.

"And who is this lovely young lady?" Hektor says.

I sniffle and peek through my lashes. He can't be talking about me. I stink of soot and sweat and have a halo of ash.

Crap, he's talking about me.

"Dad, this is Raine." Julian scrubs his face and leads his father over to me. "She's my girlfriend."

Hektor holds his hand out. I glance at it and notice way too much pale skin beyond. I fix my eyes on his forehead and flap my hand in his general direction.

Hektor chuckles. "I had forgotten the prudish nature of humans. I'm sorry, my dear. We can do proper introductions once I have some clothes on."

"Here," Nate says, approaching with a bundle of material. "This stuff was left on the steps."

Hektor pulls on Kester's trousers and suit jacket while Julian buttons the shirt, the hem drooping to cover his modesty.

"Much more civilised," Hektor says and captures my hand. "Lovely to meet you, Raine. I assume you are the reason my son has been happy these past few weeks?"

"Well, I-I… Um…"

Julian gathers me into a cuddle and I manage to stop stuttering at his father. He places a kiss on my temple.

"She's the reason," he says.

And Nate doesn't make a sound.

He really has mellowed.

51

"So… this is my bedroom."

The room is on the third floor, which seems mostly unoc-cupied, though the corridor has fancy dark panelling and is lined by thick runners. Julian pushes open a door that's been kicked in numerous times, the wood a serious splinter hazard. He waves me in front, his head bowed, his hair hiding his eyes.

Man, his nervousness is cute. He could live in a hovel and I'd still love him. Though his bedroom gives a whole new meaning to the word 'spartan'.

"Well, you did tell me your bed was the nicest thing in it," I say, my socks padding on the worn, navy carpet.

My boots are somewhere getting de-ashed by a Romanov servant. The Lessers and guards emerged as soon as they saw Hektor and Julian approaching the house. They'd hidden when Cozma's army swept into the grounds.

Funny how tyranny leads to rebellion rather than loyalty.

"My brothers would've stolen the bed with the rest of my furniture but it was too heavy, even for them." Julian's toe pokes a cardboard box filled with folded clothes out of sight.

The bed is more majestic than I imagined way back on one of our early phone calls, when he was just Jay the informant and I was the drooling weirdo. The ebony posts support a canopy of sheer black curtains tied back. The covers are bronze, patterned in gold and silver thread. I shoot a glance at Julian and he nods.

"To remind me I'll never be any of those colours. It's the only reason I have sheets or I'd be sleeping on nothing but the mattress."

I hug him and smudge more soot on Kester's shirt. "No one will ever treat you like that again."

He squeezes me tight and I struggle to breathe but who needs oxygen? He's suffered so many cruelties for something he couldn't control. All I want to do is make him happy.

Voices pass in the corridor.

Hektor invited everyone to stay the night in the mansion to get cleaned up and rest and show them not all Romanovs are evil. In fact, the remaining Romanovs are pretty darned magnificent.

Julian sneezes and eases away. "Sorry. You're dusty."

"I know. I can't believe your dad saw me like this."

"He loves you already."

I look down at myself to hide my blush. "Still, I'd like him to see me in something that's not mostly ash."

Julian lets me shower first. Alone. I'm too filthy for anything but a functional shower, the water running grey for five minutes of vigorous scrubbing. I dress in a pair of his boxer shorts and a t-shirt and the scent of him on the clothes speeds my heartbeat. He can probably hear it but maybe he'll think I'm really excited about being clean.

I swipe the fog from the mirror and stare at my reflection. Straggly, wet hair pushed back, my skin pink and glowing, the ghost of the freckles I hated as a kid dusting my nose. There's a scrape on my cheek and several bruises on my legs and arms. My muscles ache like I've had an intense session with Fabian.

We avenged his death today, alongside so many others.

Despite the events of the last few hours, I'm not tired. I'm too nervous to be tired, which is dumb. Who cares if I'm in Julian's house, in Julian's bathroom and soon to be in Julian's bed?

I splash cold water on my face and release the shower to Julian, pretending my heart doesn't leap when he grins at me wearing his clothes. He shuts the door and I fidget in the middle of the room. I can't just stand here but there's nowhere to sit. Climbing into his bed seems a bit forward.

"You're a big tough dragon hunter," I scold myself. "You slayed Lukas and Evelyn Romanov. You can do anything."

I hope Julian can't hear me babbling to myself over the hiss of the shower.

I spend another minute hopping from foot to foot like the unruffled professional I am then sidle up to the bed. I keep sidling until my leg hits the edge and I topple onto the mattress.

"Whoops," I whisper.

Good lord, the bed is magical.

I slither into the centre of the sheets and starfish a little, loving the slide of silk. It must feel glorious on bare skin…

Oh crap, I'm naked. *I'm naked in Julian's bed!*

I peer over the side to where I tossed his t-shirt and boxers in a fit of insanity.

Maybe I can reach them before he's done.

The shower shuts off. I dive under the covers and pull them over my head.

Not cool, Raine.

I tuck the sheets to my chin.

Julian's had an exhausting, awful, exhilarating day. How selfish to think he'll want to do anything but sleep. Me and my one-track mind.

The bathroom door swings open. I sit up and hug my knees to my chest beneath the covers.

Julian pauses in the doorway, wearing a t-shirt and boxers similar to my recently discarded ensemble. His wet hair clumps in spikes to his cheekbones.

Man, those cheekbones.

He cocks his head. "Your heart is beating pretty fast."

"I, um… seem to have lost my clothes."

His eyes darken. Wisps of steam creep around the door frame behind him.

"I've never had a naked woman in my bed," he says, his voice husky.

He stops at the edge of the mattress and plucks at the covers, his gaze pinning mine. Gathering the material in his hands, he slowly draws it away to reveal me curled in a ball.

This is ridiculous. Why must I feel like the virgin around him? *I* deflowered *him.* I should be sexy, confident, commanding.

He watches me in silence. My heart flutters into my throat and the damn thing won't settle no matter how hard I swallow.

"We don't have to… If you're tired," I mumble in the direction of my kneecap.

His smirk pools heat in intimate places.

"I'm not tired," he says.

He crawls onto the bed. I tell myself to keep breathing. No need to panic. He trails his fingertips up my shin. My leg flops straight and boneless. He does the same to the other until I'm fully exposed. I squirm beneath the hunger in his eyes.

"Lie down," he says, a small tremor in his voice betraying him.

The silky sheets caress my back, cool compared to the heat pulsing from my skin. His hands brush my thighs and I jump. Instead of pulling away as he would before, he rewards me with a smile.

"You're not going to last, are you?"

"Hurry up and take off your clothes," I growl.

His t-shirt flutters over the side of the bed. Violet bruises bloom from shoulder to chest, the scrapes on his arms scabbing as if they're a day old. He holds himself above me, not touching, his face inches from mine. I stroke my fingers up his ribs, and he shivers.

"Are you in pain?"

He shakes his head. "I thought I'd be dead by now. This is nothing."

"I'm glad you're not dead."

"Me, too," he whispers, his soft smile curving against my lips.

The kiss jolts my heart rate to a thousand beats per minute. I find myself pawing at his boxer shorts like a lunatic.

"But we're not safe yet," I gasp in a vain attempt to distract him and salvage my dignity. "Cozma may be gone but any one of the group leaders on that call could take her place."

"That's a problem for tomorrow. Now, my only problem is how many times I can get you to moan my name before you faint."

He wriggles out of his boxers. I almost drown in my own saliva.

"So cocky," I gulp.

He captures my mouth and kisses me until I make little whimpering noises in my throat. I grip his hips and arch my body towards him. Need pulses through me—a different, more demanding kind of ache. The kiss grows frantic—tongues, teeth, everything. Julian slides inside me and, Christ, I'm so close already. There's no way I can survive his slow, glorious torture.

"Oh, fuck," he says, his eyes desperate.

And that's it. I blast into heaven and drift around for a millennium or two. Julian collapses on top of me and his heart drums against my chest.

"Okay," he pants into my neck, "let's try that again."

And, sweet mother of orgasms, we do.

Twice.

52

"The Vanatori are in chaos," Nate says.

He strides into the living room and flops on the satin pillows of a couch that's wider than my bedroom. Or my old bedroom, anyway. Julian and I swung by my fire-damaged house to salvage my possessions from the wreckage. Adam-in-Chains was alive and treated me to a haughty expression of betta disdain. His tank now sits on a beautiful mahogany chest of drawers in Julian's bedroom. They're not the only new additions. Hektor offered Julian one of the luxurious rooms on the first floor but Julian decided he liked his room, though he accepted some redecorating and some furniture.

And I've moved in but so have Nate, Sofia and Dustan. The Romanov mansion is the new Titan Group headquarters extraordinaire. We've simply clarified our mission statement— kill the bad dragons, protect the good dragons.

"The latest vote dissolved into bickering," Nate continues. "Devaki Kala has Farouk on her side but Haralda supports Negus. The other leaders don't have a clue."

I snuggle closer to Julian on the chaise longue. The thing looks like half a sleigh and is decorated in silver leaf. Sunlight streams through the French doors and sparkles on an honest-to-god chandelier that has more crystals than Swarovski.

Julian wasn't allowed in the room before, as if he were a dog that would dirty the furniture.

"If any of the four heads are voted in, it's not an improvement on Cozma," I say.

"No, but the dissent and confusion among the other groups will damage their position. Hell, it's the only reason I'm tolerated at the meetings. There are enough people talking about the Romanov mission. We get new supporters every day."

I check my watch. "Sofia and Dustan should be reporting back on that soon."

The loss of Cozma and her elite hunters, including the best of the best from the four largest groups, has weakened the hold they have on the rest of us, helped by the surviving witnesses spreading the word of Drakul aiding Vanatori. No one saw me accidentally (or subconsciously on purpose) shoot Cozma but everyone knows I killed Evelyn Romanov, which makes me a legend.

Even if I am sleeping with a dragon.

A Lesser servant enters carrying a tea tray and sets it on the glass coffee table. She pours three mugs, her frame as delicate as the porcelain. She bows to Julian and slips from the room.

Every servant and guard approached him in the days following the battle. They, like his father, asked for his forgiveness. Evelyn Romanov forbade them to speak to or wait on him and they were too terrified to disobey. Julian accepted their apologies with his usual grace while I sniffled at the sight of him surrounded by people—*his people*—smiling at him, touching him. He offered them their freedom and not a single one chose to leave.

Nate rises and adds a dollop of honey to two cups, passing

them to me and Julian. I inhale the fragrant steam, Julian keeping one arm wrapped around me.

"When's Hektor due in?" Nate scoops the last mug and returns to the couch. He scowls at the contents and places the cup on a side table worth more than my Mazda.

"Should be any minute now," Julian says. "He didn't expect his talks with some of the families to last very long."

Nate snorts but says nothing.

A muffled thump echoes from the hall and Sofia's voice drifts through the archway. "I will have some nice, strong coffee, *por favor*. None of that flowery tea rubbish."

She sweeps in ahead of Dustan and drops her bag by the couch, the plush rug muffling the clank of weapons and handcuffs and probably a can of hair-spray, knowing Sofia.

She packs the essentials.

"We come bearing good news," she says and curtsies at Julian, "your Lordship."

He grins at her and I slurp my tea instead of swooning. Our future is still uncertain, our safety not assured, but his face glows with happiness.

Sofia smooths her red sweater dress under her legs and sits on the couch. "Your situation is not as rare and shocking as Cozma had us believe."

"You should hear some of these stories, Raine." Dustan slouches next to Sofia. "We lost so many Vanatori, so many opportunities for allies, from Cozma's unflinching doctrine."

"She killed them?" I say.

I shouldn't be surprised since she tried to do the same to me.

"The Lessers and Drakul, yes. She retrained most of the hunters but some were too broken. Others committed suicide." Dustan shakes his head and Sofia puts her arm around his skinny waist.

They never told me the details of their 'retraining', only that it was a form of brainwashing and they were glad it was cut short.

"How did she keep it so quiet?" I say.

"Threats, and by making them too ashamed to speak of it."

"Bottom line is"—Sofia accepts her coffee from the servant with a grateful smile—"we have a core group of about fifty Vanatori who want to join us."

Nate's normal scowly expression lifts to a dark smile. "That's enough to cause problems. With the ones adding their voice after the Romanov battle, they won't have an easy time silencing us."

We finish our various beverages and the Lesser woman slips in to clear everything away.

Julian squeezes my arm. "My dad's home."

It's at least thirty seconds before I hear a flurry of activity from the hall. Julian probably heard the cars as soon as they crested the rise of the long driveway. Hektor enters alone, dapper in a plum suit that makes his peridot eyes more striking.

"Ah, good afternoon, my fellow rebels!" He helps himself to a snifter of brandy from the sideboard and rests his hand on Julian's shoulder. "My son. Miss… Raine."

He wanted to address me as Miss Waller for propriety's sake but it reminded me too much of Cozma. He's still getting used to the idea.

He perches on the Chesterfield, one leg crossed over the other, his hand drifting to where Julian's elbow rests on the side of the chaise longue.

Hektor spent a lot of years unable to touch his son. He's making up for it now.

"I had a fascinating morning of Drakul politics but it all went exactly as expected," he says and sips his brandy.

"The Morrisons and Vanderbelts?" Julian says.

"Have pledged their allegiance as have my family, of course. The others enjoy the status quo. I didn't bother approaching the Della Valles."

Julian stiffens beside me.

I would like to punch a certain Della Valle right in the mouth. And maybe I will, someday, since her family are still the enemy. Rich, powerful and brutal.

"You did a great job, Dad, but… I guess I was hoping for more. The weakest from the powerful families. Aren't they tired of the way they're treated?"

"They'll come around. They just need time. And I left the most interesting for last. It's something of a coup." He takes a long, slow drink and I struggle not to fidget. "At this very moment, a third of the Lessers from every powerful family are making themselves comfortable in the throne room. I'll have to update the facilities—beds and plumbing and such."

"Way to go, Mr Romanov!" Sofia whoops.

Julian's arm tightens around me. "Is it enough? With support from the Vanatori, is it enough to keep us safe?"

"Almost, my son. Now we have consolidated our power, we need to present a strong front."

"What do you mean?"

Hektor stands to place his empty glass on the sideboard. "We need a new Romanov matriarch."

I suck in a breath before I can stop myself. Nate looks at Hektor with dark, wary eyes.

Does Hektor need to search for another wife, a non-psychotic female Drakul if such a beast exists? Or… will Julian have to choose a female as the heir to the Romanovs? And what will I become—the mistress? No, I can't handle it, even if it's pretend. A new matriarch could threaten our fledgling empire.

And a strange growly thing happens in my chest at the thought of another woman touching him.

Julian slides out from underneath me and rolls onto one knee, my hand gripped in his. I vaguely hear Sofia squeal in the background while I blink at him.

"What are you doing?" I squeak.

He stuns me with a tender smile. "I can think of no better person."

"I can't be the matriarch. I'm not a Drakul."

He shrugs. "Aren't rebels supposed to make their own rules?"

I seem to have trouble breathing. Julian watches me with his steady, different-coloured eyes.

"Does her heart always do that?" Hektor says.

"Yes." Julian's thumb skims my knuckles. "It bounces around all over the place when she's nervous."

"There's no need to be nervous, my dear. You can't possibly be worse than the last one, may she roast in hell."

I stare at Julian. When did I last speak? Maybe being the matriarch isn't what I think it means.

"I'm asking you to marry me, Raine," Julian says softly.

Holy crap. Oh holy crap. Oh—

Julian swallows hard and his hand trembles in mine. My heart swells to a gazillion times its normal size. I slide bonelessly to the floor and collapse into him.

"Julian," I sob into his neck, "of course I will."

And just like that, I take Evelyn Romanov's place as the matriarch. Soon-to-be Mrs Raine Romanov, head of the most powerful Drakul family in Scotland.

The Queen is dead.

Long live the Queen.

Let Me Know What You Think!

Thank you for reading my book! I love hearing from my readers so please leave me a review.
Can't wait to hear from you!

To get a free character sheet for everyone in the Vanatori's Titan Group, join my mailing list at http://nadinelittle.com/character-sheet by scanning the QR code below:

Buy the Next Book in the Series: *To Tame a Monster*
You'd think being the golden daughter of the most powerful
Drakul family after the fall of the Romanovs would mean life
is pretty easy. But when you have to pretend to fit in, it can
be a bit of a nightmare. Especially when one wrong move
could destroy everything.
Just ask Madisyn Della Valle.

About the Author

Nadine Little lives in Scotland and is an ecologist, though her specialism is botany, not dragons (unfortunately). She loves dragons so much, she has a tattoo of Julian's dragon form on her back, rainbow wings and all. She thinks this is perfectly normal. When she's not writing steamy science fiction and paranormal romance, she can be found falling over in bogs and into the occasional pond.

One day, she hopes to be a famous writer who lives in the woods.

You can connect with me on:
- https://nadinelittle.com
- https://twitter.com/Nadine_Little_
- https://www.facebook.com/nadinelittleauthor

Subscribe to my newsletter:
- https://nadinelittle.com/character-sheet